Clockwork Curandera

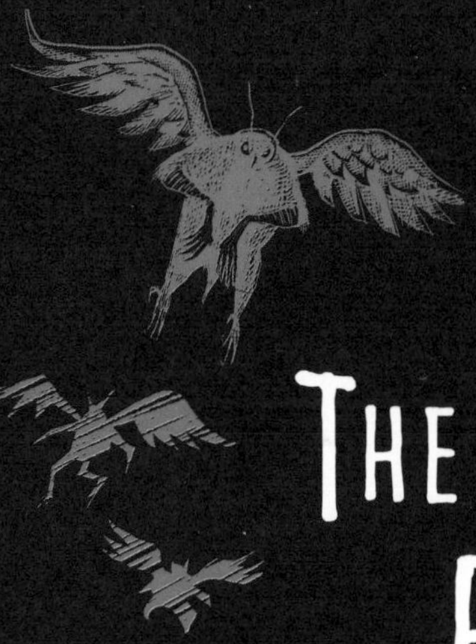

Volume I

The Witch Owl Parliament

CLOCKWORK CURANDERA

Volume I
THE WITCH OWL PARLIAMENT

CREATED BY
David Bowles & Raúl the Third

COLORS BY **Stacey Robinson**
LETTERING BY **Damian Duffy**

TU BOOKS

AN IMPRINT OF LEE & LOW BOOKS INC.

NEW YORK

To Mamá Petrita, our family curandera.
Que en paz descanse
—D.B.

To my Abuelita Susana,
la Curandera del Mercado Cuauhtémoc
—R.G.III

Text copyright © 2021 by David Bowles
Illustrations copyright © 2021 by Raúl Gonzalez III

TU BOOKS, an imprint of LEE & LOW BOOKS Inc.
95 Madison Avenue, New York, NY 10016 | leeandlow.com

Manufactured in China by RR Donnelley | Printed on paper from responsible sources

Edited by Stacy Whitman | Book design by Abhi Alwar | Colors by Stacey Robinson
Lettering by Damian Duffy | Book production by The Kids at Our House | The text is set in
Architect's Daughter | The illustrations are rendered in ink
10 9 8 7 6 5 4 3 2
First Edition

Library of Congress Cataloging-in-Publication Data

Names: Bowles, David (David O.), author. | Raúl the Third, 1976- author. | Robinson, Stacey, 1972- colourist. | Duffy, Damian, letterer.
Title: The witch owl parliament / created by David Bowles & Raúl the Third ; colors by Stacey Robinson ; lettering by Damian Duffy.
Description: First edition. | New York : Tu Books, an imprint of Lee & Low Books Inc., [2021] | Series: Clockwork curandera ;
volume 1 | Audience: Ages 12 and up. | Audience: Grades 7-9. | Summary: Resurrected by her brother using a forbidden combination
of alchemy and engineering, apprentice curandera Cristina vows to protect the Republic of Santander against the lechuzas terrorizing
immigrants and plaguing the country.
Identifiers: LCCN 2021010532 | ISBN 9781620145920 (v. 1 ; paperback) | ISBN 9781620145937 (v. 1 ; epub)
Subjects: LCSH: Graphic novels. | CYAC: Graphic novels. | Cyborgs--Fiction. |
Brothers and sisters--Fiction. | Shapeshifting--Fiction. | Magic--Fiction.
Classification: LCC PZ7.7.B715 Wi 2021 | DDC 741.5/973--dc23
LC record available at https://lccn.loc.gov/2021010532

1865 North America in the

Clockwork Curandera

Universe

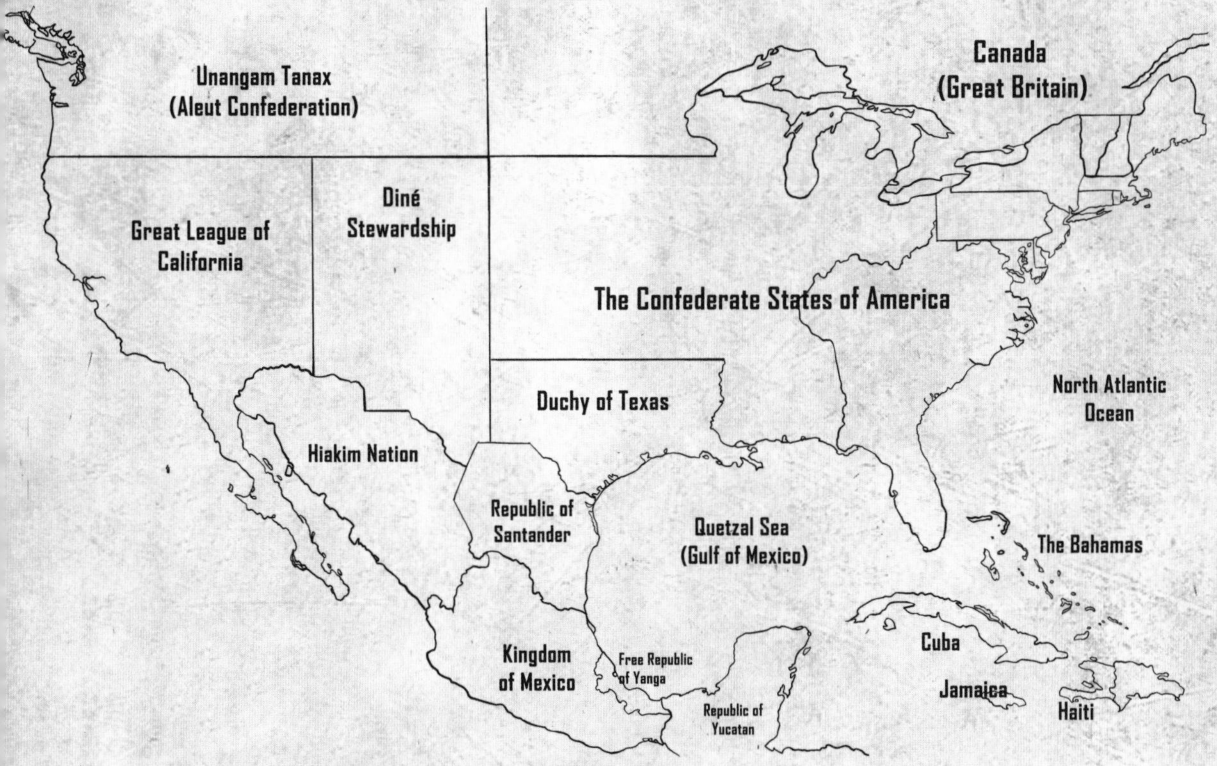
Unangam Tanax
(Aleut Confederation)
Canada
(Great Britain)
Great League of
California
Diné
Stewardship
The Confederate States of America
Duchy of Texas
North Atlantic
Ocean
Hiakim Nation
Republic of
Santander
Quetzal Sea
(Gulf of Mexico)
The Bahamas
Cuba
Kingdom
of Mexico
Free Republic
of Yanga
Jamaica
Haiti
Republic of
Yucatan

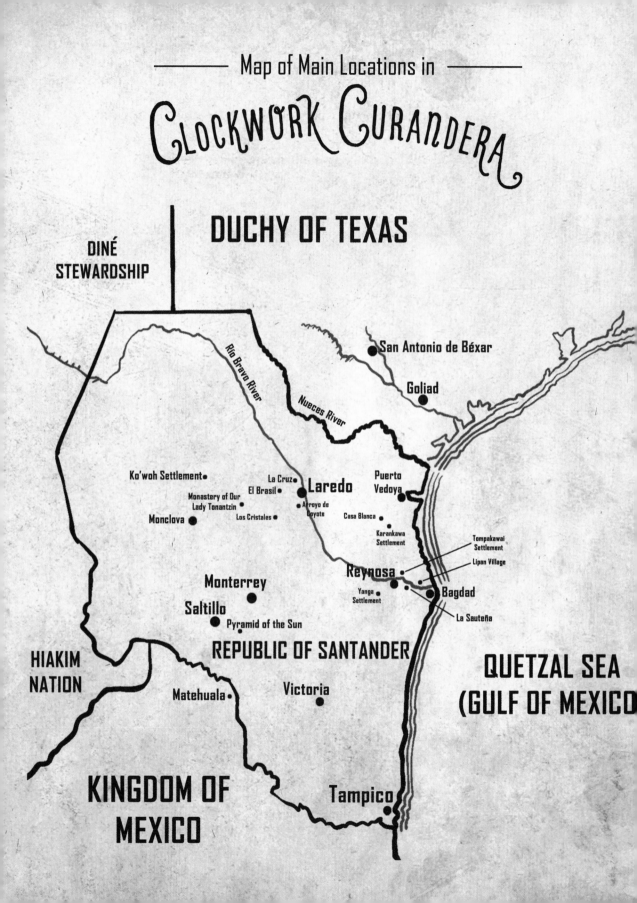

Map of Main Locations in

Clockwork Curandera

DUCHY OF TEXAS

DINÉ
STEWARDSHIP

Rio Bravo River

San Antonio de Béxar

Goliad

Nueces River

Ko'woh Settlement

La Cruz
El Brasil
Laredo

Puerto
Vedoya

Monastery of Our
Lady Tonantzin

Arroyo de
Coyote

Los Cristales

Casa Blanca

Monclova

Karankawa
Settlement

Tompakawai
Settlement

Lipan Village

Reynosa

Monterrey

Yanga
Settlement

Bagdad

Saltillo

La Sauteña

Pyramid of the Sun

REPUBLIC OF SANTANDER

HIAKIM
NATION

**QUETZAL SEA
(GULF OF MEXICO**

Matehuala

Victoria

KINGDOM OF
MEXICO

Tampico

PROLOGUE

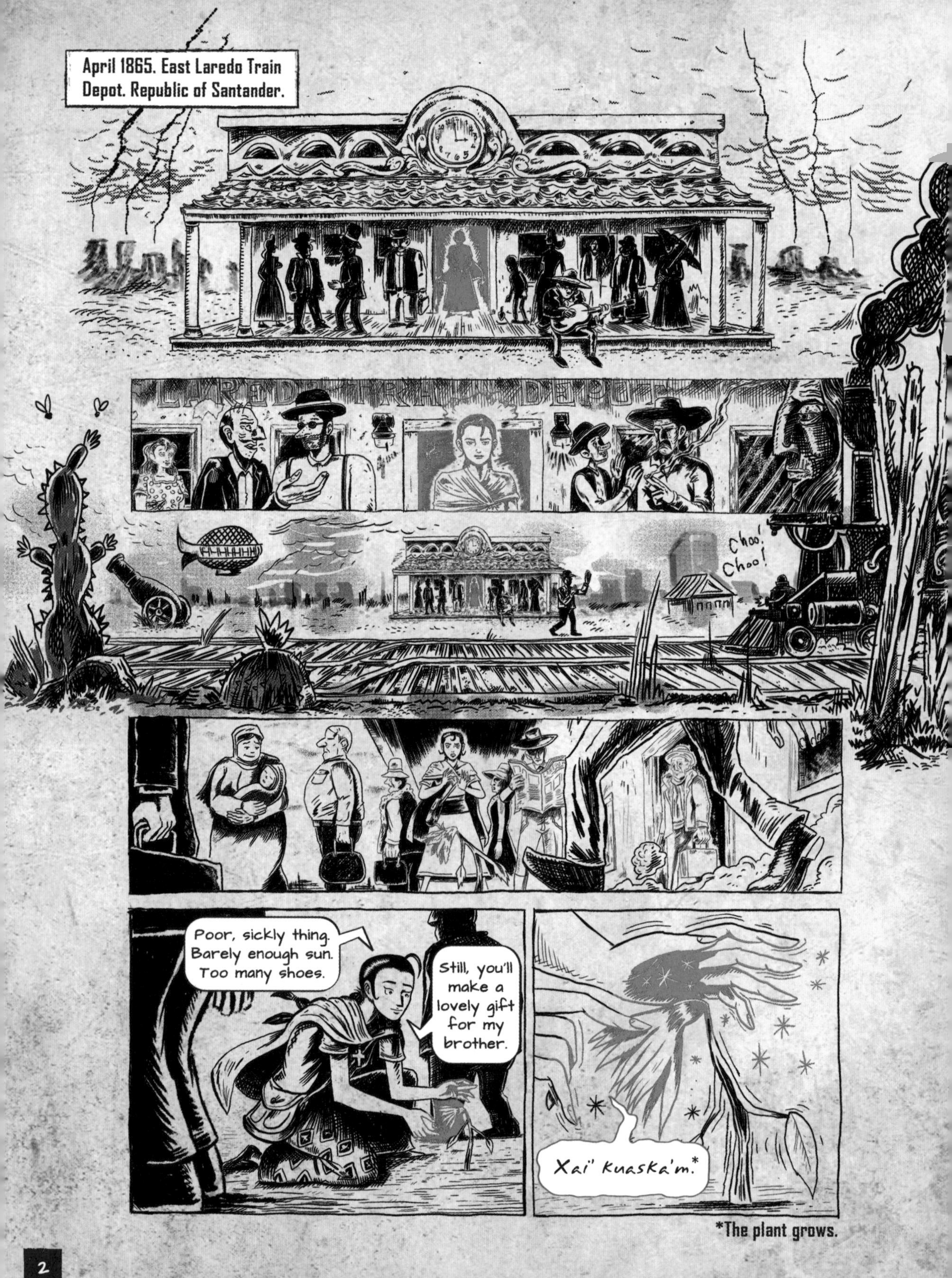
April 1865. East Laredo Train Depot. Republic of Santander.
Choo! Choo!
Poor, sickly thing. Barely enough sun. Too many shoes.
Still, you'll make a lovely gift for my brother.
Xai' kuaska'm.*

*The plant grows.

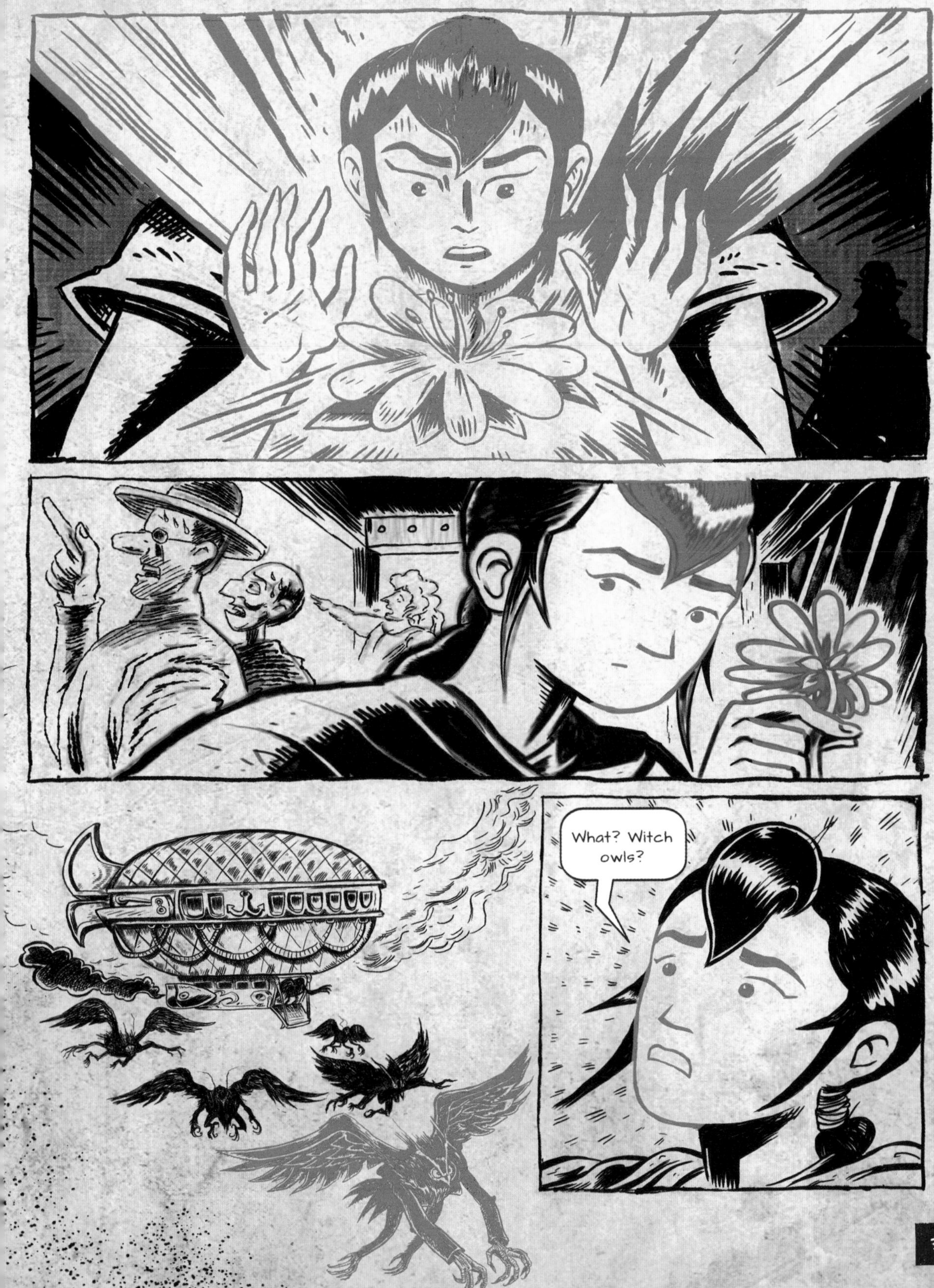
What? Witch owls?

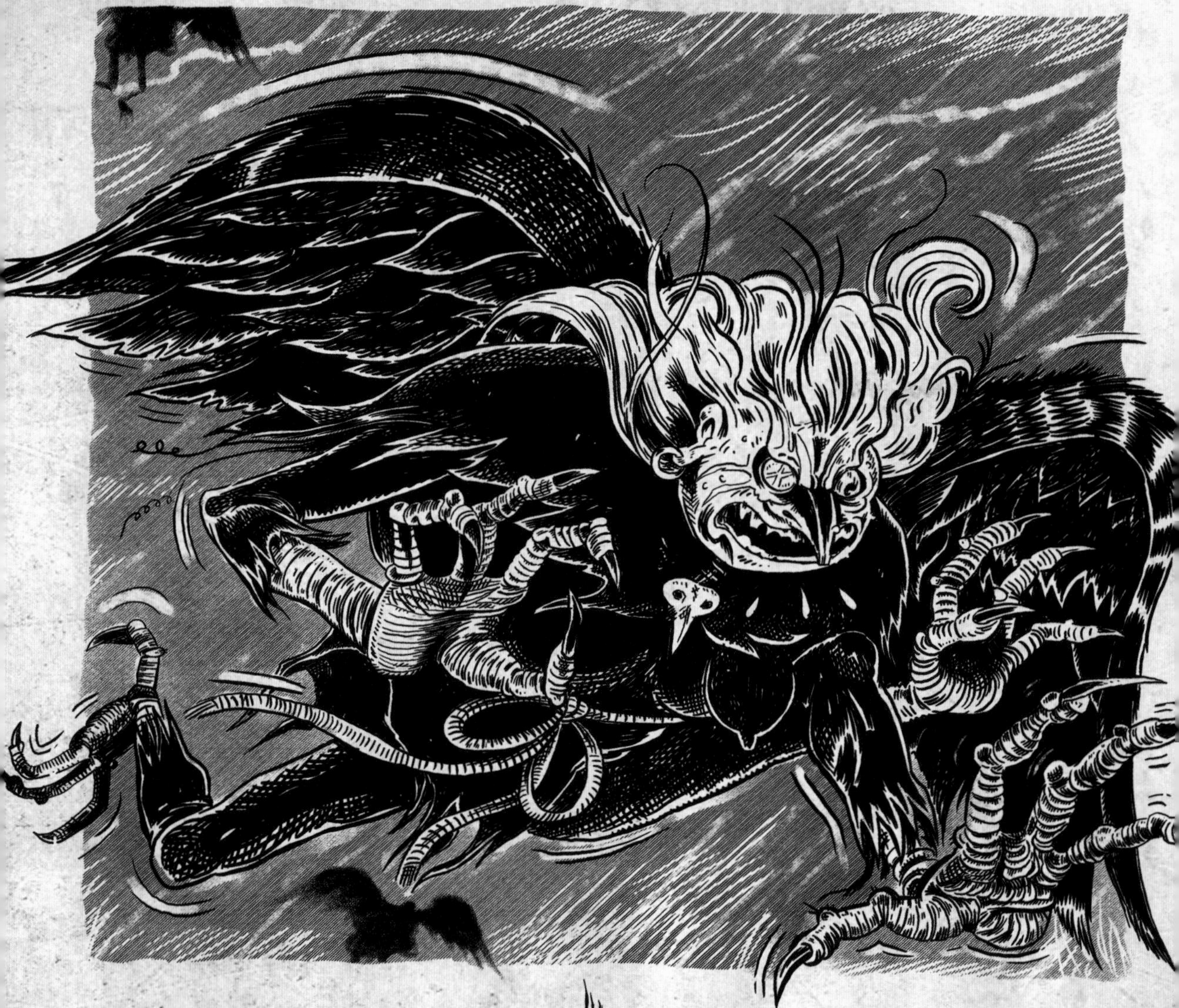

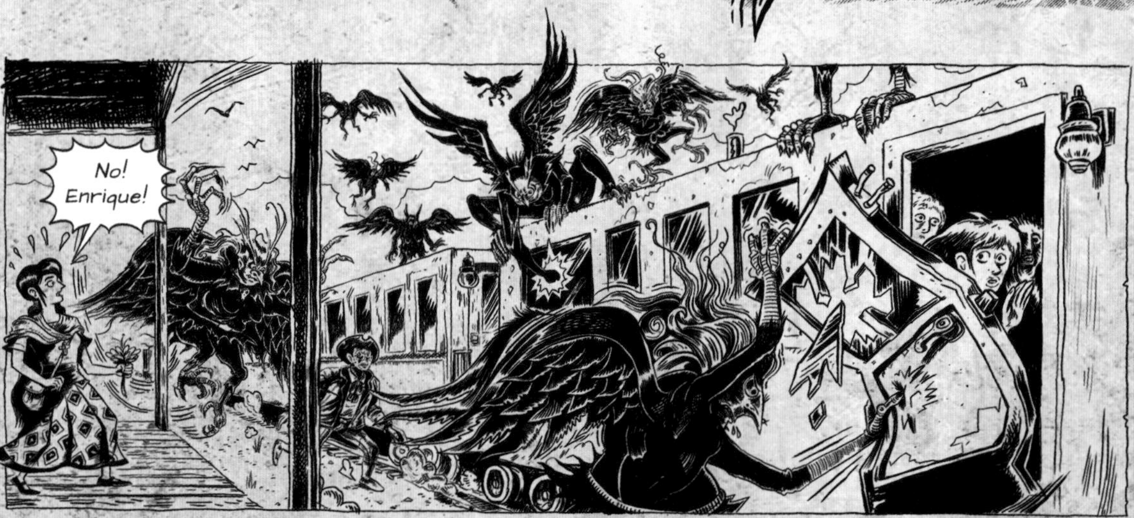
No! Enrique!

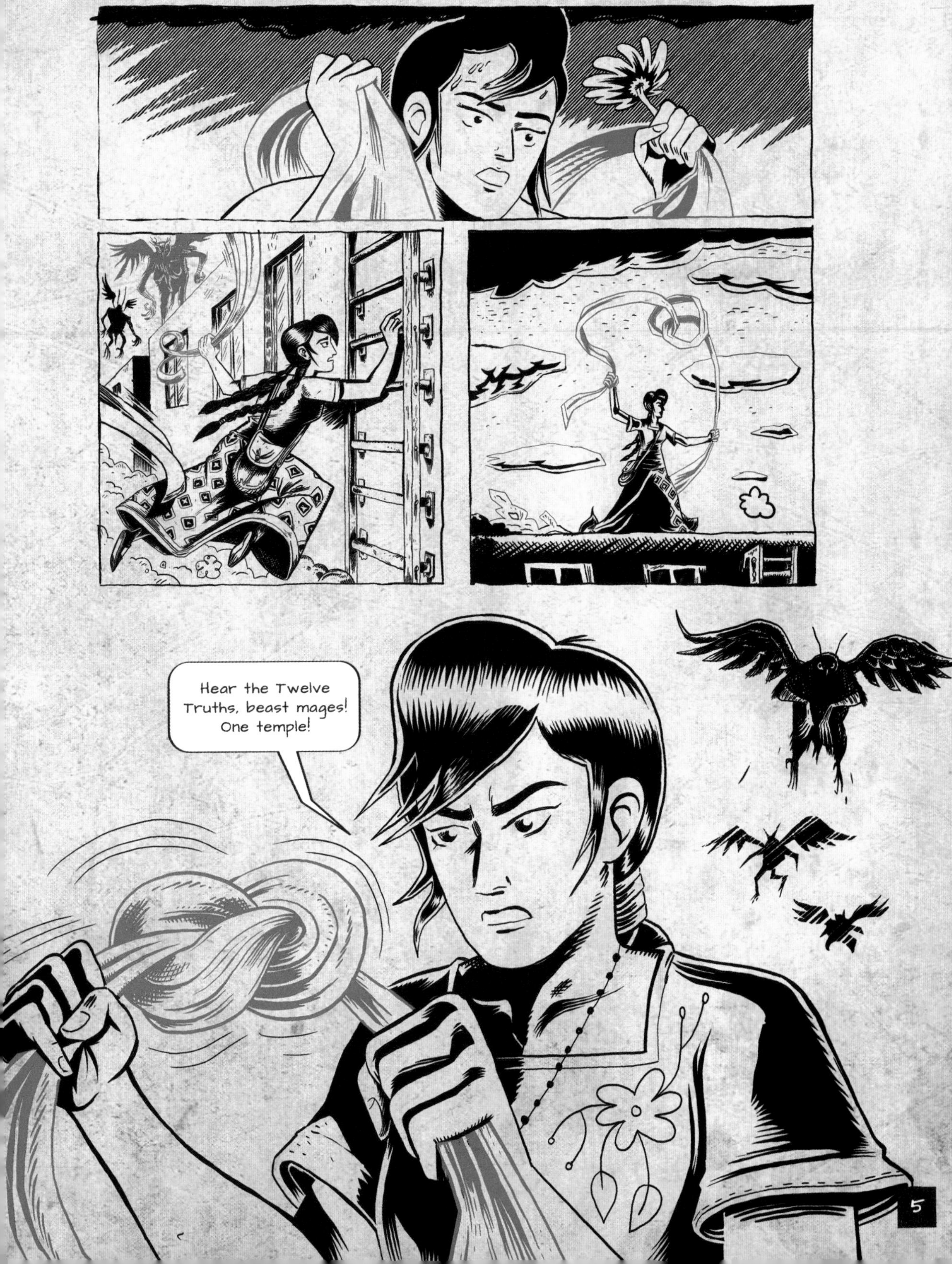
Hear the Twelve Truths, beast mages! One temple!

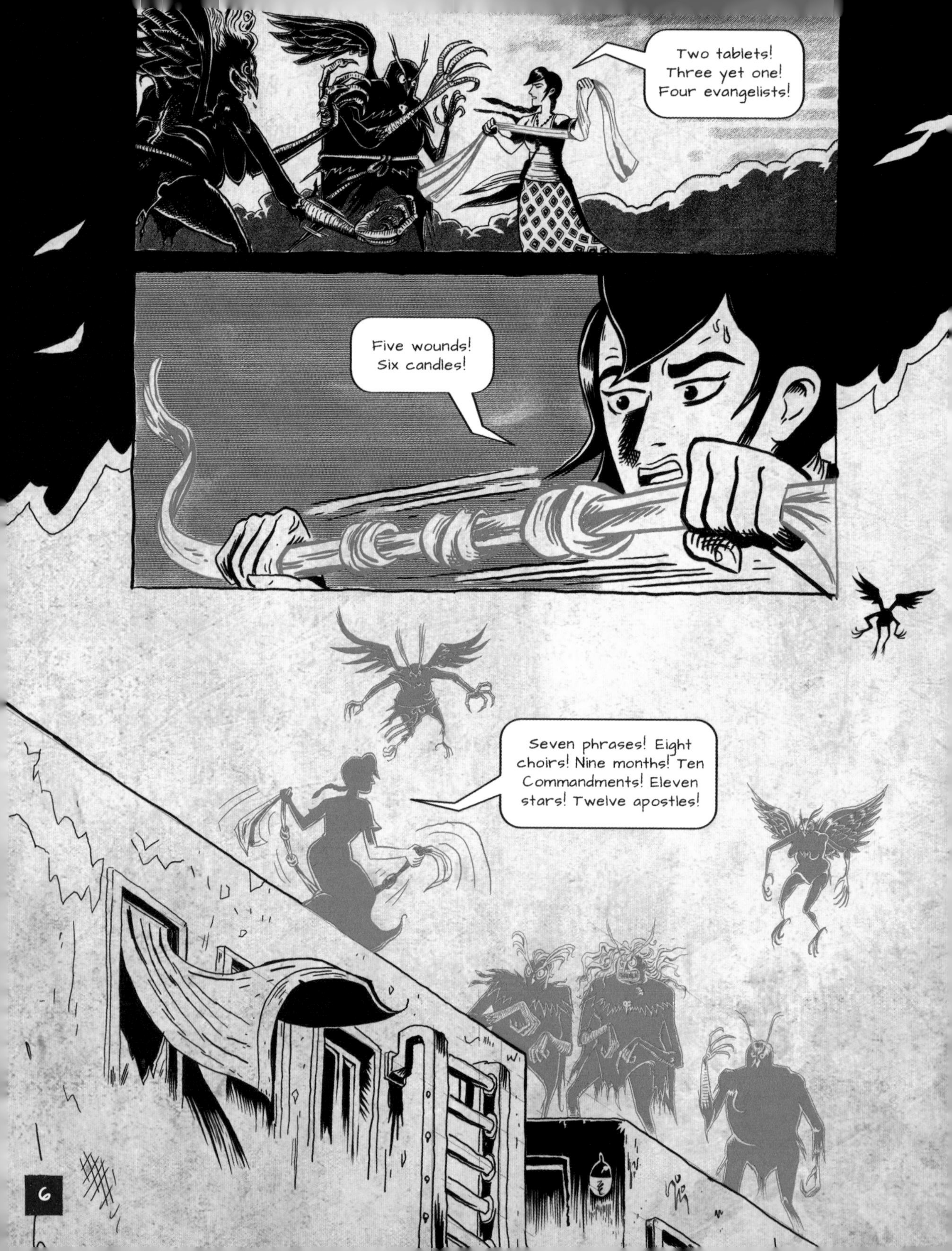
Two tablets! Three yet one! Four evangelists!
Five wounds! Six candles!
Seven phrases! Eight choirs! Nine months! Ten Commandments! Eleven stars! Twelve apostles!

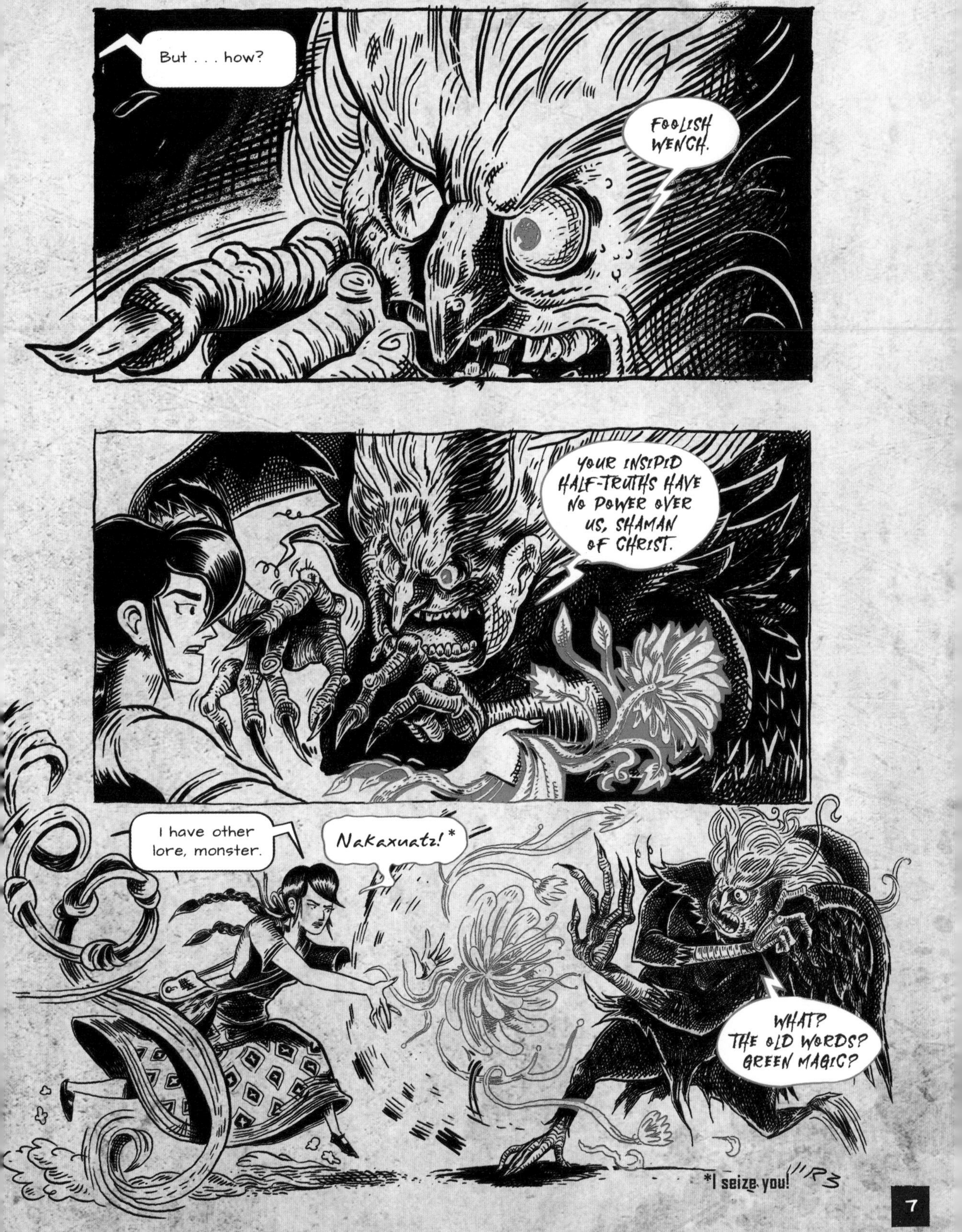
But . . . how?
FOOLISH WENCH.
YOUR INSIPID HALF-TRUTHS HAVE NO POWER OVER US, SHAMAN OF CHRIST.
I have other lore, monster.
Nakaxuatz!*
WHAT? THE OLD WORDS? GREEN MAGIC?
*I seize you!

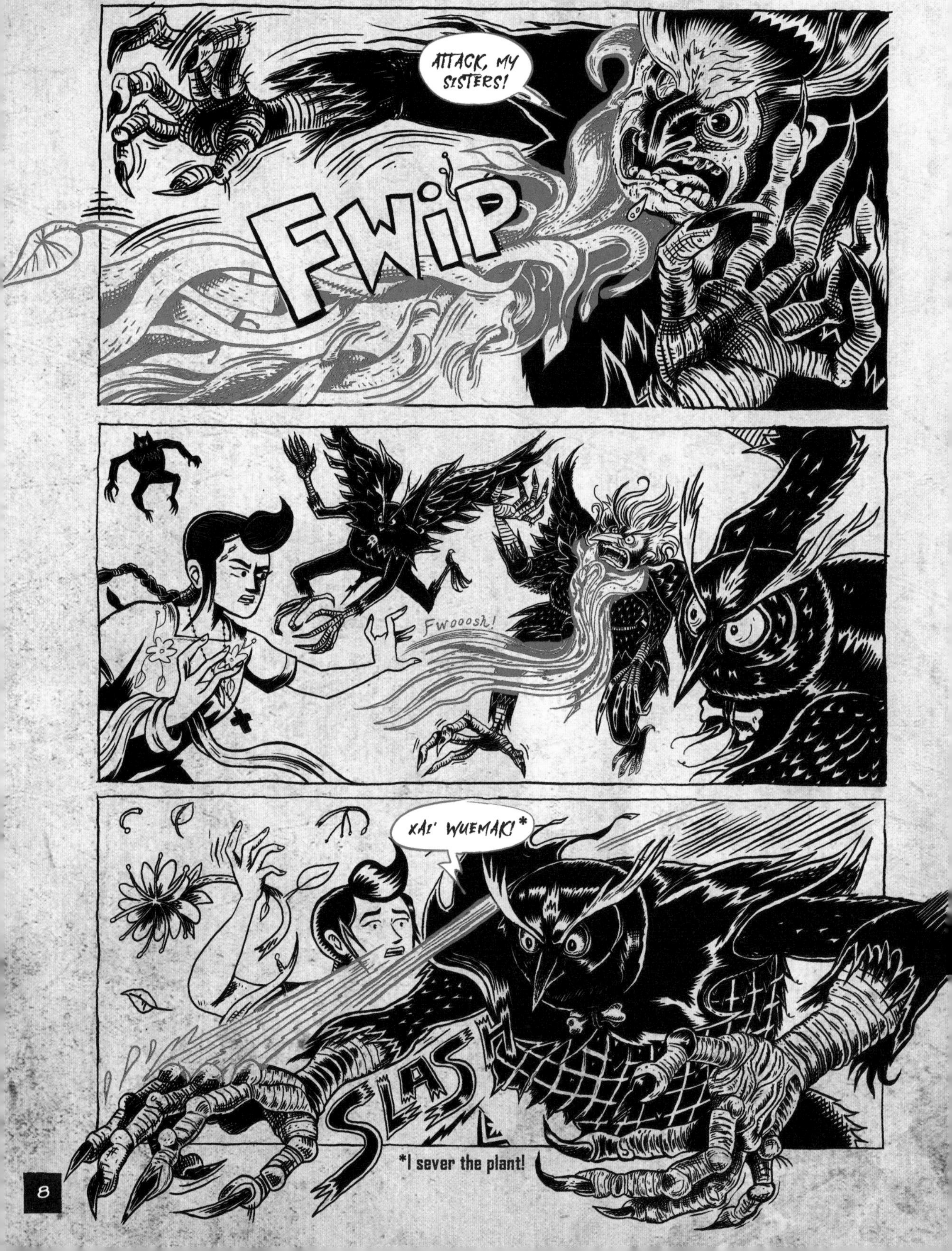
ATTACK, MY SISTERS!
FWIP
Fwooosh!
XAI' WUEMAK!*
SLASH

*I sever the plant!

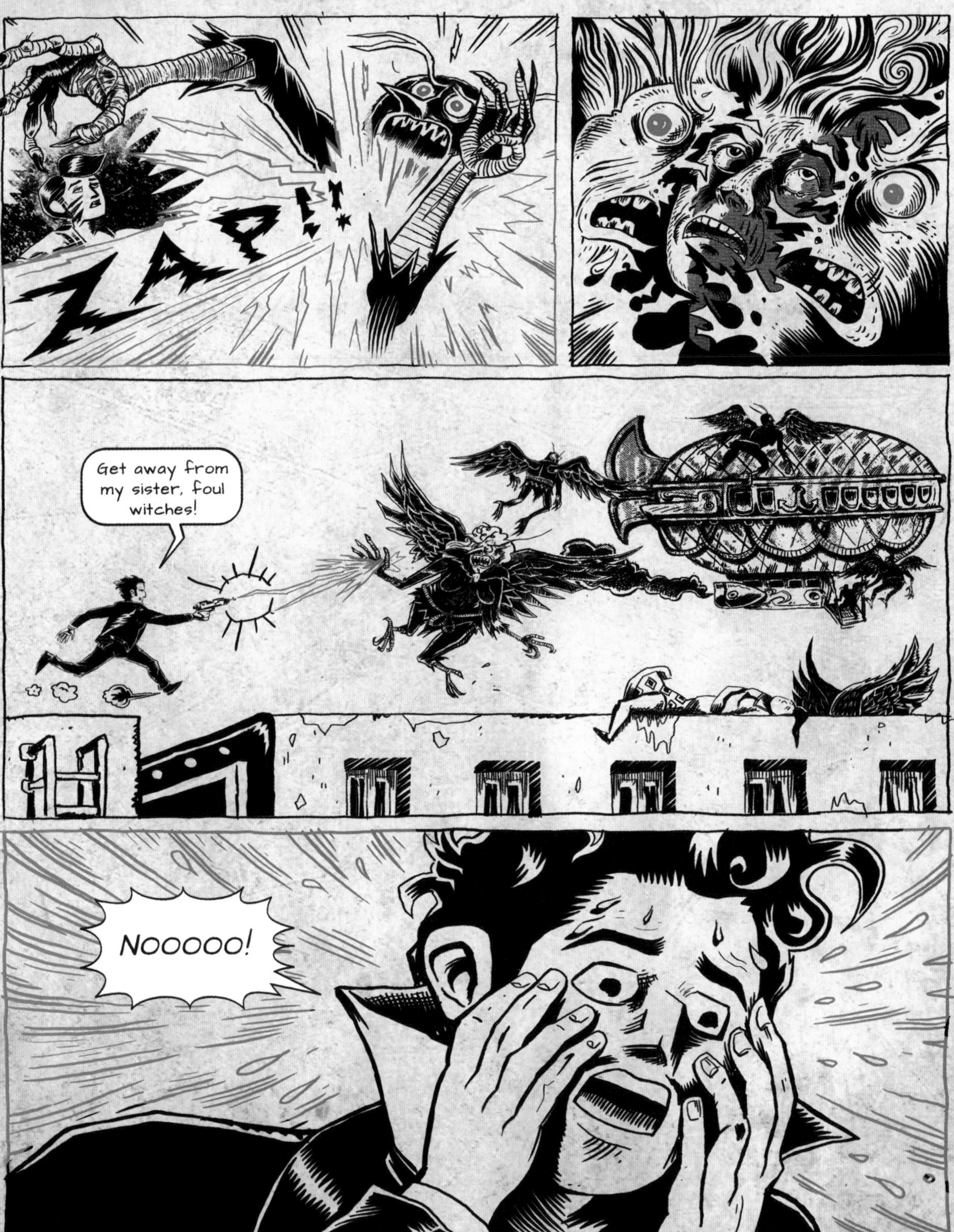
ZAP!!
Get away from my sister, foul witches!
NOOOOO!

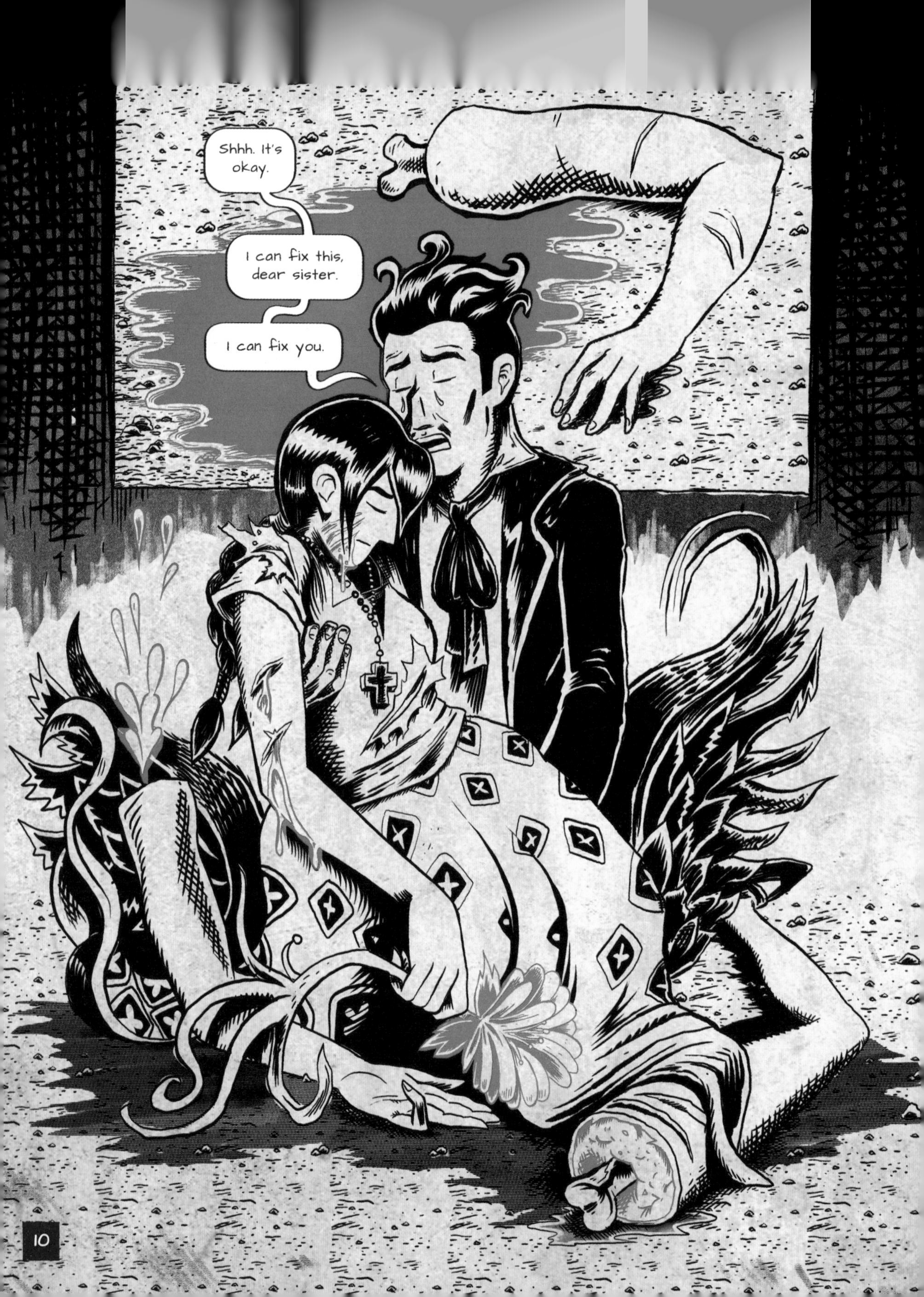
Shhh. It's okay.
I can fix this, dear sister.
I can fix you.

CHAPTER 1

RESURRECTION

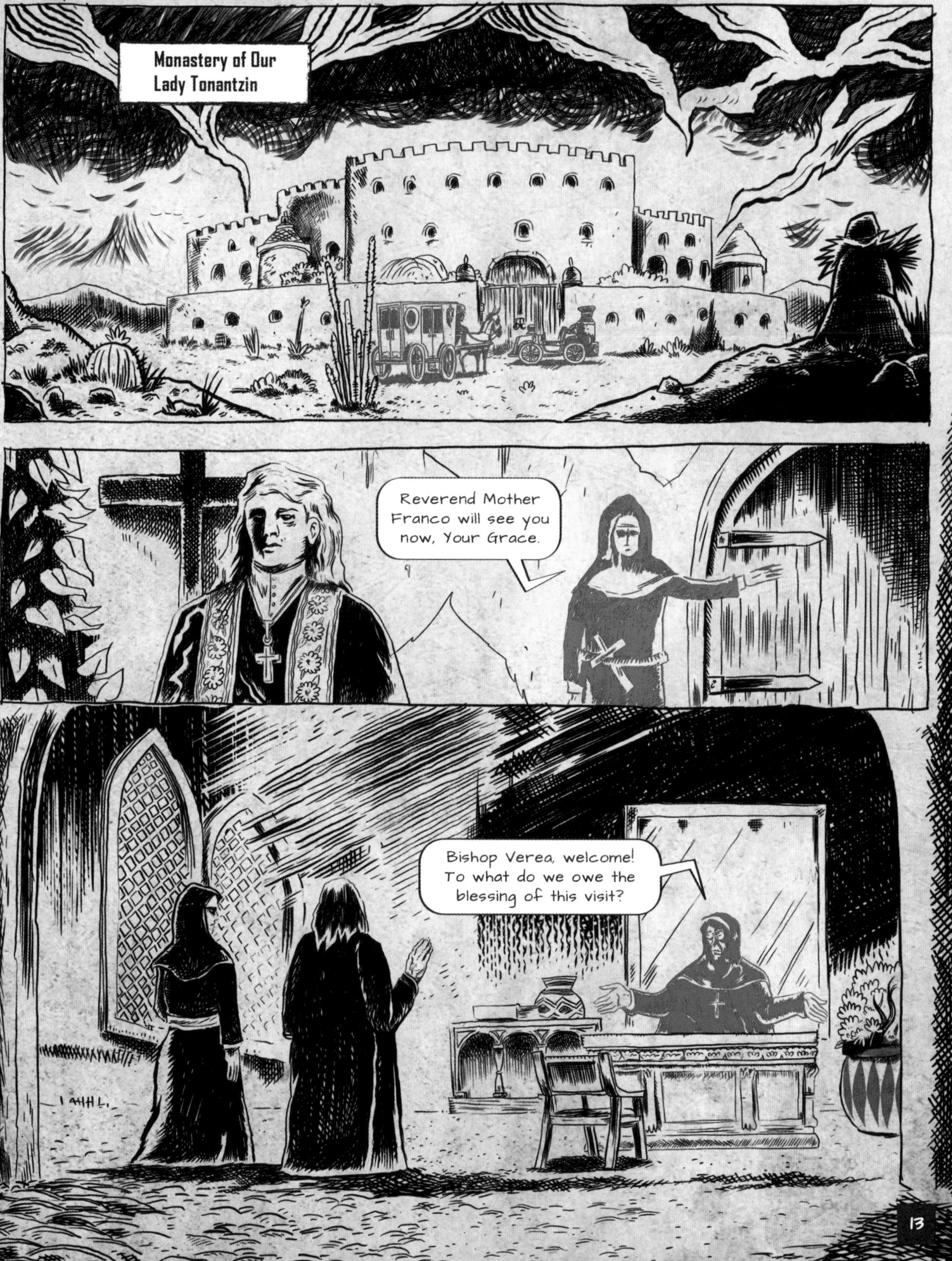
Monastery of Our Lady Tonantzin
Reverend Mother Franco will see you now, Your Grace.
Bishop Verea, welcome! To what do we owe the blessing of this visit?

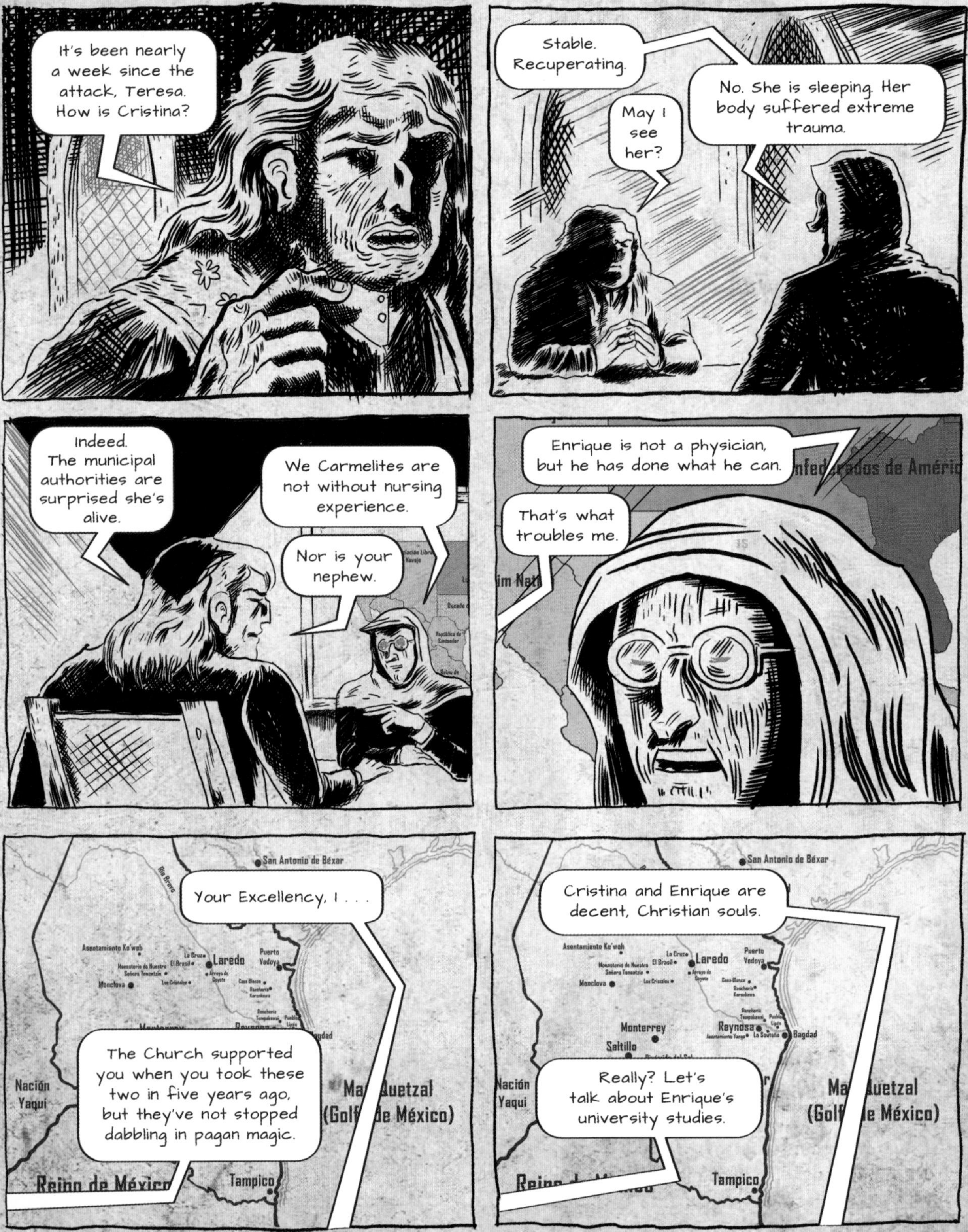
It's been nearly a week since the attack, Teresa. How is Cristina?
Stable. Recuperating.
May I see her?
No. She is sleeping. Her body suffered extreme trauma.
Indeed. The municipal authorities are surprised she's alive.
We Carmelites are not without nursing experience.
Nor is your nephew.
Enrique is not a physician, but he has done what he can.
That's what troubles me.
San Antonio de Béxar
Laredo
Monclova
Nación Yaqui
Tampico
Your Excellency, I . . .
The Church supported you when you took these two in five years ago, but they've not stopped dabbling in pagan magic.
Monterrey
Saltillo
Reynosa
Bagdad
Cristina and Enrique are decent, Christian souls.
Really? Let's talk about Enrique's university studies.

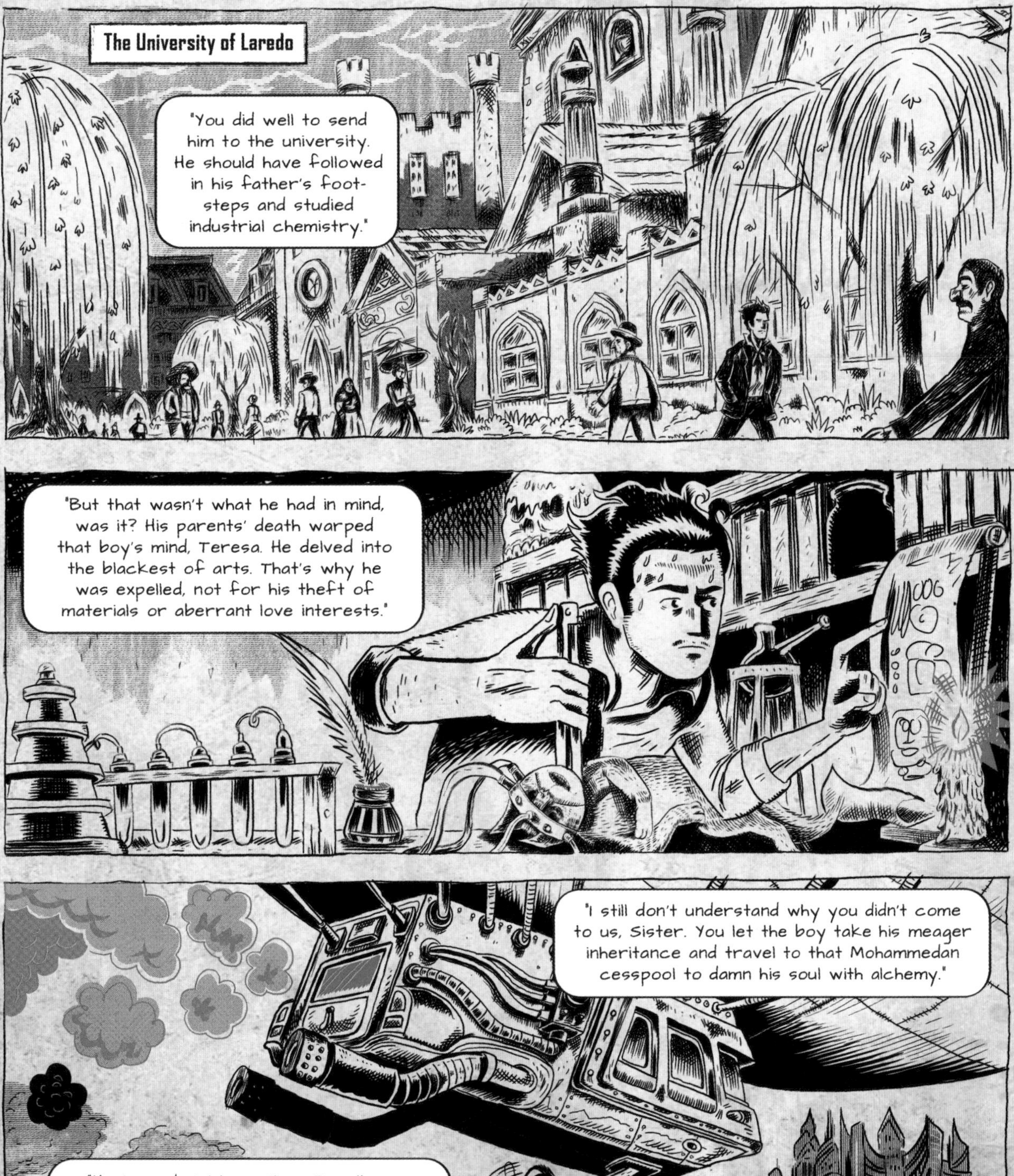
The University of Laredo
"You did well to send him to the university. He should have followed in his father's foot-steps and studied industrial chemistry."
"But that wasn't what he had in mind, was it? His parents' death warped that boy's mind, Teresa. He delved into the blackest of arts. That's why he was expelled, not for his theft of materials or aberrant love interests."
"I still don't understand why you didn't come to us, Sister. You let the boy take his meager inheritance and travel to that Mohammedan cesspool to damn his soul with alchemy."
"He turned eighteen, Your Excellency, legally entitled to claim his funds and go. And Mayurqa is one of the most tolerant, enlightened nations on earth."
The Taifa of Mayurqa

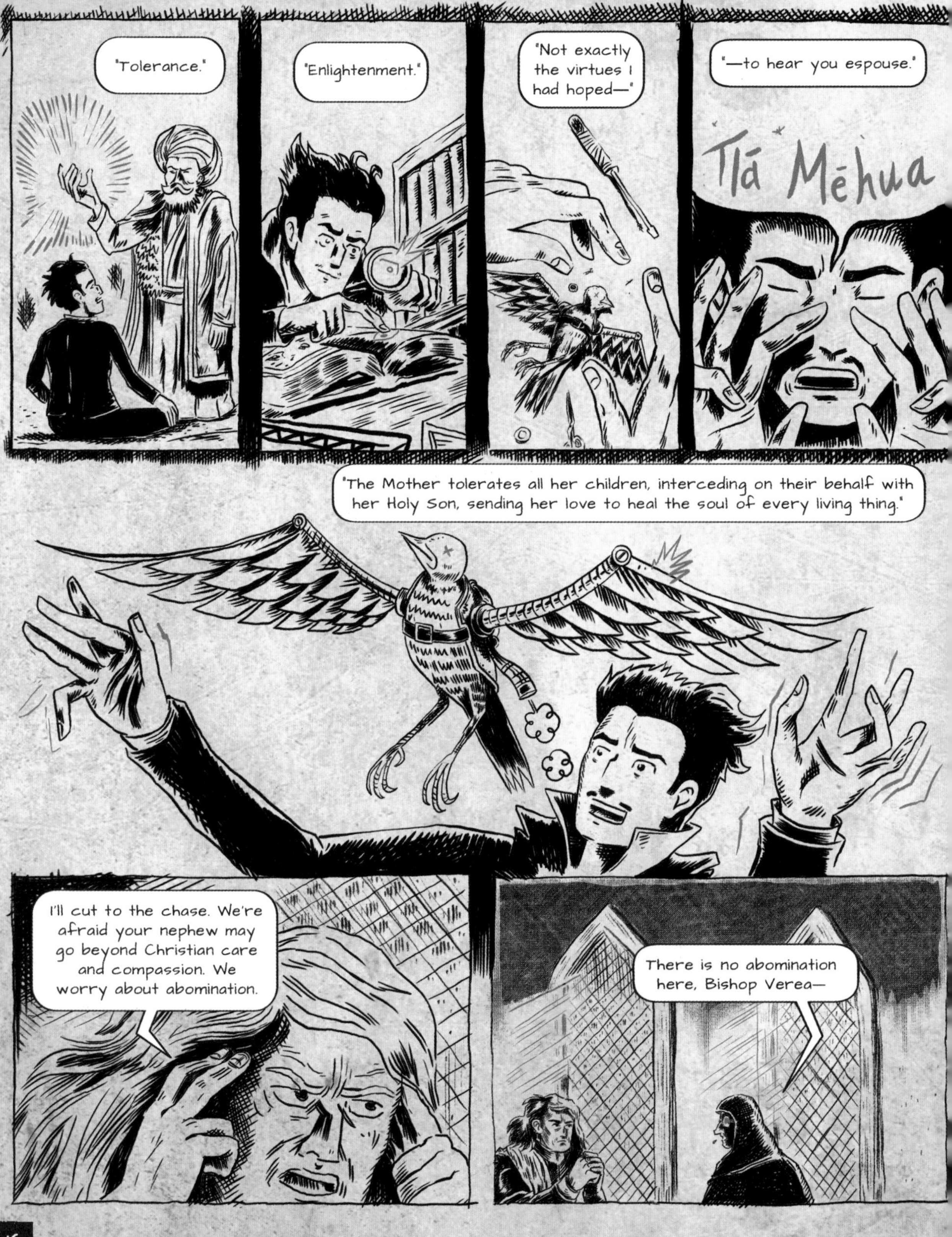
"Tolerance."
"Enlightenment."
"Not exactly the virtues I had hoped—"
"—to hear you espouse."
Tlā Mēhua
"The Mother tolerates all her children, interceding on their behalf with her Holy Son, sending her love to heal the soul of every living thing."
I'll cut to the chase. We're afraid your nephew may go beyond Christian care and compassion. We worry about abomination.
There is no abomination here, Bishop Verea—

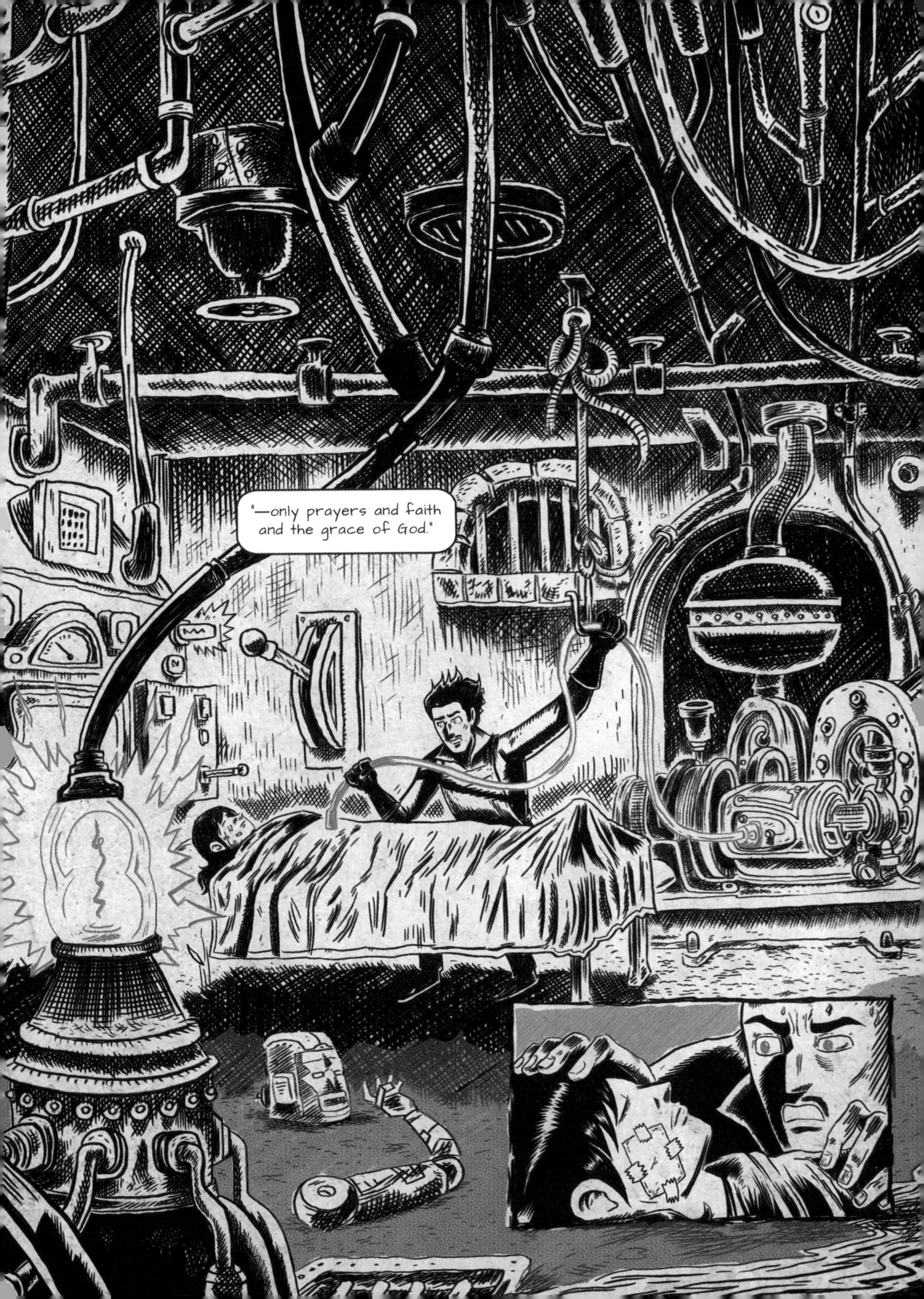
"—only prayers and faith and the grace of God."

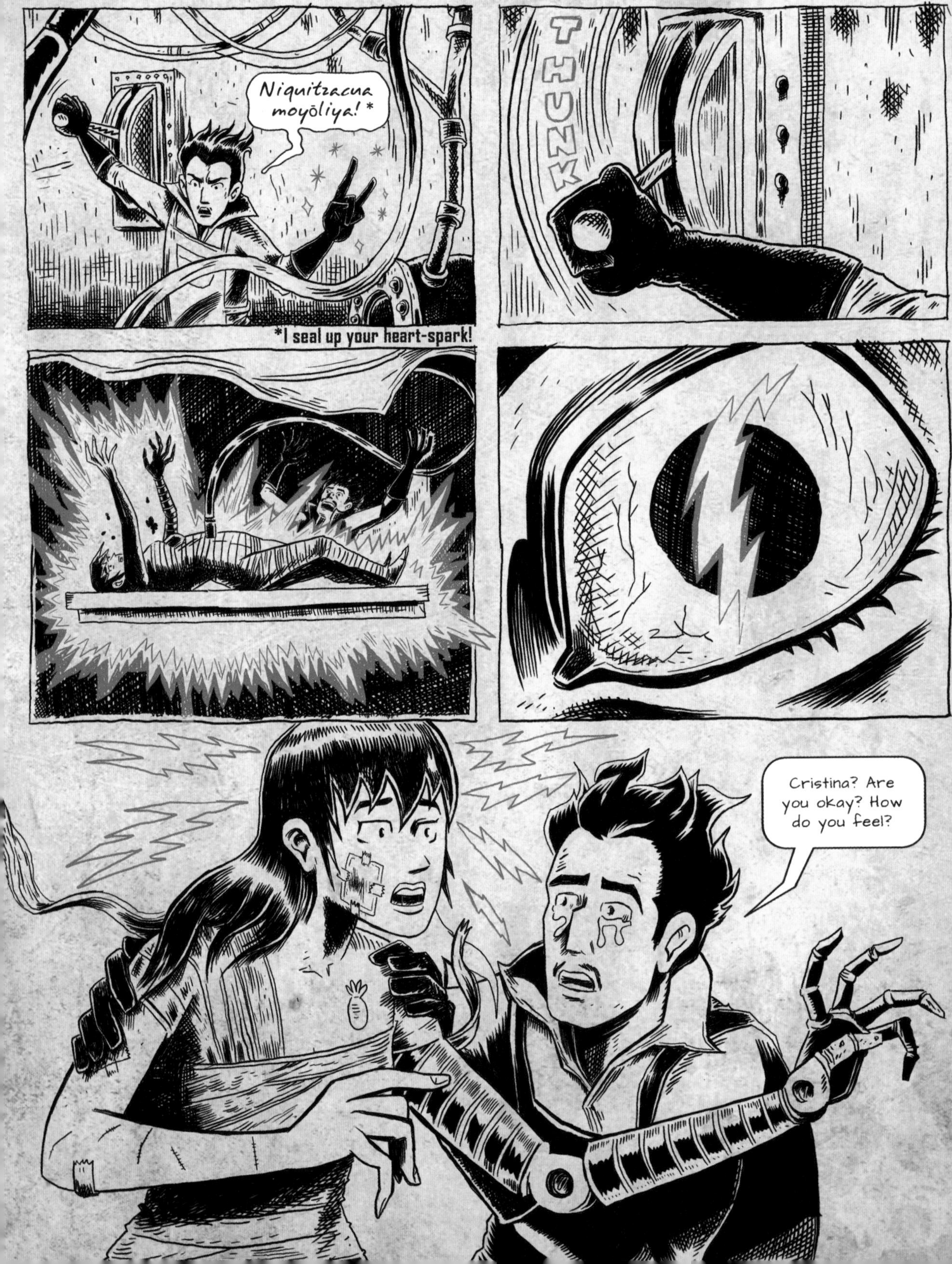
Niquitzacua moyōliya!*
*I seal up your heart-spark!
THUNK
Cristina? Are you okay? How do you feel?

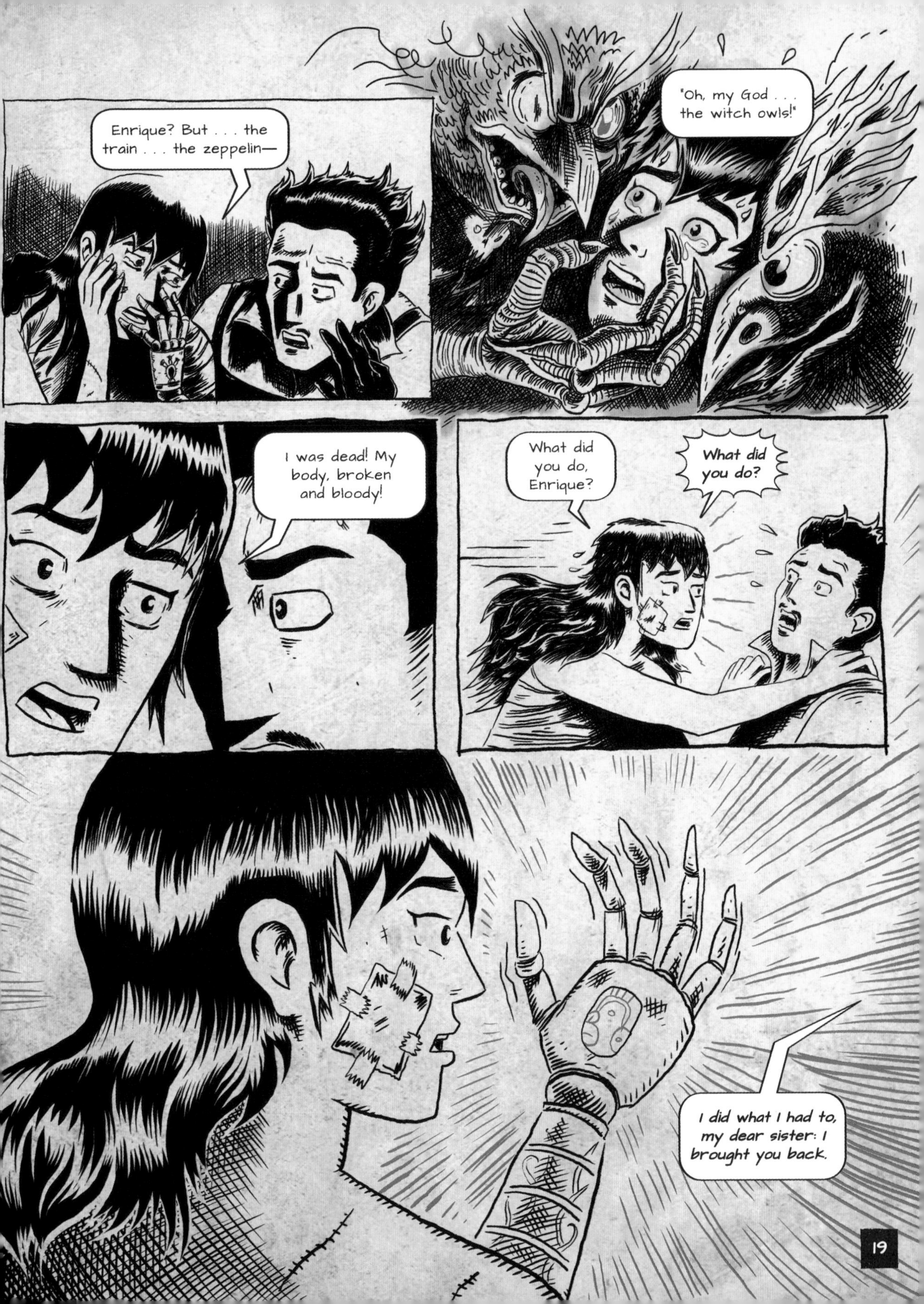
Enrique? But . . . the train . . . the zeppelin—
"Oh, my God . . . the witch owls!"
I was dead! My body, broken and bloody!
What did you do, Enrique?
What did you do?
I did what I had to, my dear sister: I brought you back.

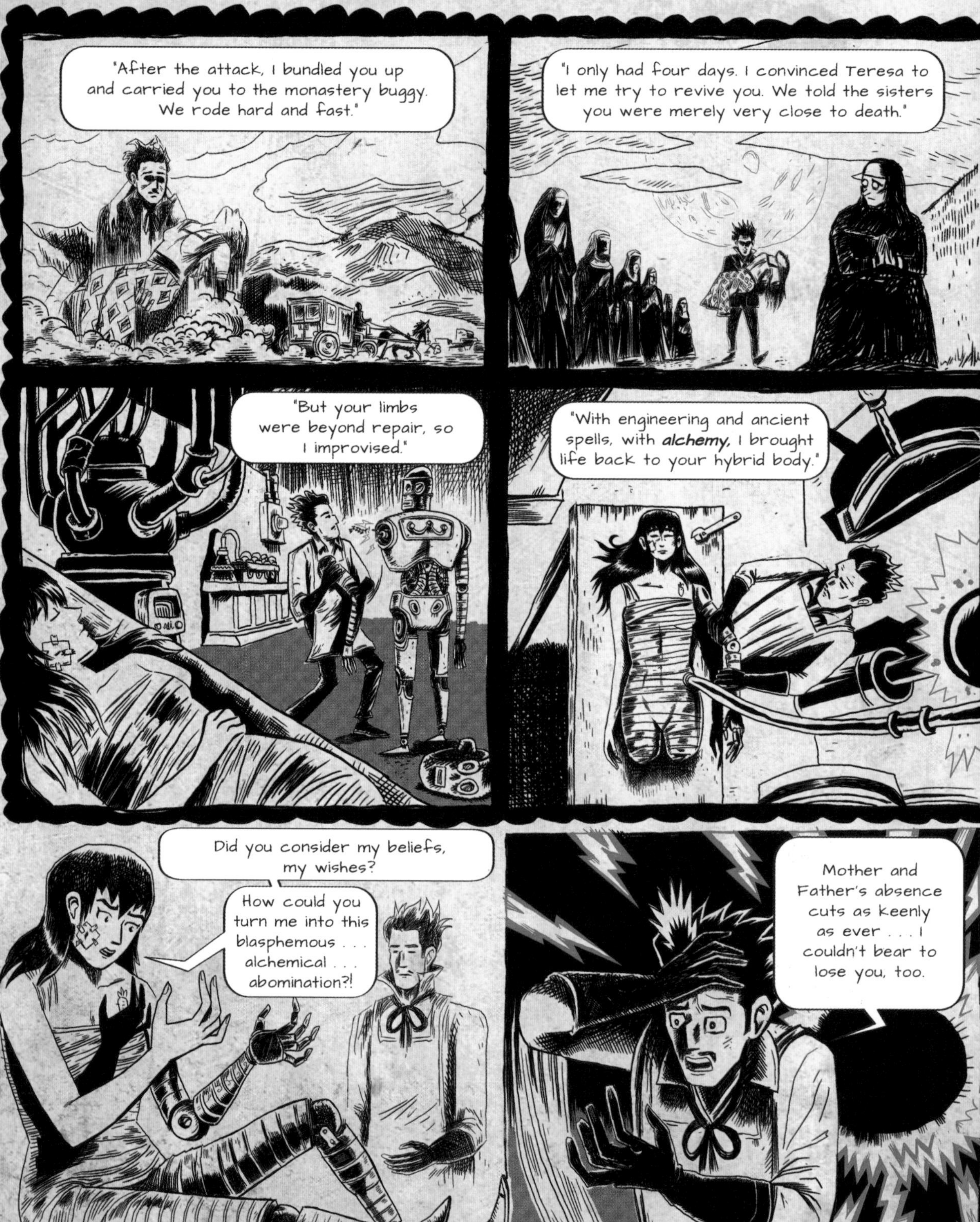
"After the attack, I bundled you up and carried you to the monastery buggy. We rode hard and fast."
"I only had four days. I convinced Teresa to let me try to revive you. We told the sisters you were merely very close to death."
"But your limbs were beyond repair, so I improvised."
"With engineering and ancient spells, with alchemy, I brought life back to your hybrid body."
Did you consider my beliefs, my wishes?
How could you turn me into this blasphemous . . . alchemical . . . abomination?!
Mother and Father's absence cuts as keenly as ever . . . I couldn't bear to lose you, too.

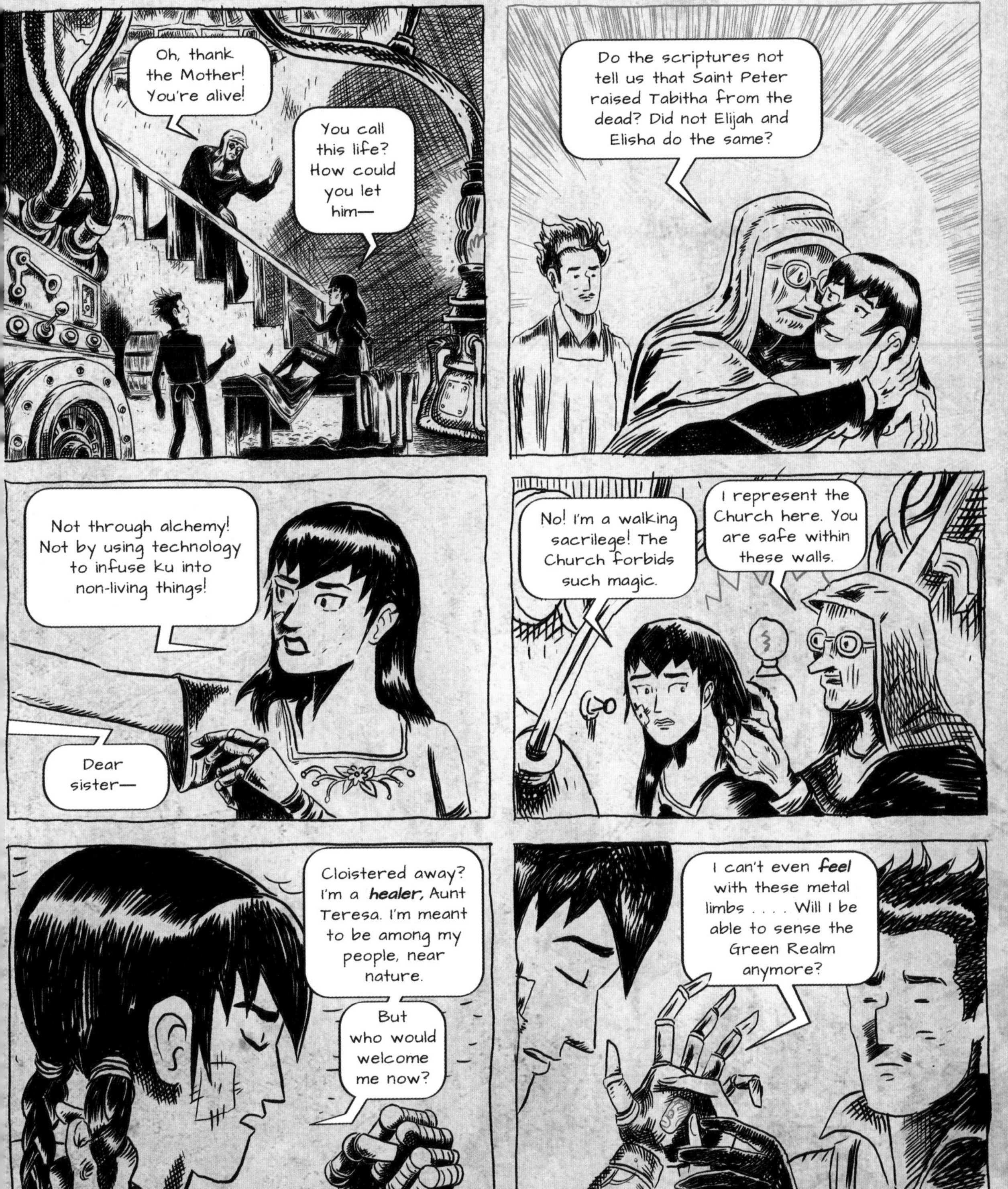
Oh, thank the Mother! You're alive!
You call this life? How could you let him—
Do the scriptures not tell us that Saint Peter raised Tabitha from the dead? Did not Elijah and Elisha do the same?
Not through alchemy! Not by using technology to infuse ku into non-living things!
Dear sister—
No! I'm a walking sacrilege! The Church forbids such magic.
I represent the Church here. You are safe within these walls.
Cloistered away? I'm a ***healer,*** Aunt Teresa. I'm meant to be among my people, near nature.
But who would welcome me now?
I can't even ***feel*** with these metal limbs . . . . Will I be able to sense the Green Realm anymore?

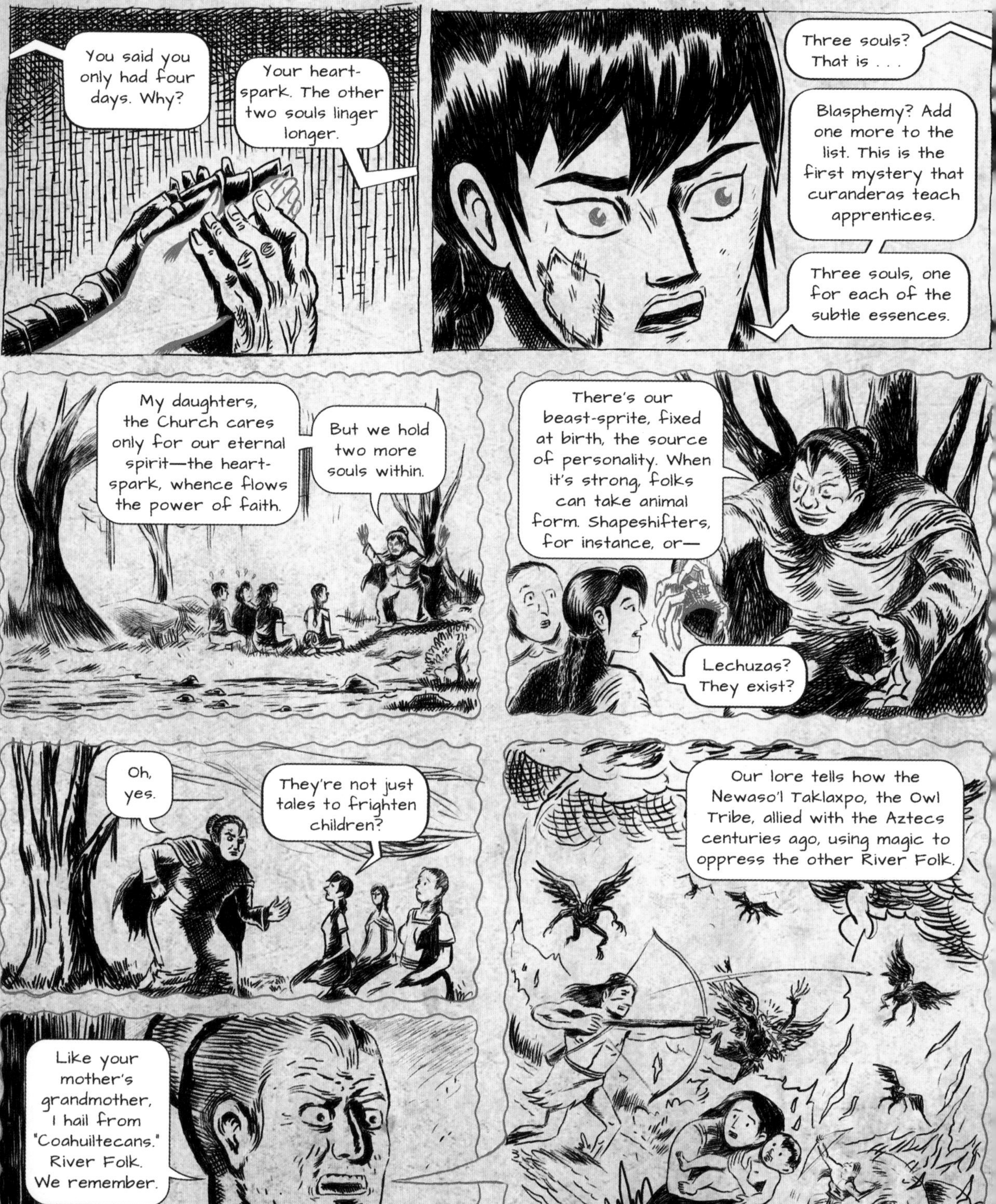
You said you only had four days. Why?
Your heart-spark. The other two souls linger longer.
Three souls? That is . . .
Blasphemy? Add one more to the list. This is the first mystery that curanderas teach apprentices.
Three souls, one for each of the subtle essences.
My daughters, the Church cares only for our eternal spirit—the heart-spark, whence flows the power of faith.
But we hold two more souls within.
There's our beast-sprite, fixed at birth, the source of personality. When it's strong, folks can take animal form. Shapeshifters, for instance, or—
Lechuzas? They exist?
Oh, yes.
They're not just tales to frighten children?
Like your mother's grandmother, I hail from "Coahuiltecans." River Folk. We remember.
Our lore tells how the Newaso'l Taklaxpo, the Owl Tribe, allied with the Aztecs centuries ago, using magic to oppress the other River Folk.

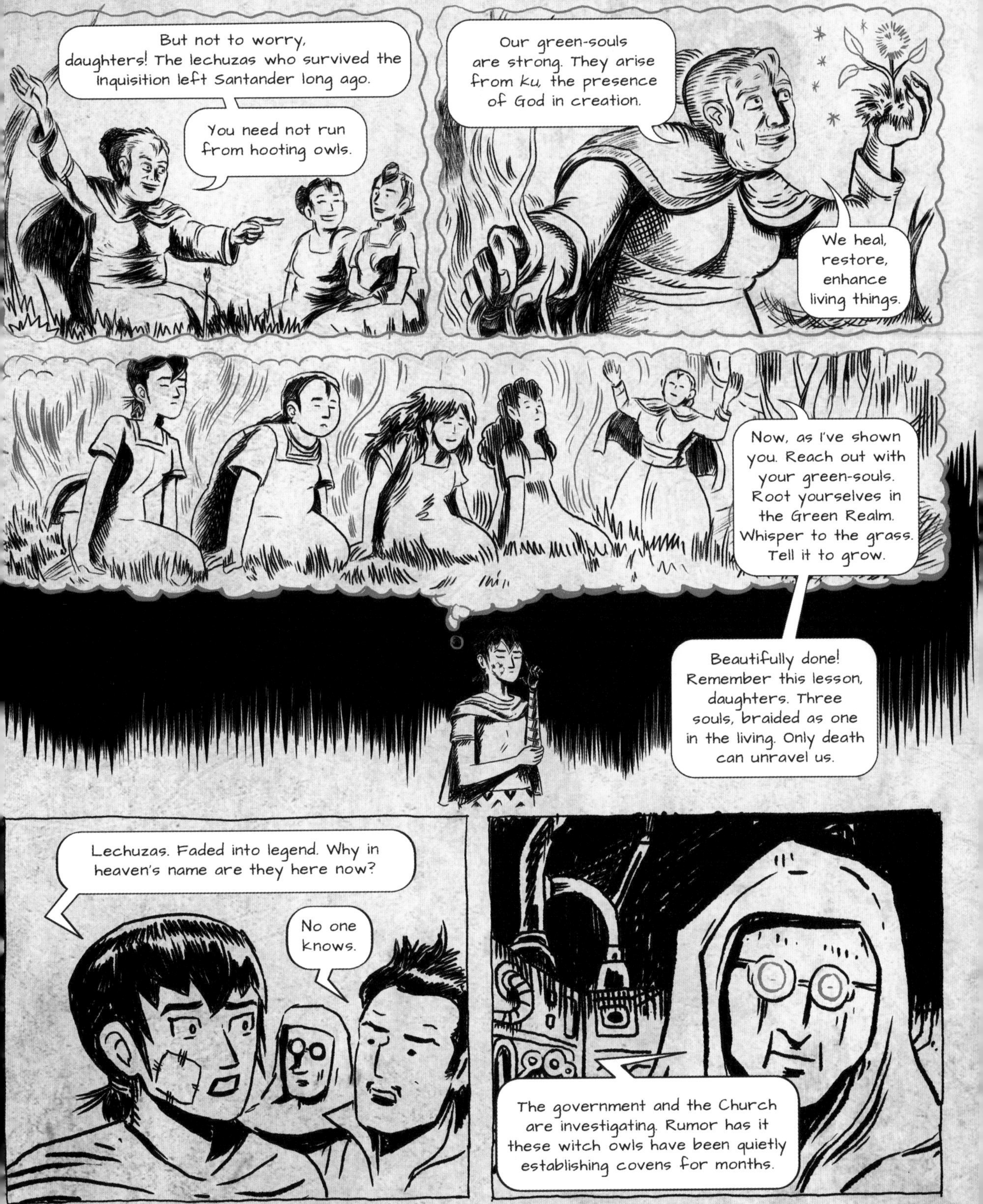
But not to worry, daughters! The lechuzas who survived the Inquisition left Santander long ago.
You need not run from hooting owls.
Our green-souls are strong. They arise from ku, the presence of God in creation.
We heal, restore, enhance living things.
Now, as I've shown you. Reach out with your green-souls. Root yourselves in the Green Realm. Whisper to the grass. Tell it to grow.
Beautifully done! Remember this lesson, daughters. Three souls, braided as one in the living. Only death can unravel us.
Lechuzas. Faded into legend. Why in heaven's name are they here now?
No one knows.
The government and the Church are investigating. Rumor has it these witch owls have been quietly establishing covens for months.

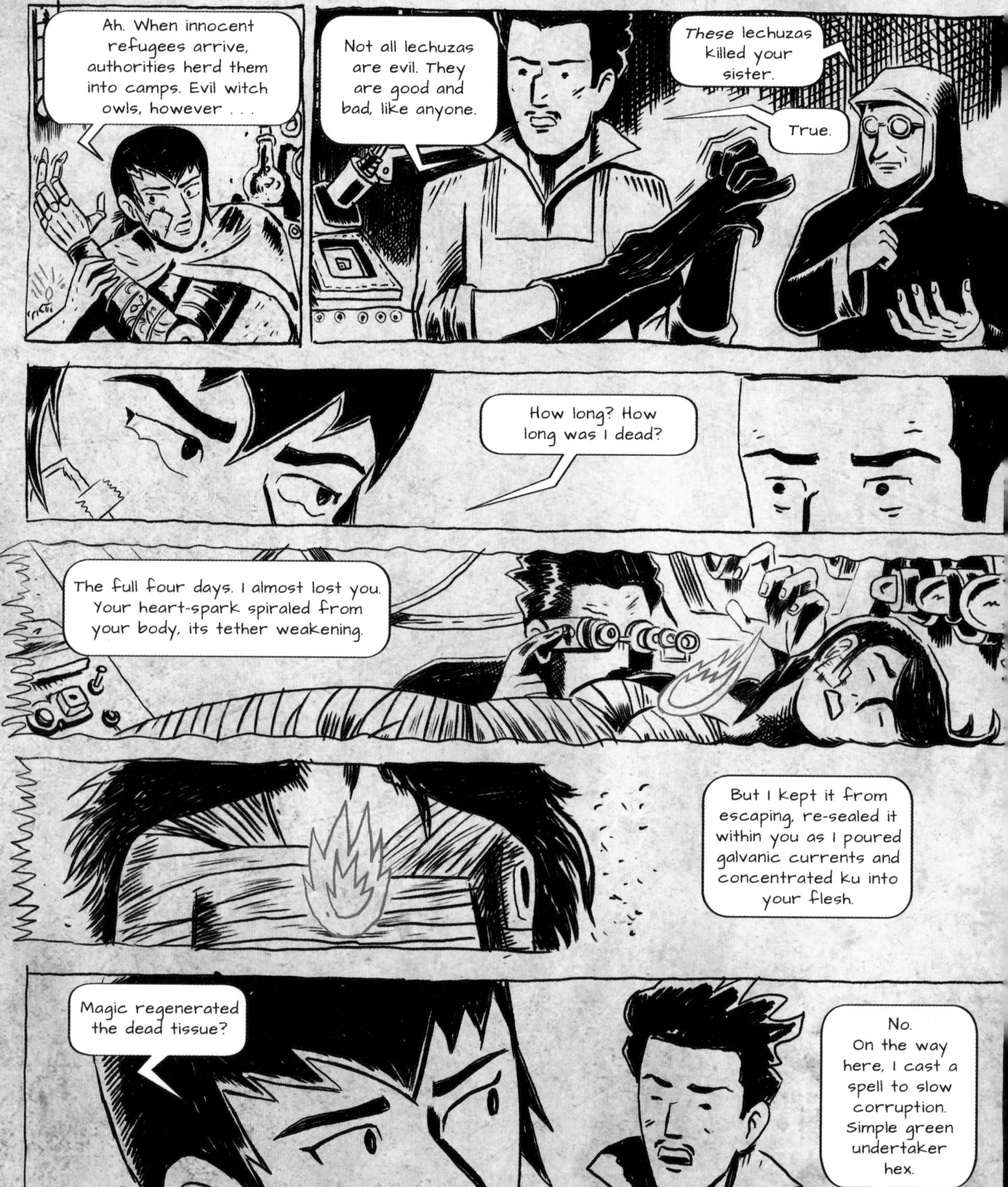
Ah. When innocent refugees arrive, authorities herd them into camps. Evil witch owls, however . . .
Not all lechuzas are evil. They are good and bad, like anyone.
These lechuzas killed your sister.
True.
How long? How long was I dead?
The full four days. I almost lost you. Your heart-spark spiraled from your body, its tether weakening.
But I kept it from escaping, re-sealed it within you as I poured galvanic currents and concentrated ku into your flesh.
Magic regenerated the dead tissue?
No. On the way here, I cast a spell to slow corruption. Simple green undertaker hex.

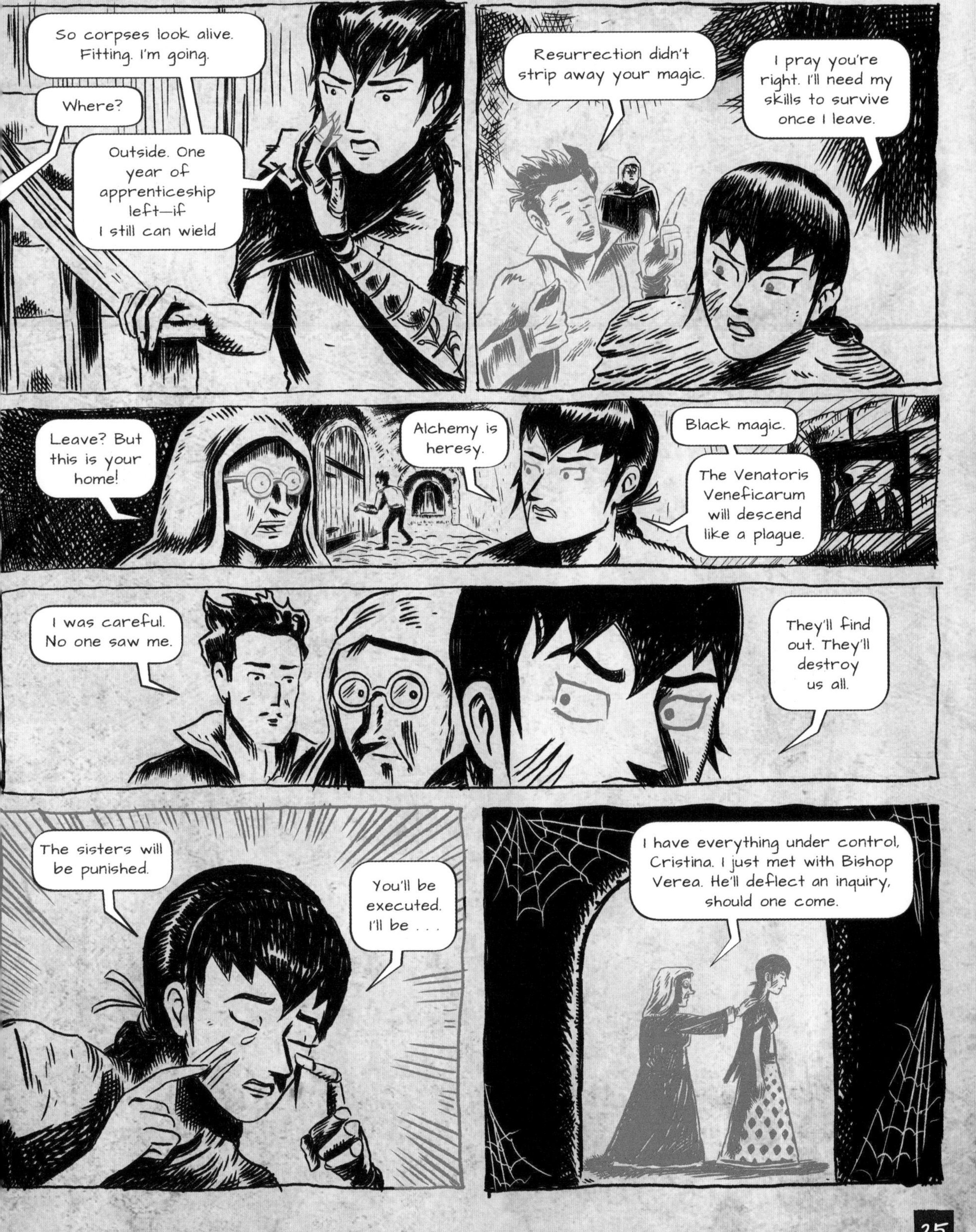

So corpses look alive. Fitting. I'm going.
Where?
Outside. One year of apprenticeship left—if I still can wield
Resurrection didn't strip away your magic.
I pray you're right. I'll need my skills to survive once I leave.
Leave? But this is your home!
Alchemy is heresy.
Black magic.
The Venatoris Veneficarum will descend like a plague.
I was careful. No one saw me.
They'll find out. They'll destroy us all.
The sisters will be punished.
You'll be executed. I'll be . . .
I have everything under control, Cristina. I just met with Bishop Verea. He'll deflect an inquiry, should one come.

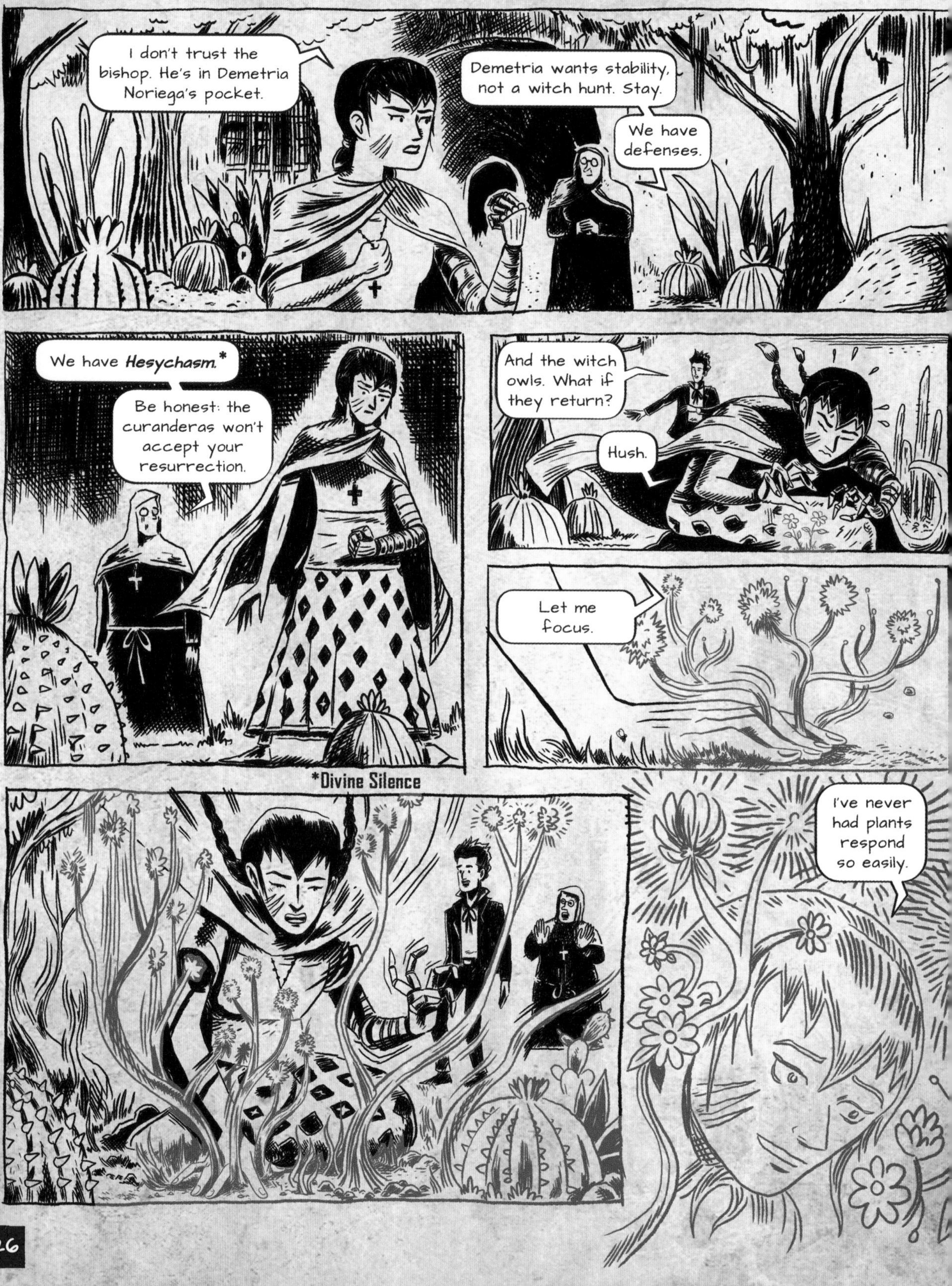
I don't trust the bishop. He's in Demetria Noriega's pocket.
Demetria wants stability, not a witch hunt. Stay.
We have defenses.
We have **Hesychasm.***
Be honest: the curanderas won't accept your resurrection.
*Divine Silence
And the witch owls. What if they return?
Hush.
Let me focus.
I've never had plants respond so easily.

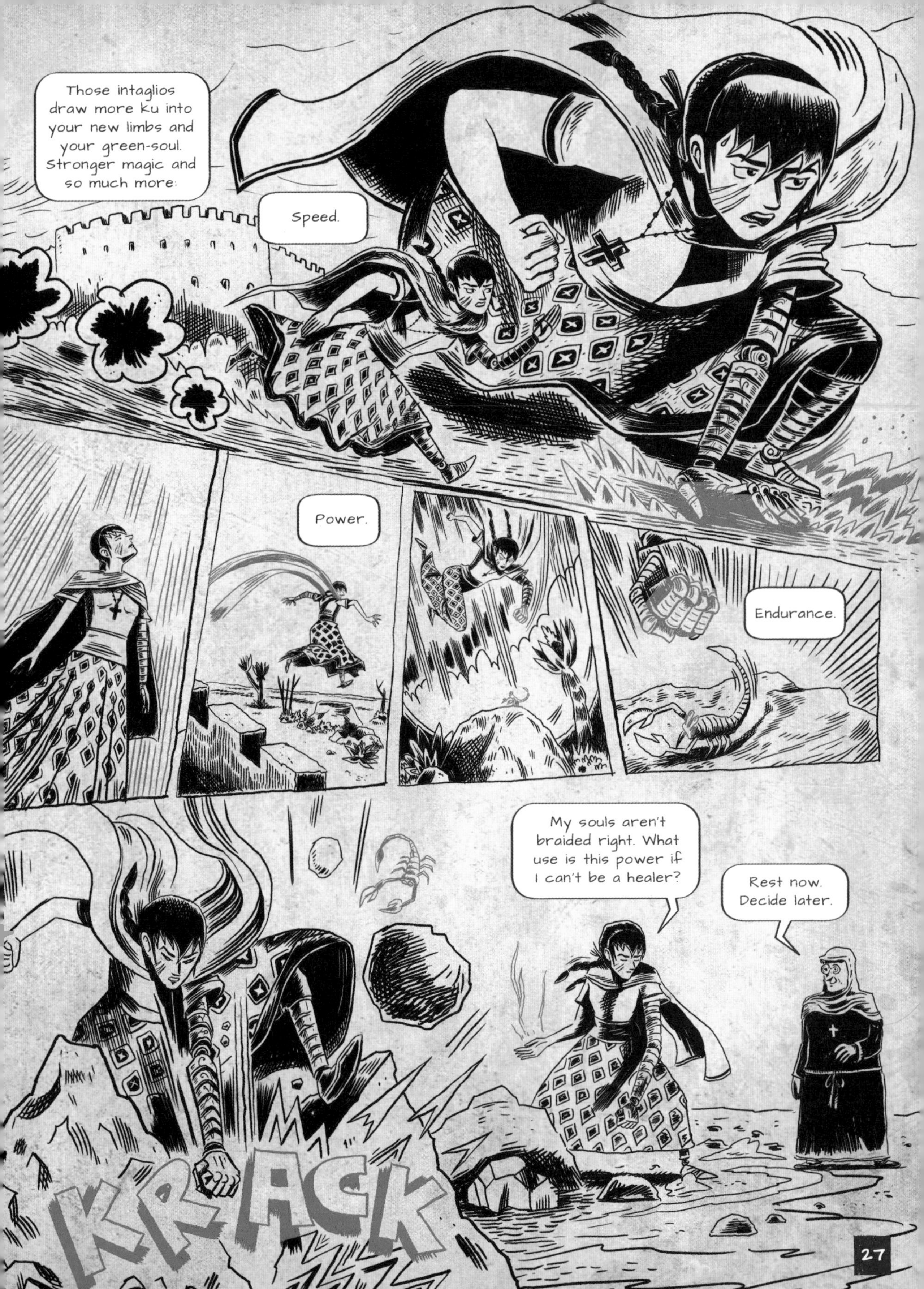

Those intaglios draw more ku into your new limbs and your green-soul. Stronger magic and so much more:
Speed.
Power.
Endurance.
KRACK
My souls aren't braided right. What use is this power if I can't be a healer?
Rest now. Decide later.

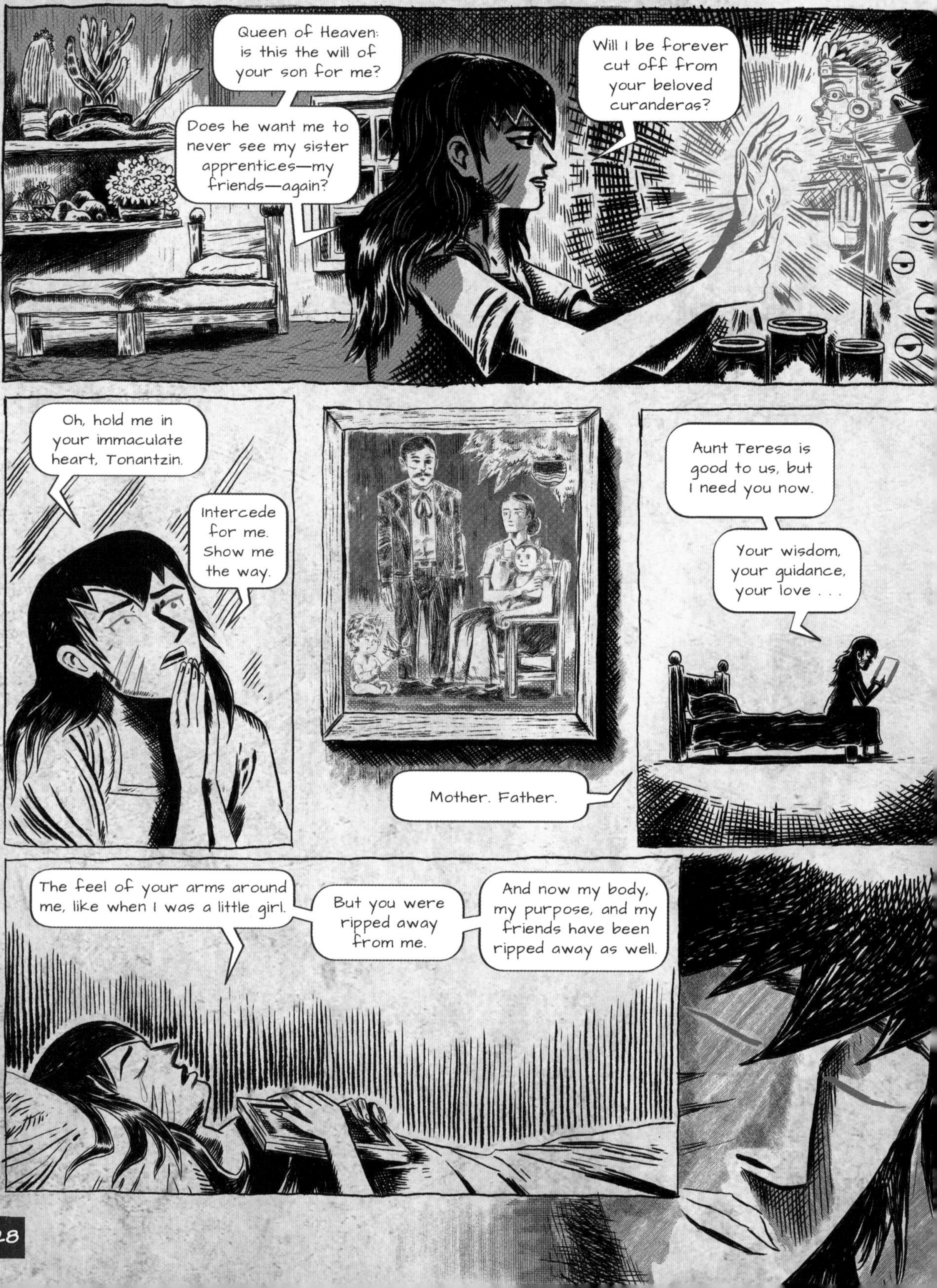

Queen of Heaven: is this the will of your son for me?
Does he want me to never see my sister apprentices—my friends—again?
Will I be forever cut off from your beloved curanderas?
Oh, hold me in your immaculate heart, Tonantzin.
Intercede for me. Show me the way.
Mother. Father.
Aunt Teresa is good to us, but I need you now.
Your wisdom, your guidance, your love . . .
The feel of your arms around me, like when I was a little girl.
But you were ripped away from me.
And now my body, my purpose, and my friends have been ripped away as well.

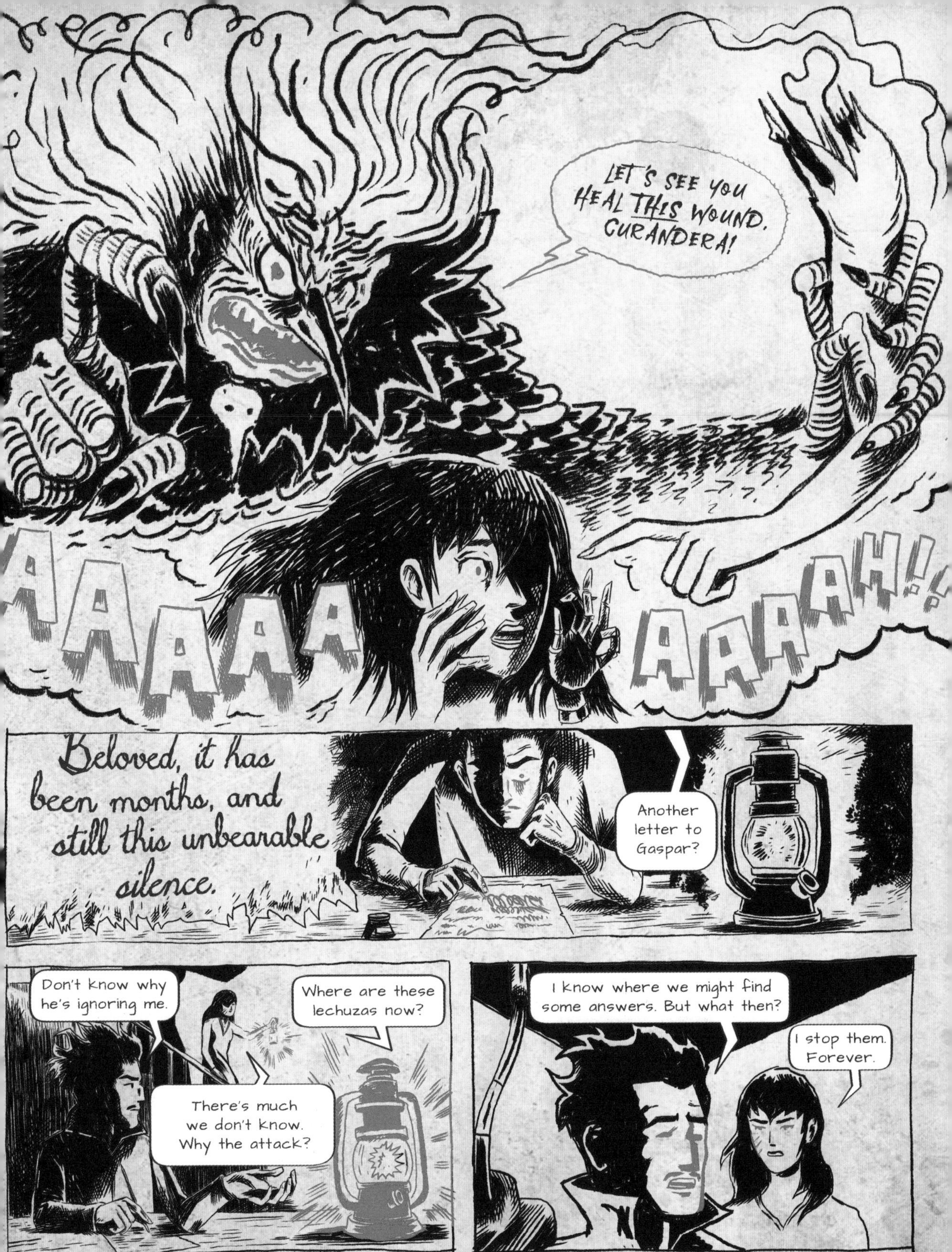

LET'S SEE YOU HEAL THIS WOUND, CURANDERA!
AAAAAAAAAH!!
Beloved, it has been months, and still this unbearable silence.
Another letter to Gaspar?
Don't know why he's ignoring me.
Where are these lechuzas now?
There's much we don't know. Why the attack?
I know where we might find some answers. But what then?
I stop them. Forever.

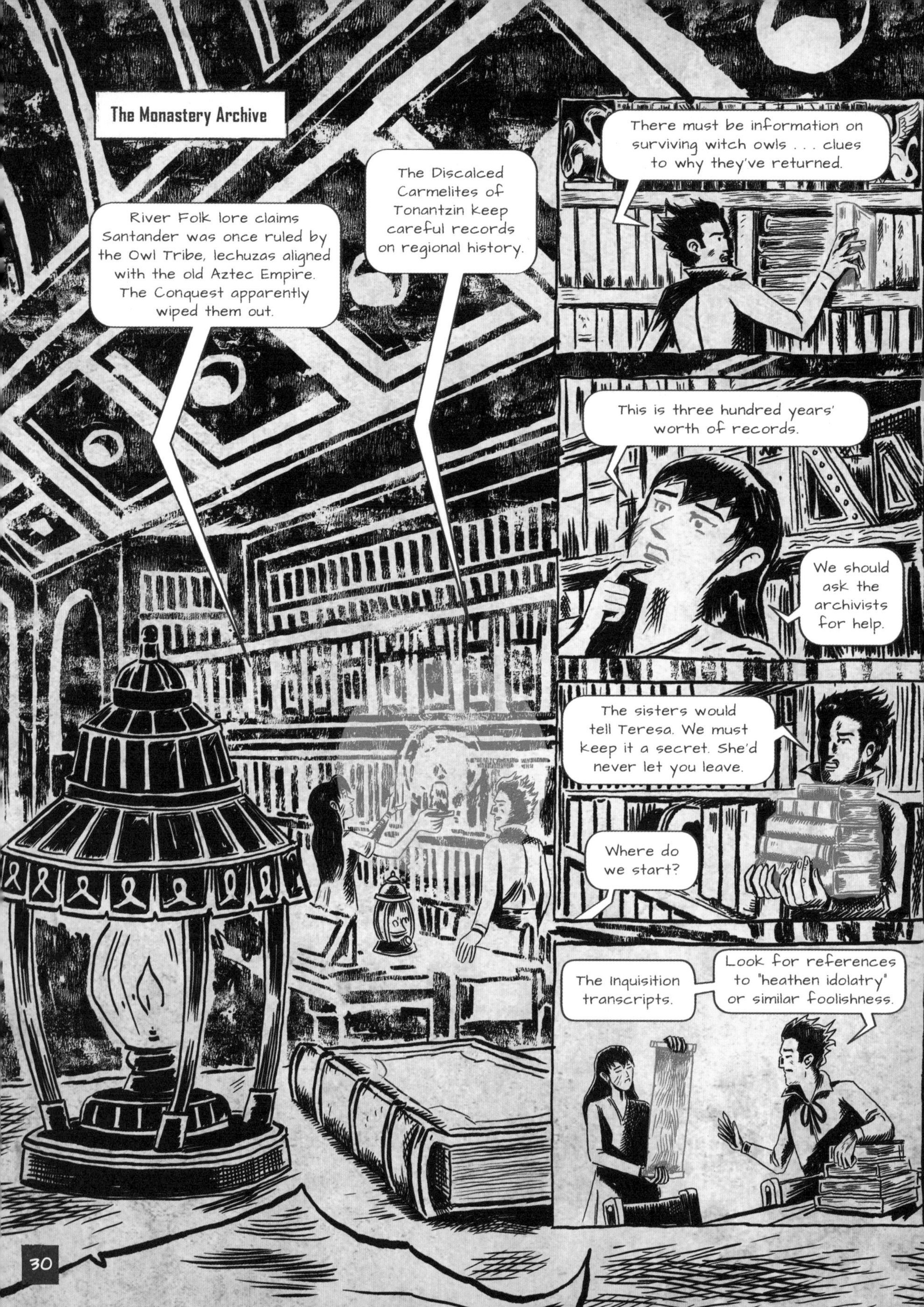
The Monastery Archive
River Folk lore claims Santander was once ruled by the Owl Tribe, lechuzas aligned with the old Aztec Empire. The Conquest apparently wiped them out.
The Discalced Carmelites of Tonantzin keep careful records on regional history.
There must be information on surviving witch owls . . . clues to why they've returned.
This is three hundred years' worth of records.
We should ask the archivists for help.
The sisters would tell Teresa. We must keep it a secret. She'd never let you leave.
Where do we start?
The Inquisition transcripts.
Look for references to "heathen idolatry" or similar foolishness.

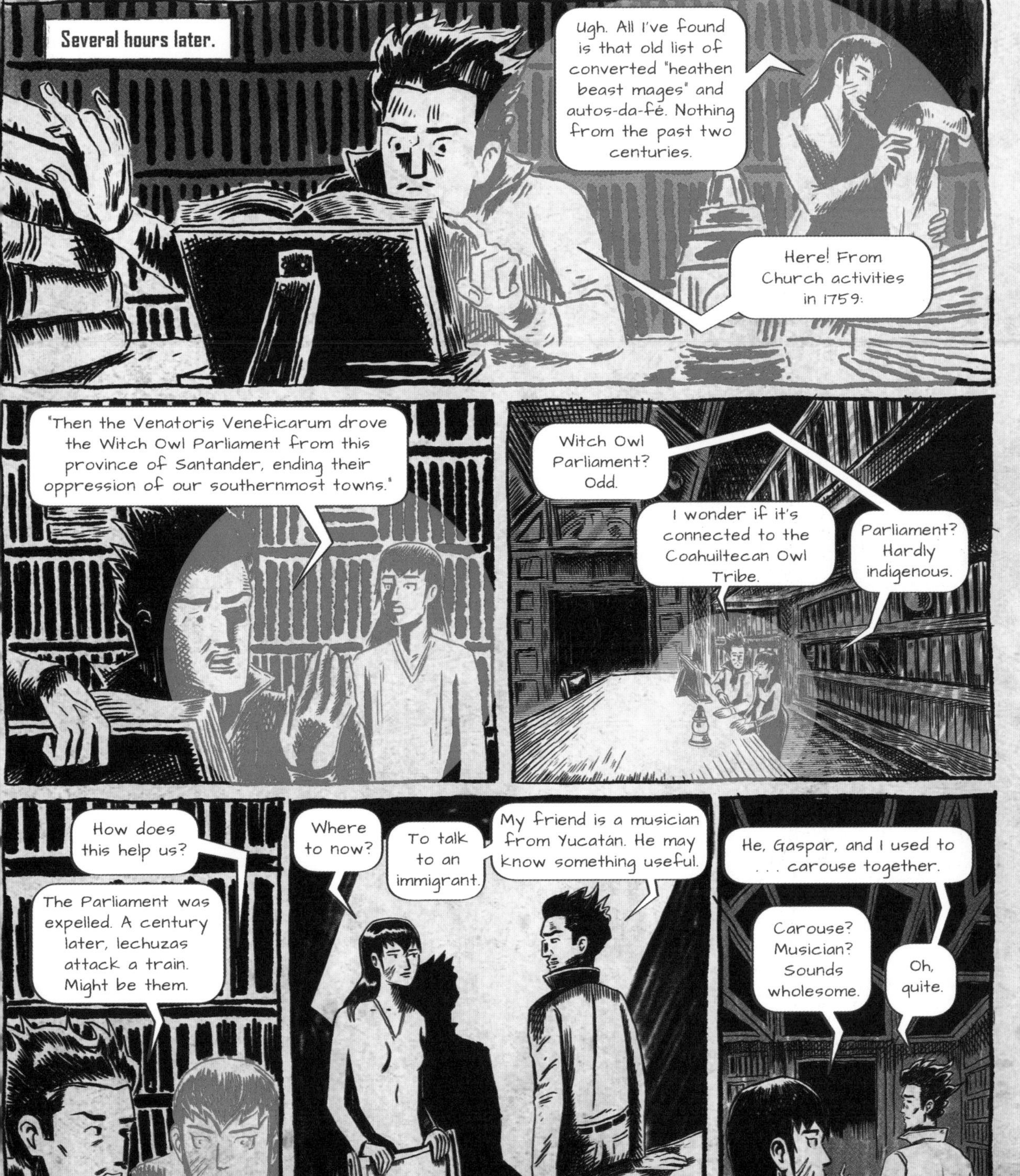

Several hours later.
Ugh. All I've found is that old list of converted "heathen beast mages" and autos-da-fé. Nothing from the past two centuries.
Here! From Church activities in 1759:
"Then the Venatoris Veneficarum drove the Witch Owl Parliament from this province of Santander, ending their oppression of our southernmost towns."
Witch Owl Parliament? Odd.
I wonder if it's connected to the Coahuiltecan Owl Tribe.
Parliament? Hardly indigenous.
How does this help us?
The Parliament was expelled. A century later, lechuzas attack a train. Might be them.
Where to now?
To talk to an immigrant.
My friend is a musician from Yucatán. He may know something useful.
He, Gaspar, and I used to . . . carouse together.
Carouse? Musician? Sounds wholesome.
Oh, quite.

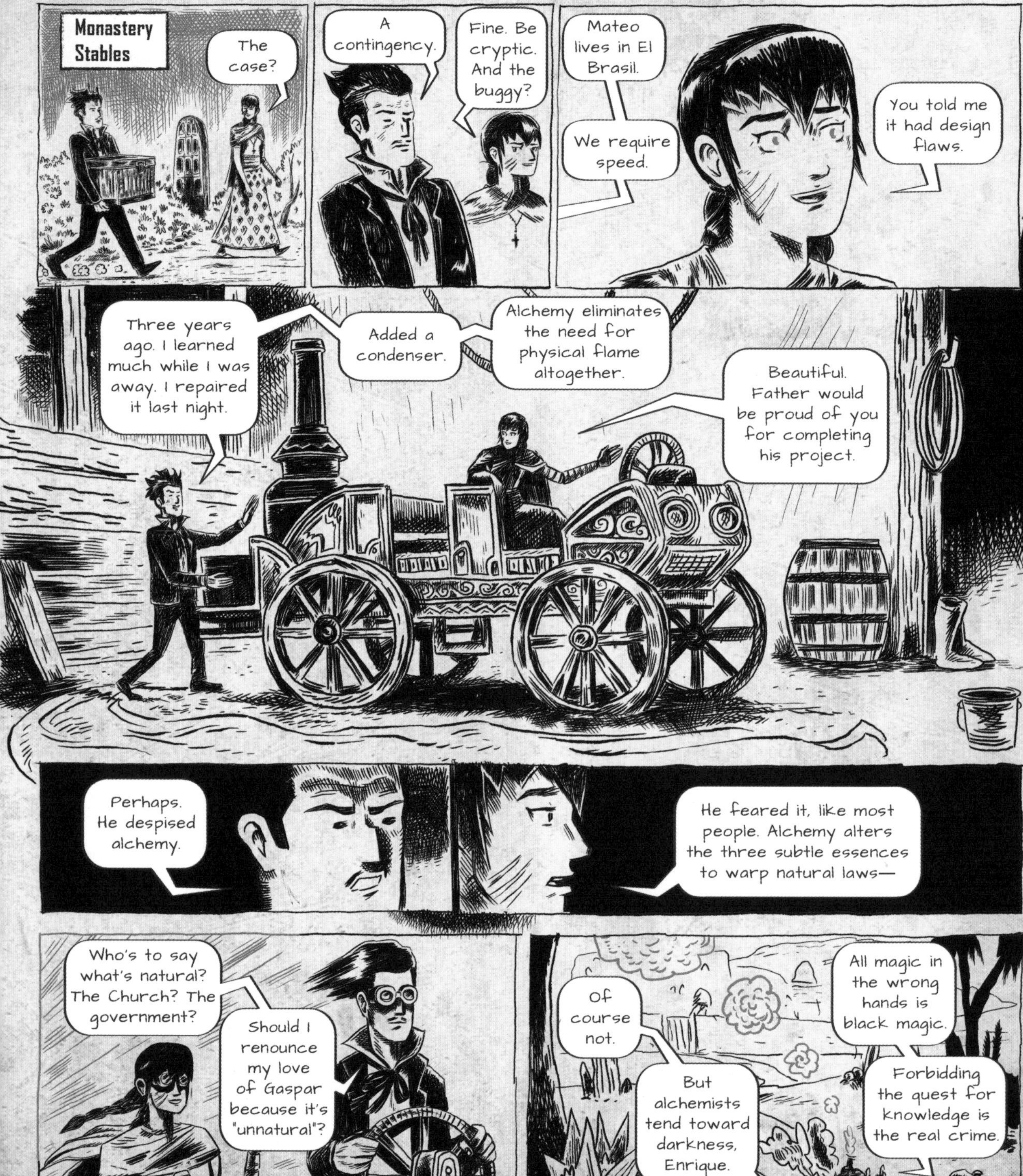

Monastery Stables
The case?
A contingency.
Fine. Be cryptic. And the buggy?
Mateo lives in El Brasil.
We require speed.
You told me it had design flaws.
Three years ago. I learned much while I was away. I repaired it last night.
Added a condenser.
Alchemy eliminates the need for physical flame altogether.
Beautiful. Father would be proud of you for completing his project.
Perhaps. He despised alchemy.
He feared it, like most people. Alchemy alters the three subtle essences to warp natural laws—
Who's to say what's natural? The Church? The government?
Should I renounce my love of Gaspar because it's "unnatural"?
Of course not.
But alchemists tend toward darkness, Enrique.
All magic in the wrong hands is black magic.
Forbidding the quest for knowledge is the real crime.

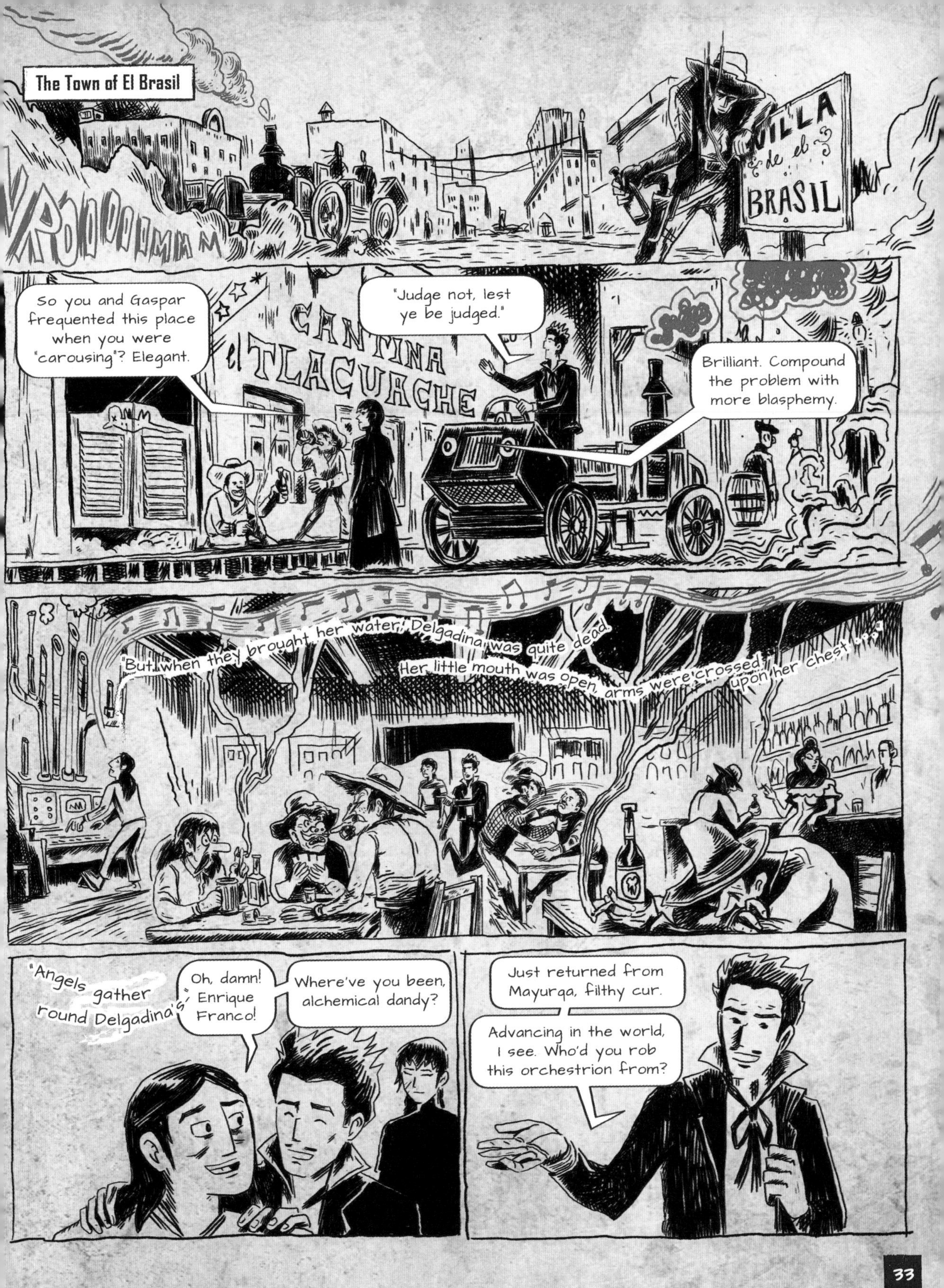
The Town of El Brasil
VROOOOOMMMM
VILLA de el BRASIL
CANTINA el TLACUACHE
So you and Gaspar frequented this place when you were "carousing"? Elegant.
"Judge not, lest ye be judged."
Brilliant. Compound the problem with more blasphemy.
"But when they brought her water, Delgadina was quite dead.
Her little mouth was open, arms were crossed . . . upon her chest . . ."
"Angels gather 'round Delgadina's"
Oh, damn! Enrique Franco!
Where've you been, alchemical dandy?
Just returned from Mayurqa, filthy cur.
Advancing in the world, I see. Who'd you rob this orchestrion from?

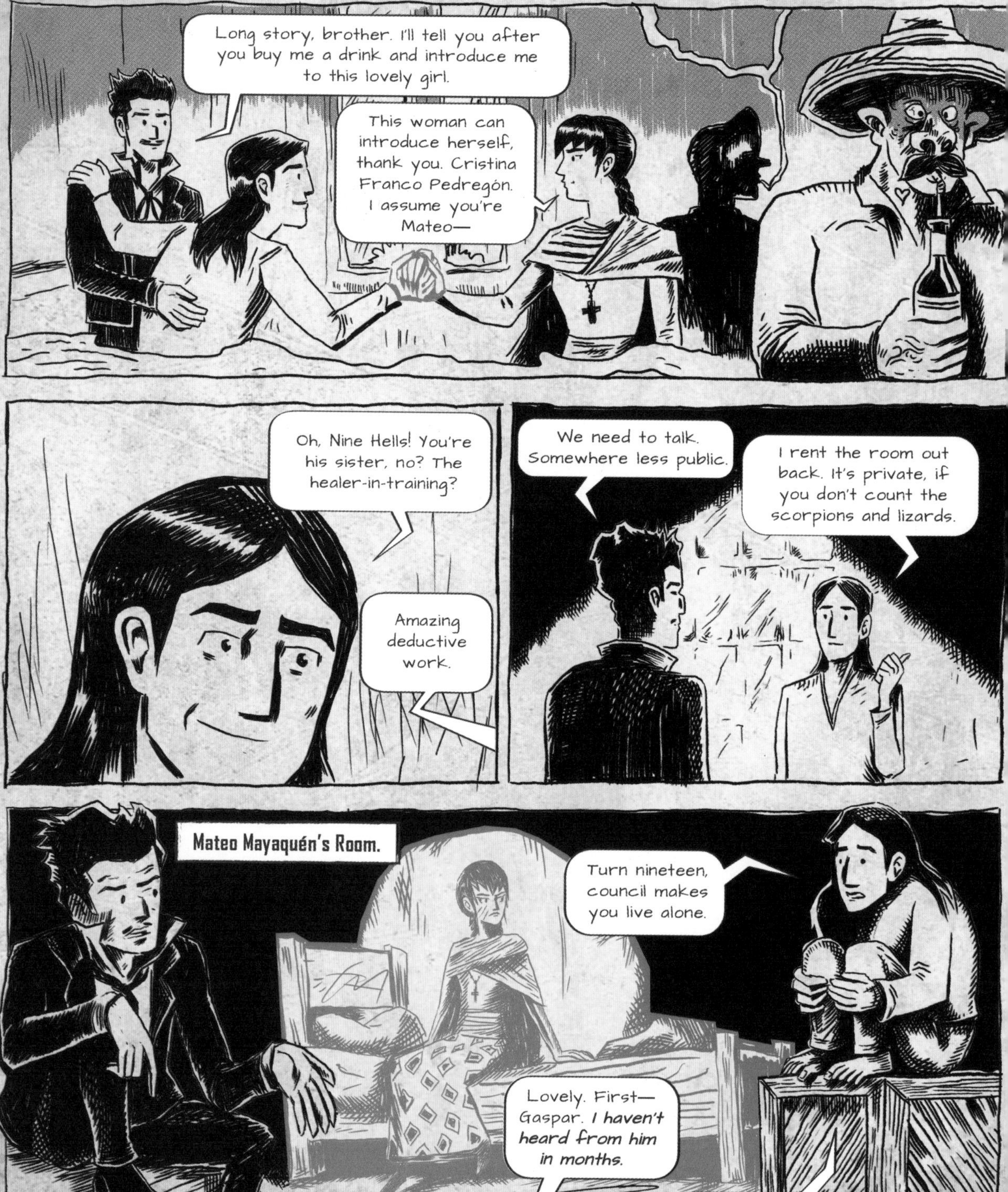
Long story, brother. I'll tell you after you buy me a drink and introduce me to this lovely girl.
This woman can introduce herself, thank you. Cristina Franco Pedregón. I assume you're Mateo—
Oh, Nine Hells! You're his sister, no? The healer-in-training?
Amazing deductive work.
We need to talk. Somewhere less public.
I rent the room out back. It's private, if you don't count the scorpions and lizards.
Mateo Mayaquén's Room.
Turn nineteen, council makes you live alone.
Lovely. First— Gaspar. *I haven't heard from him in months.*
Me neither. He's not in Laredo.

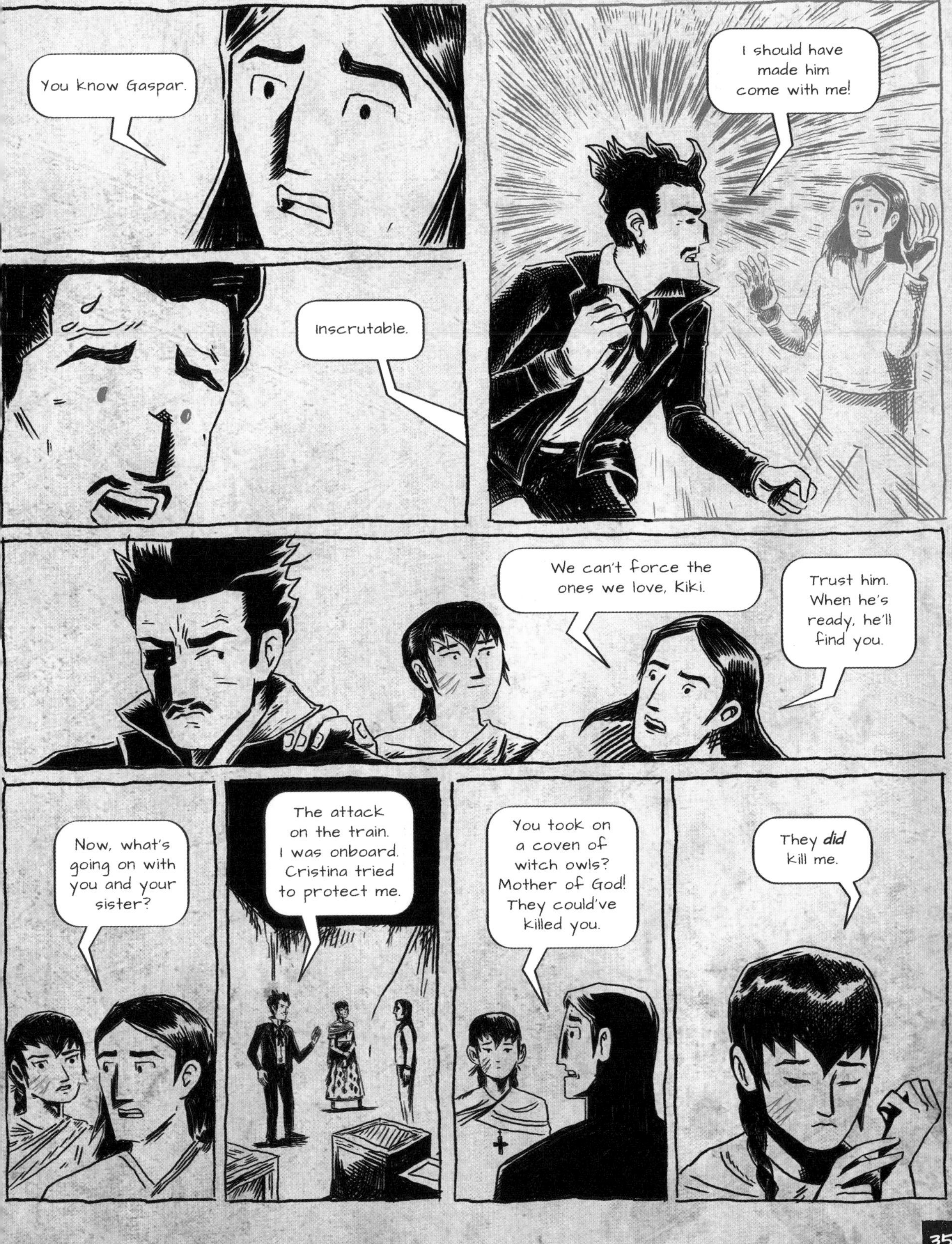
You know Gaspar.
Inscrutable.
I should have made him come with me!
We can't force the ones we love, Kiki.
Trust him. When he's ready, he'll find you.
Now, what's going on with you and your sister?
The attack on the train. I was onboard. Cristina tried to protect me.
You took on a coven of witch owls? Mother of God! They could've killed you.
They *did* kill me.

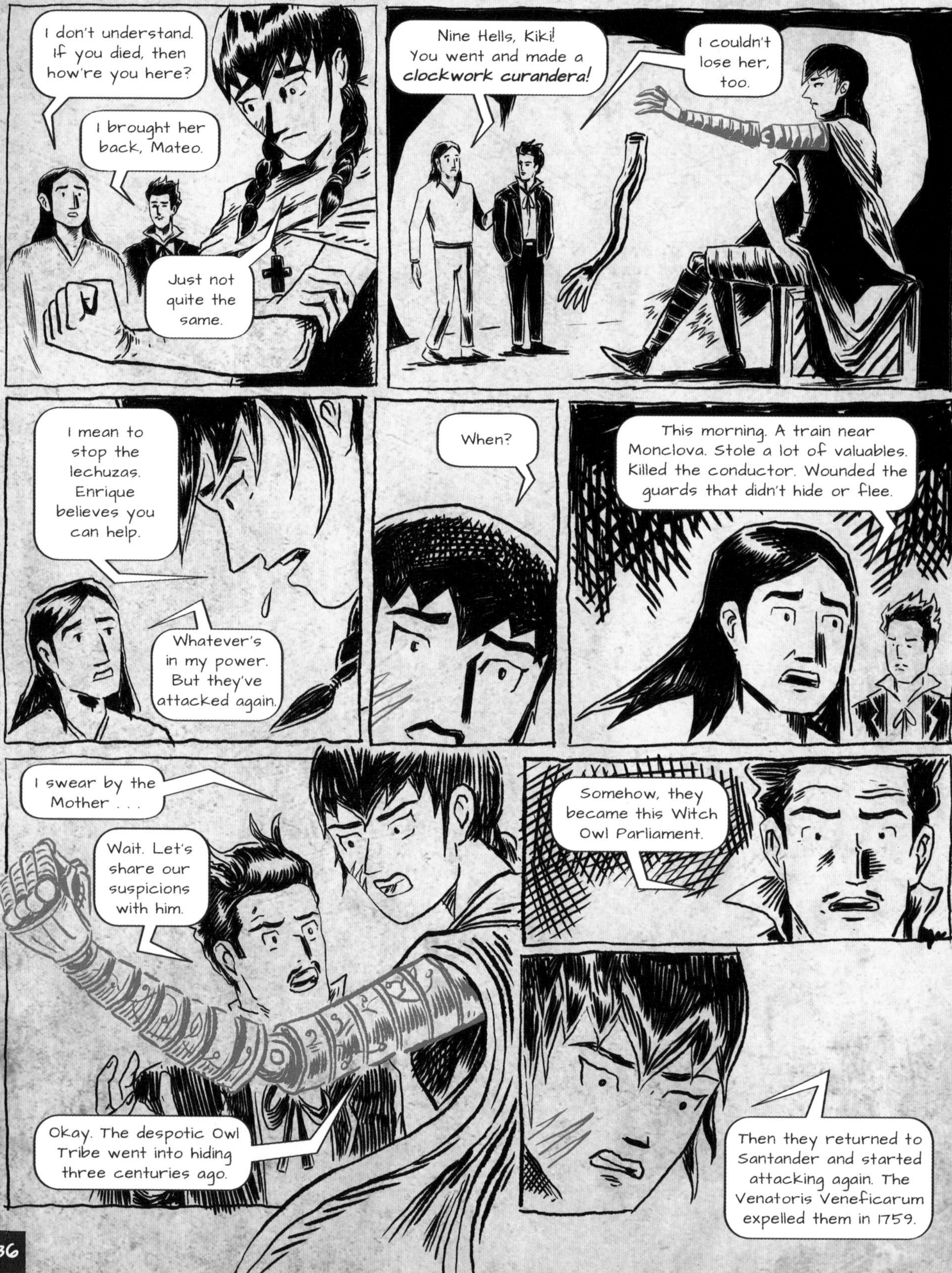
I don't understand. If you died, then how're you here?
I brought her back, Mateo.
Just not quite the same.
Nine Hells, Kiki! You went and made a **clockwork curandera!**
I couldn't lose her, too.
I mean to stop the lechuzas. Enrique believes you can help.
Whatever's in my power. But they've attacked again.
When?
This morning. A train near Monclova. Stole a lot of valuables. Killed the conductor. Wounded the guards that didn't hide or flee.
I swear by the Mother . . .
Wait. Let's share our suspicions with him.
Okay. The despotic Owl Tribe went into hiding three centuries ago.
Somehow, they became this Witch Owl Parliament.
Then they returned to Santander and started attacking again. The Venatoris Veneficarum expelled them in 1759.

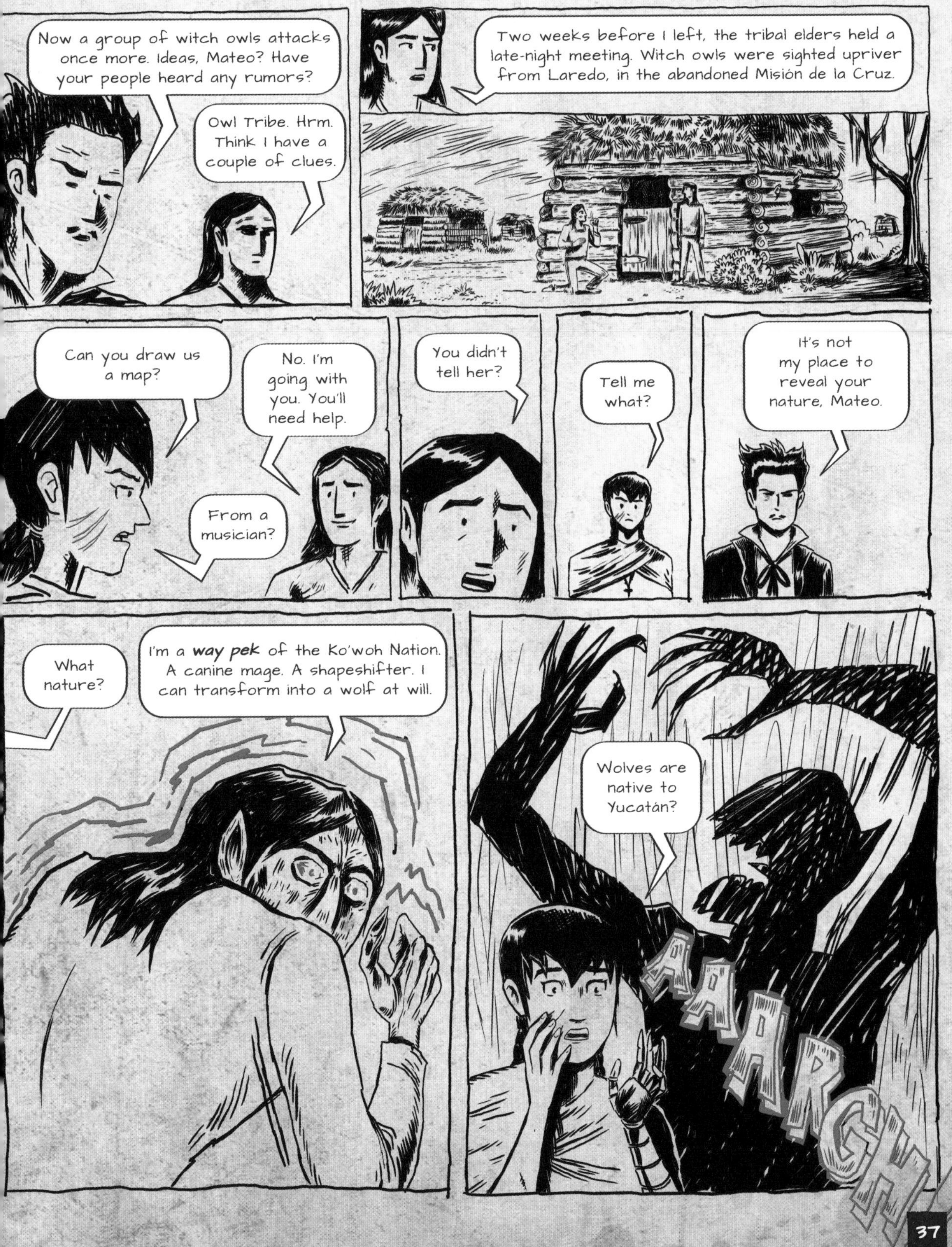
Now a group of witch owls attacks once more. Ideas, Mateo? Have your people heard any rumors?
Owl Tribe. Hrm. Think I have a couple of clues.
Two weeks before I left, the tribal elders held a late-night meeting. Witch owls were sighted upriver from Laredo, in the abandoned Misión de la Cruz.
Can you draw us a map?
No. I'm going with you. You'll need help.
From a musician?
You didn't tell her?
Tell me what?
It's not my place to reveal your nature, Mateo.
What nature?
I'm a **way pek** of the Ko'woh Nation. A canine mage. A shapeshifter. I can transform into a wolf at will.
Wolves are native to Yucatán?
AAARGH!!

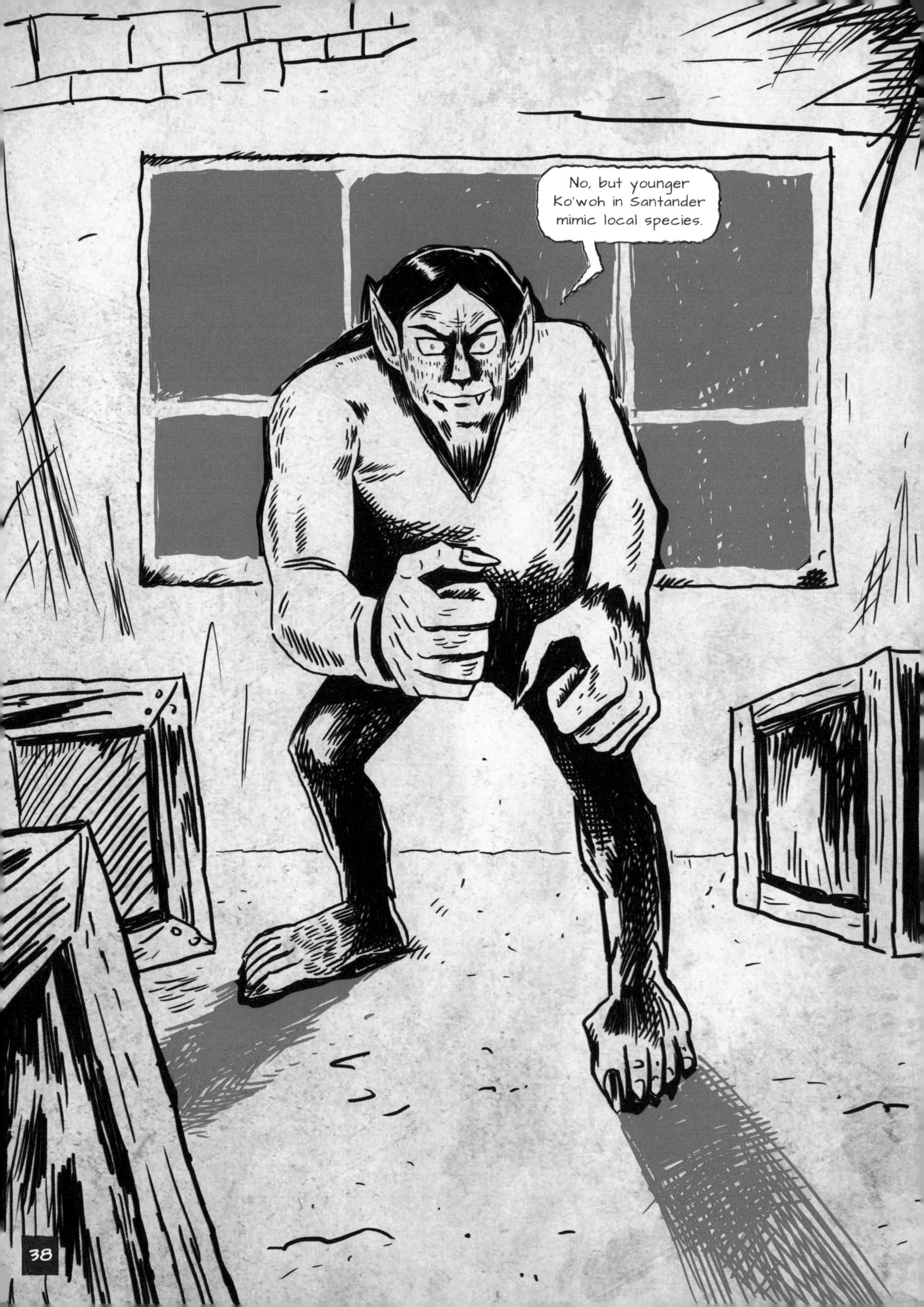
No, but younger Ko'woh in Santander mimic local species.

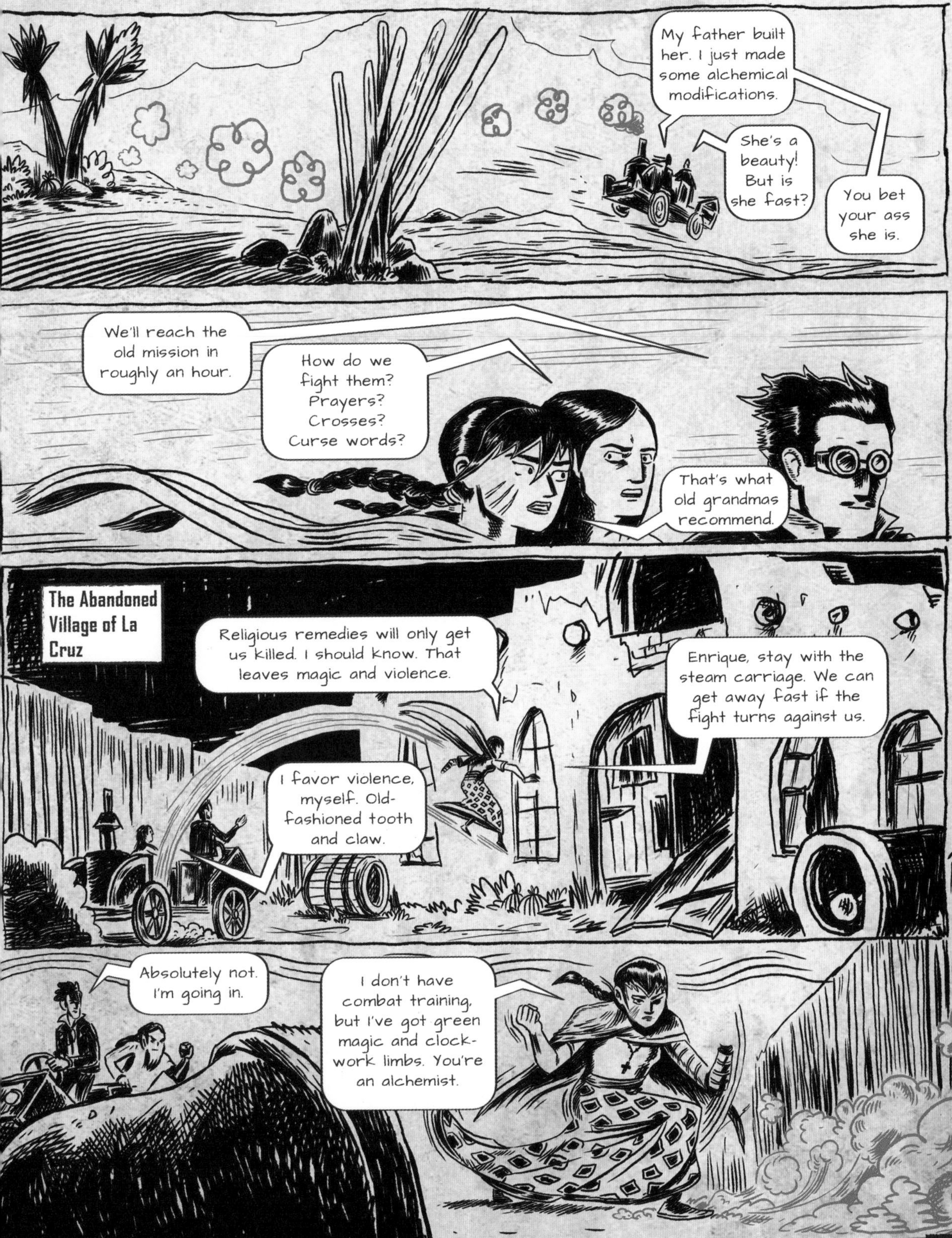

My father built her. I just made some alchemical modifications.
She's a beauty! But is she fast?
You bet your ass she is.
We'll reach the old mission in roughly an hour.
How do we fight them? Prayers? Crosses? Curse words?
That's what old grandmas recommend.
The Abandoned Village of La Cruz
Religious remedies will only get us killed. I should know. That leaves magic and violence.
Enrique, stay with the steam carriage. We can get away fast if the fight turns against us.
I favor violence, myself. Old-fashioned tooth and claw.
Absolutely not. I'm going in.
I don't have combat training, but I've got green magic and clock-work limbs. You're an alchemist.

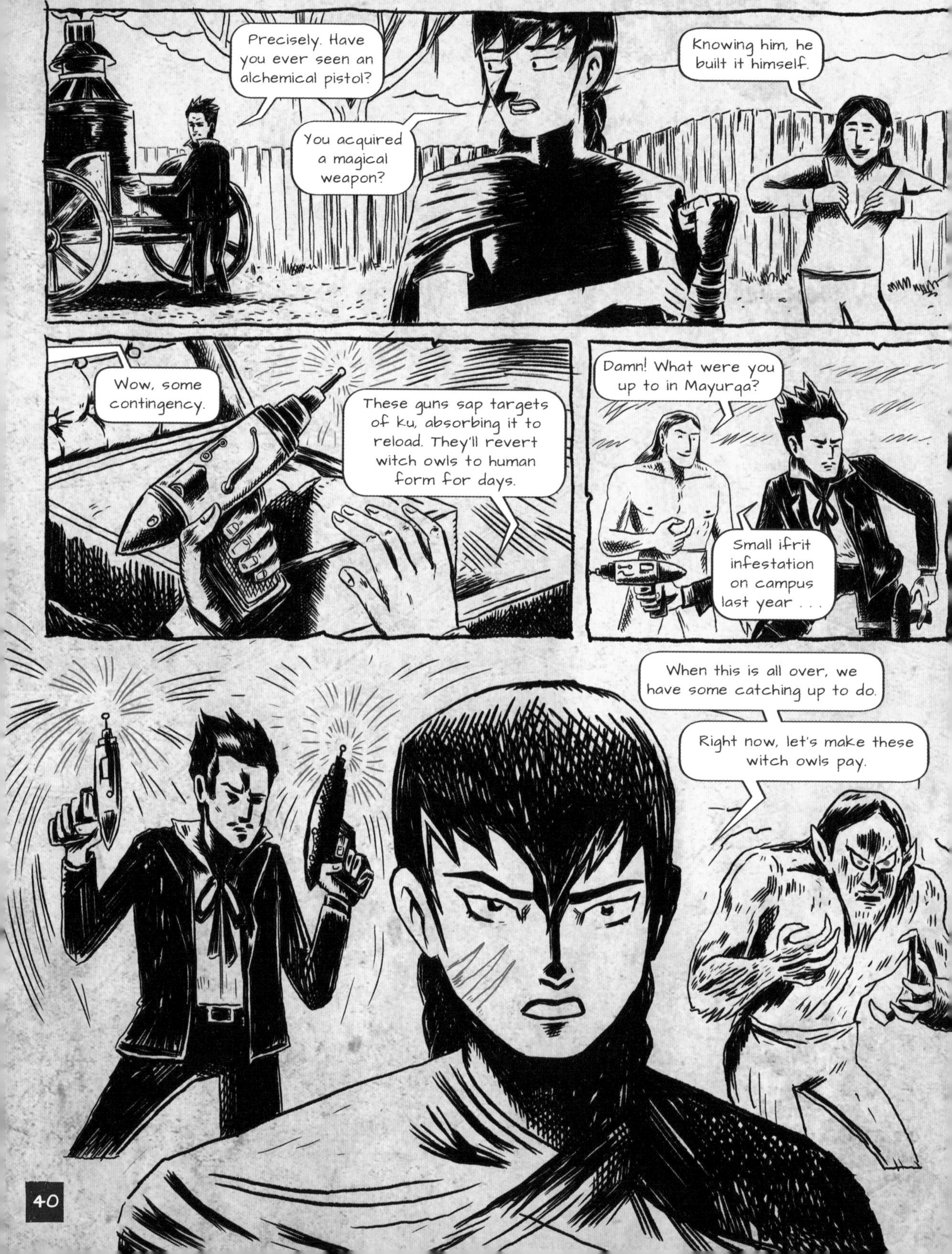
Precisely. Have you ever seen an alchemical pistol?
You acquired a magical weapon?
Knowing him, he built it himself.
Wow, some contingency.
These guns sap targets of ku, absorbing it to reload. They'll revert witch owls to human form for days.
Damn! What were you up to in Mayurqa?
Small ifrit infestation on campus last year . . .
When this is all over, we have some catching up to do.
Right now, let's make these witch owls pay.

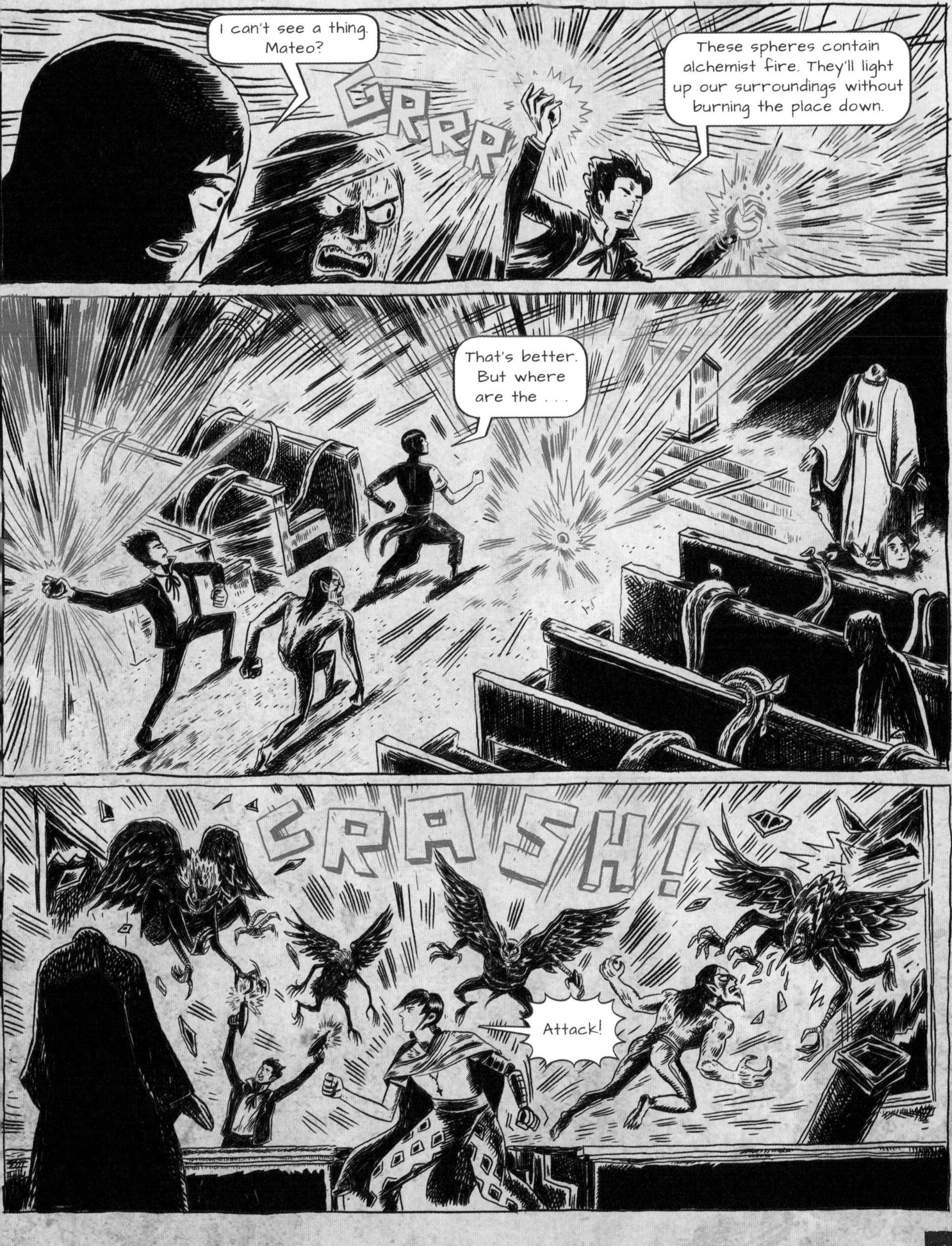
I can't see a thing. Mateo?
GRRR
These spheres contain alchemist fire. They'll light up our surroundings without burning the place down.
That's better. But where are the . . .
CRASH!
Attack!

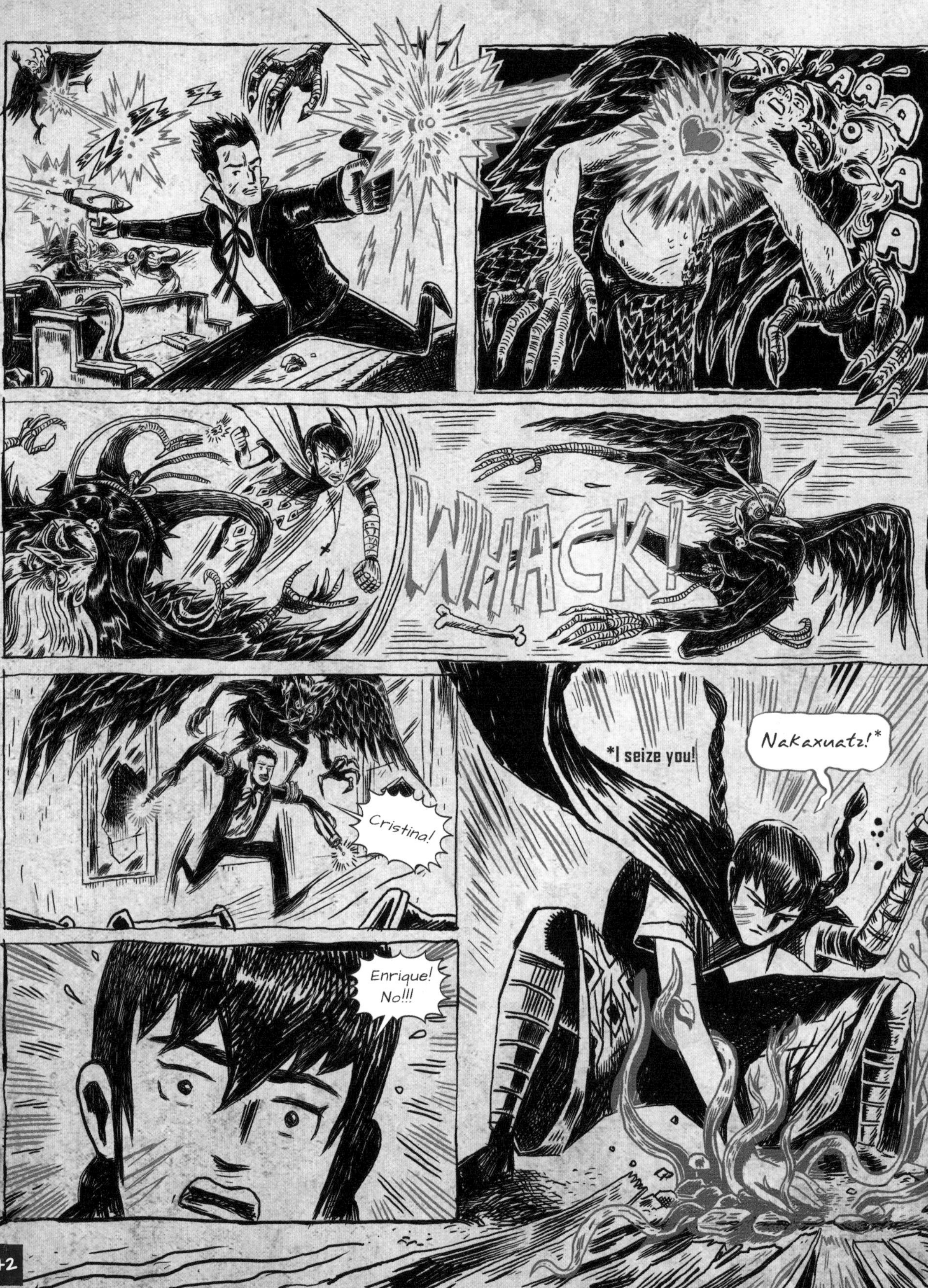
WHACK!
Cristina!
Enrique! No!!!
Nakaxuatz!*
*I seize you!

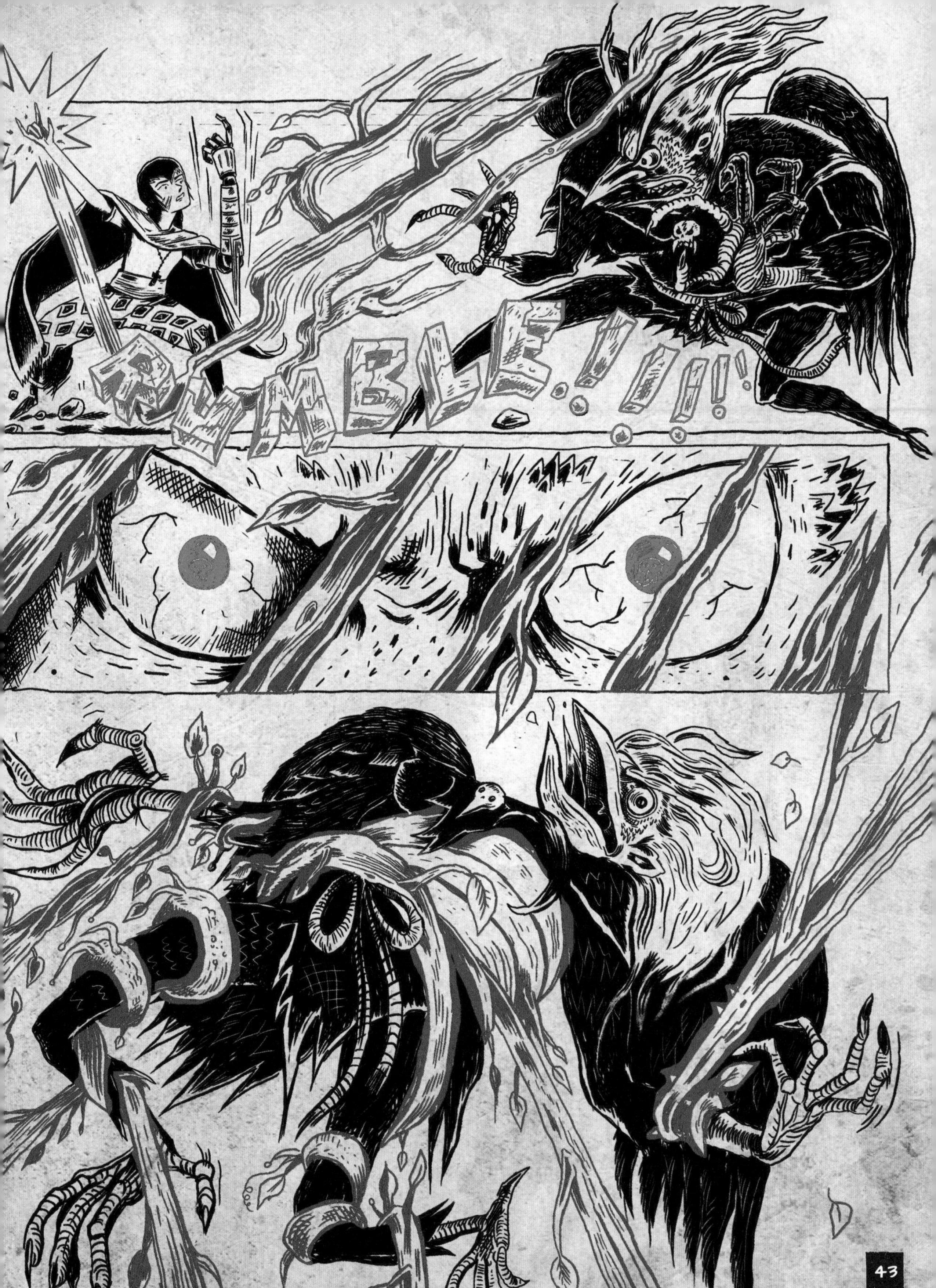
RUMBLE!!!!!

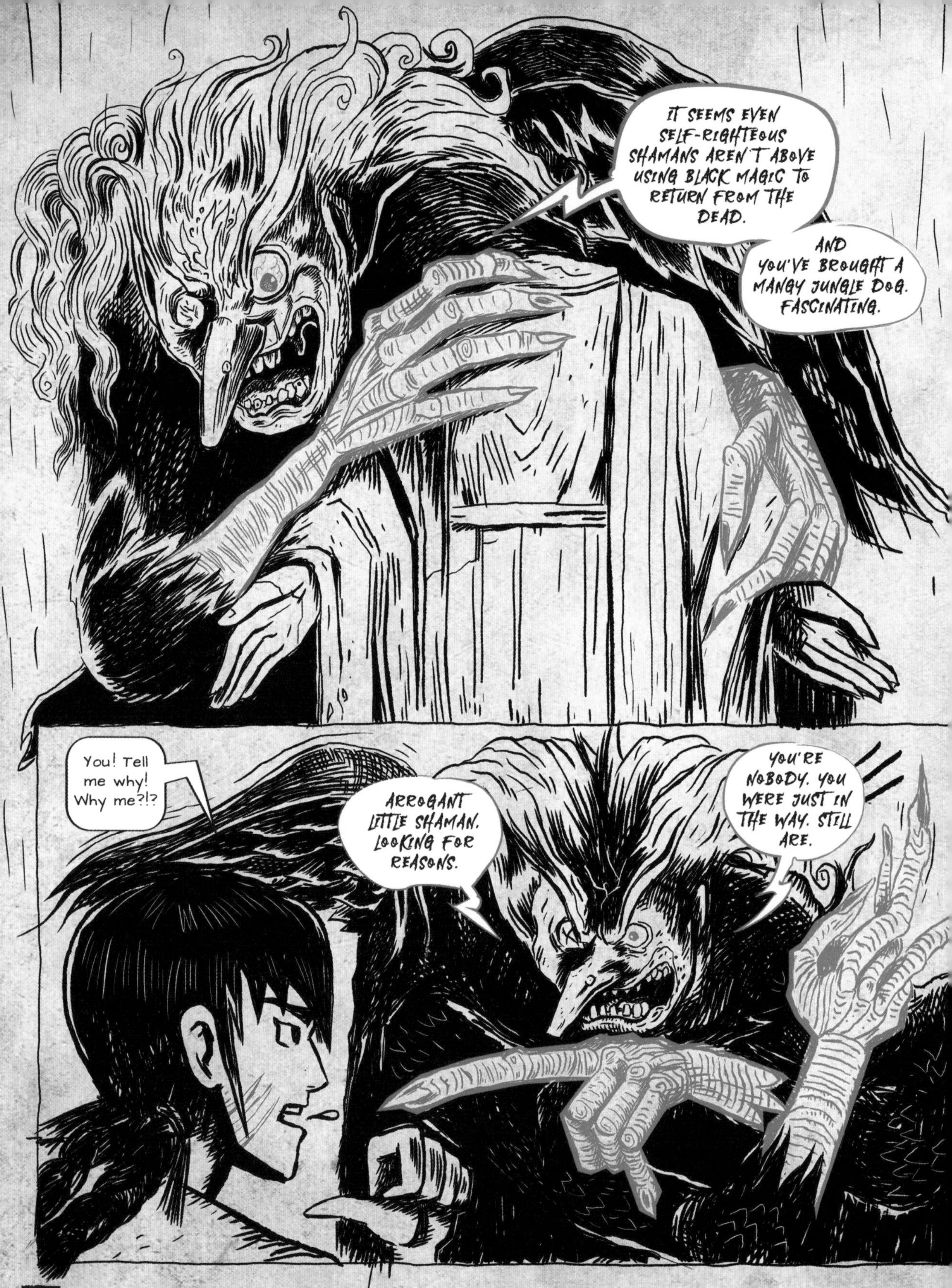
IT SEEMS EVEN SELF-RIGHTEOUS SHAMANS AREN'T ABOVE USING BLACK MAGIC TO RETURN FROM THE DEAD.
AND YOU'VE BROUGHT A MANGY JUNGLE DOG. FASCINATING.
You! Tell me why! Why me?!?
ARROGANT LITTLE SHAMAN. LOOKING FOR REASONS.
YOU'RE NOBODY. YOU WERE JUST IN THE WAY. STILL ARE.

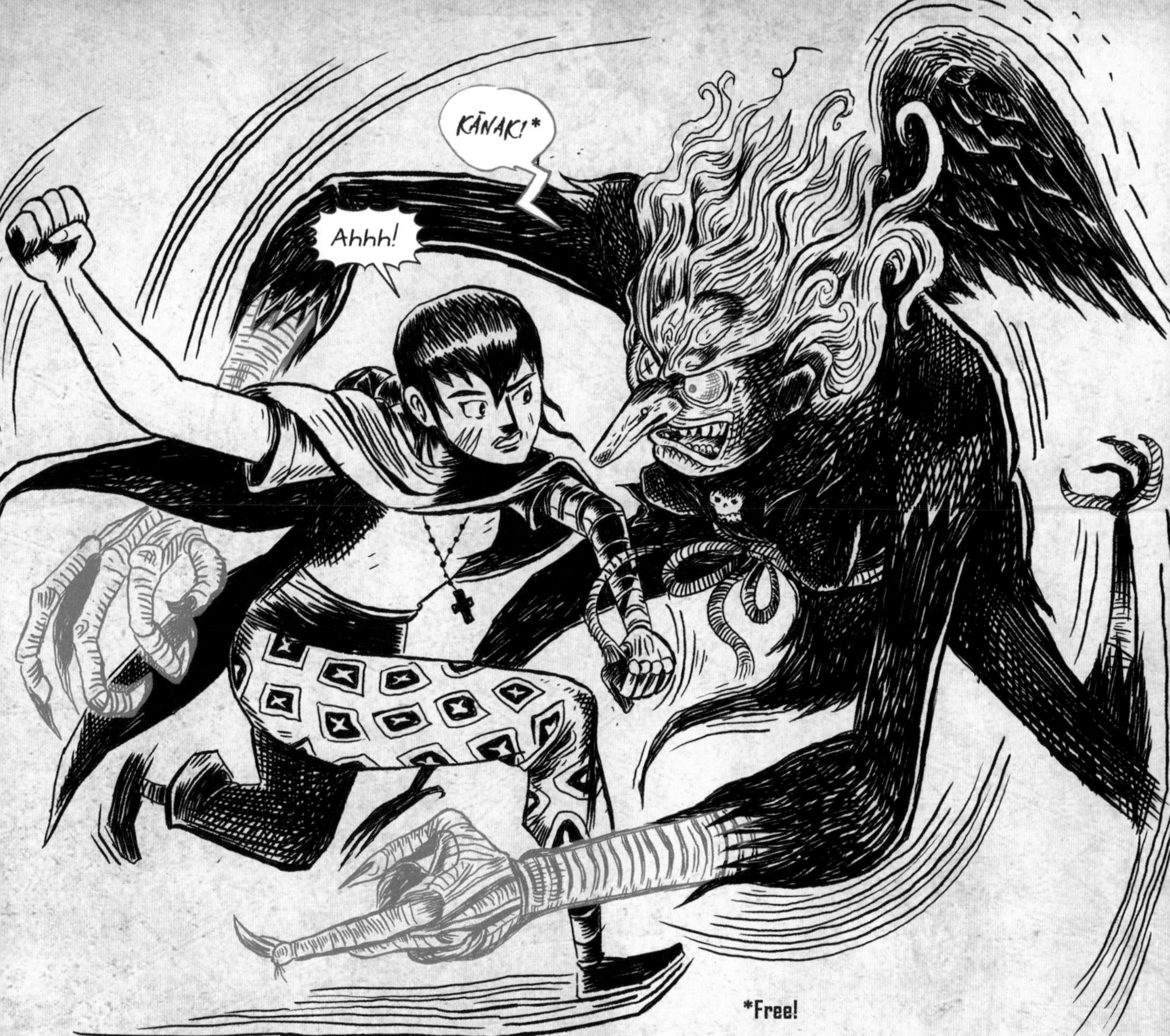
KĀNAK!*
Ahhh!

*Free!

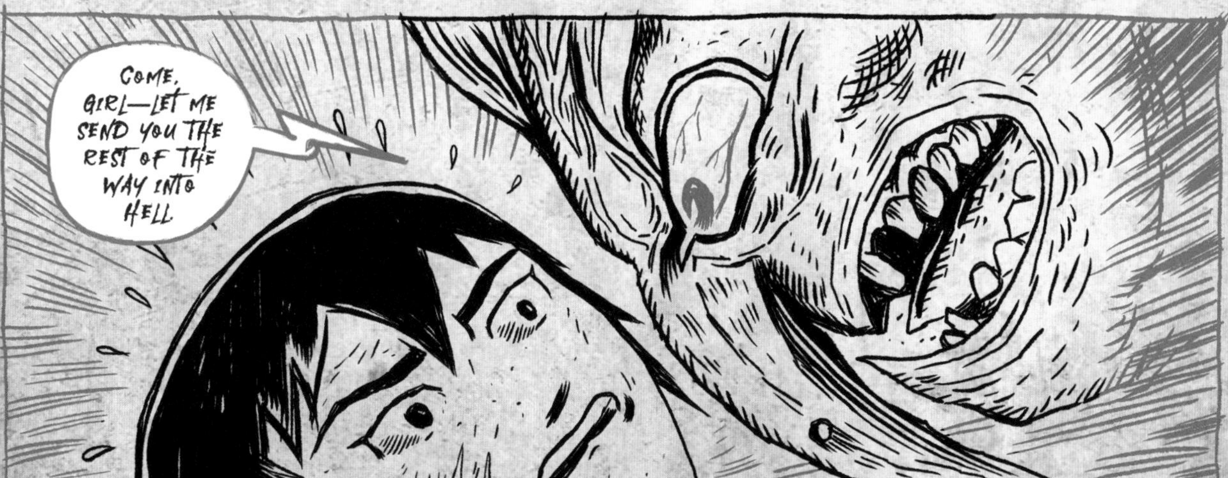
COME, GIRL—LET ME SEND YOU THE REST OF THE WAY INTO HELL.

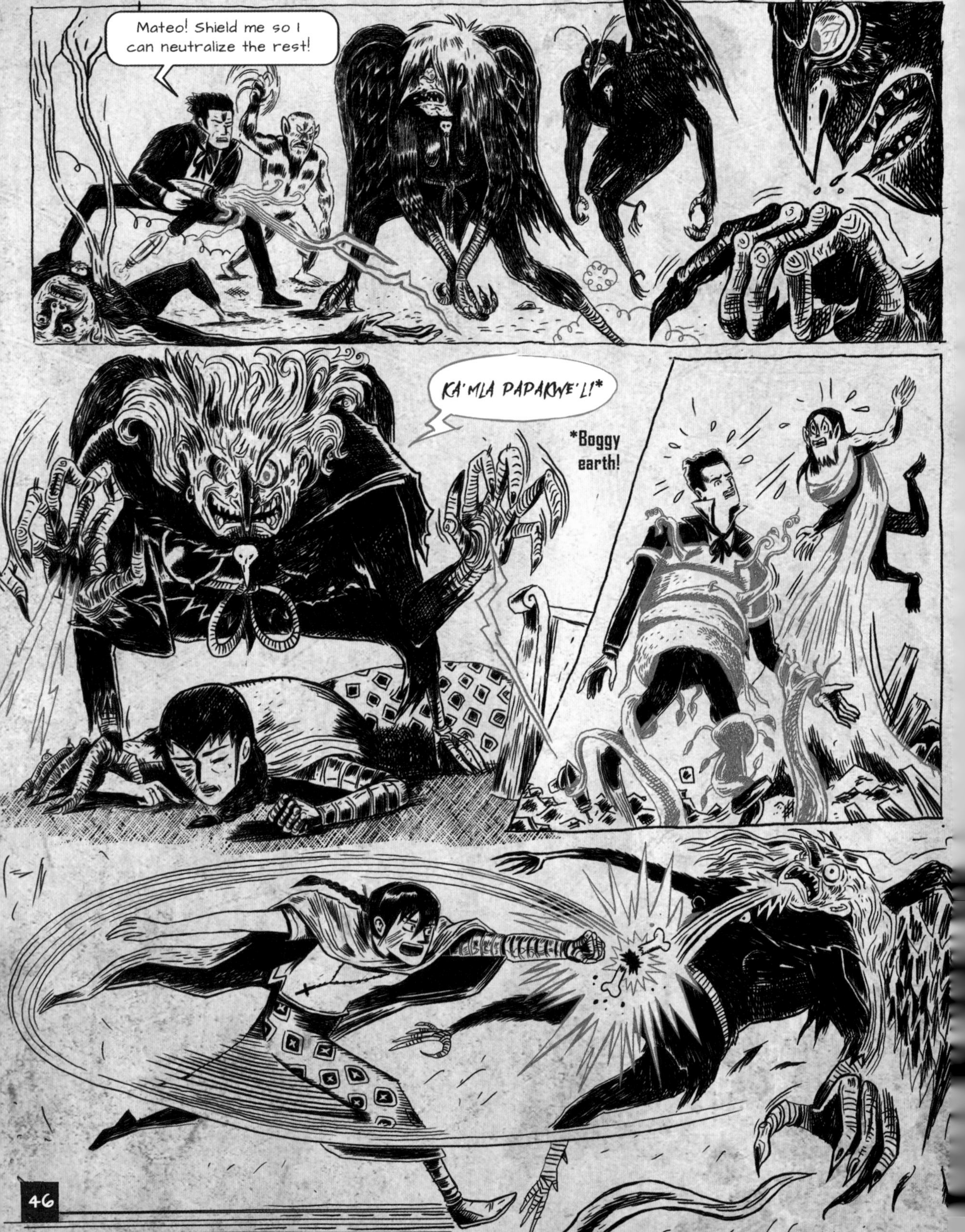
Mateo! Shield me so I can neutralize the rest!
KA'MLA PAPAKWE'L!*
*Boggy earth!

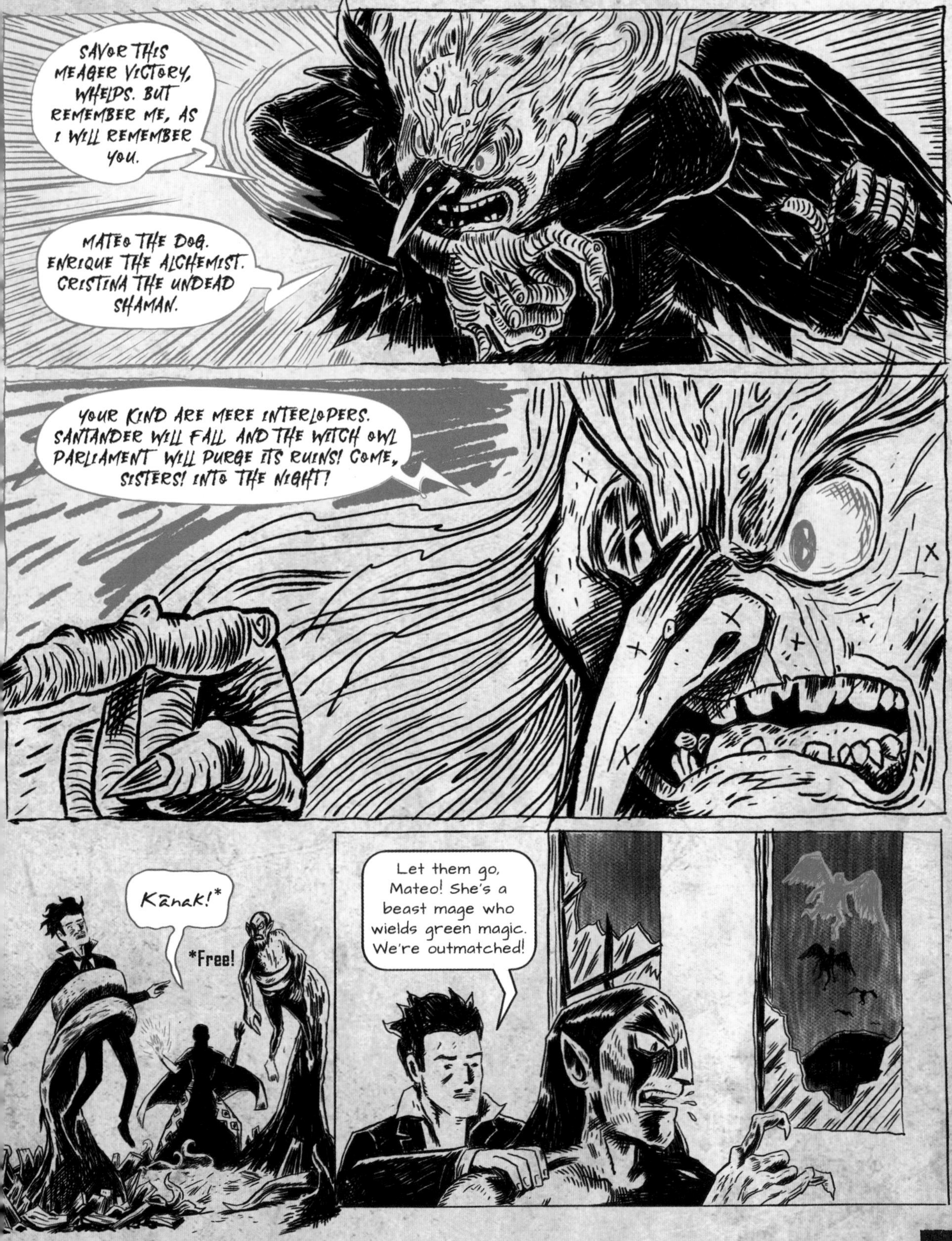
SAVOR THIS MEAGER VICTORY, WHELPS. BUT REMEMBER ME, AS I WILL REMEMBER YOU.
MATEO THE DOG. ENRIQUE THE ALCHEMIST. CRISTINA THE UNDEAD SHAMAN.
YOUR KIND ARE MERE INTERLOPERS. SANTANDER WILL FALL AND THE WITCH OWL PARLIAMENT WILL PURGE ITS RUINS! COME, SISTERS! INTO THE NIGHT!
Kānak!*
*Free!
Let them go, Mateo! She's a beast mage who wields green magic. We're outmatched!

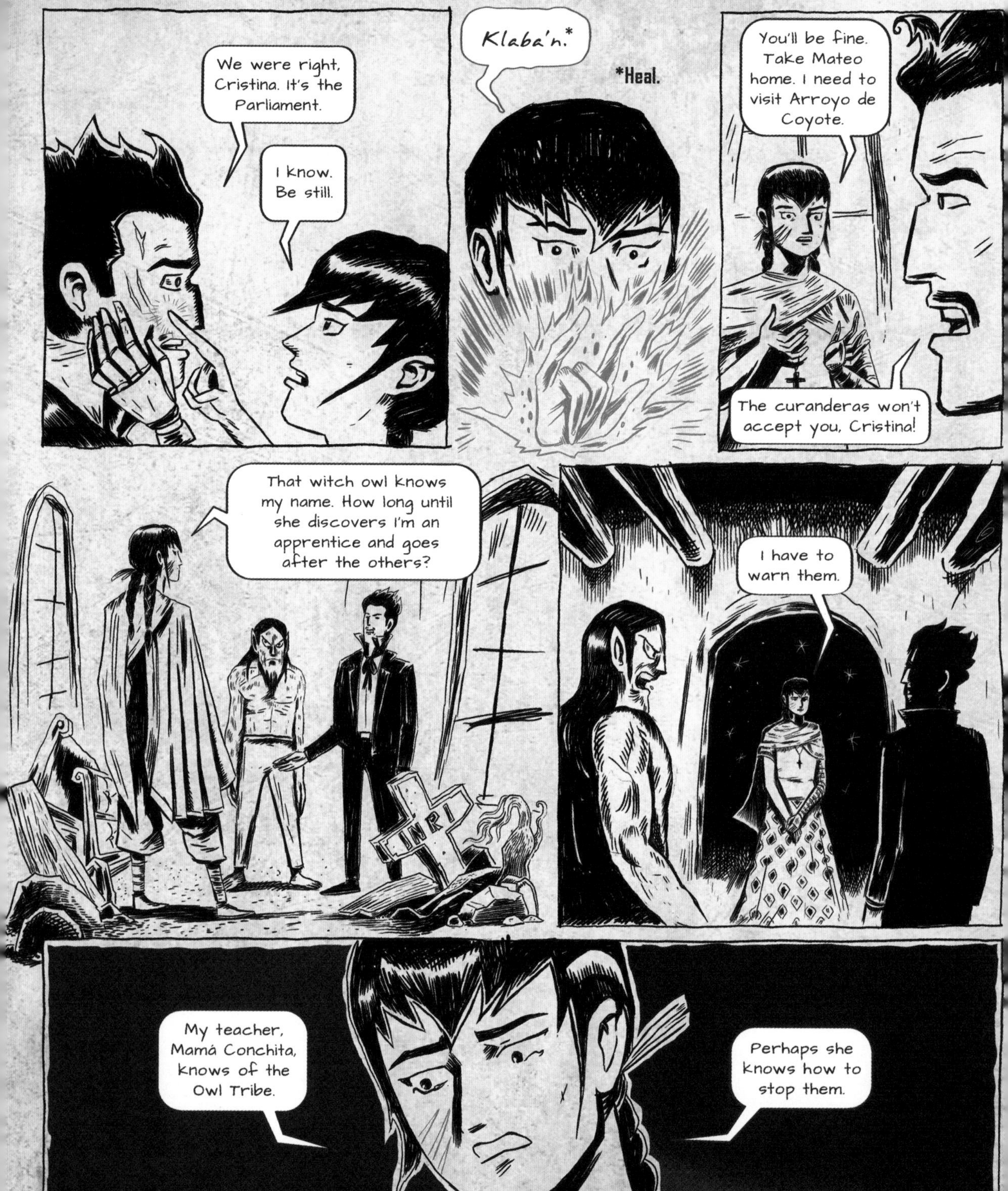
We were right, Cristina. It's the Parliament.
I know. Be still.
Klaba'n.*
*Heal.
You'll be fine. Take Mateo home. I need to visit Arroyo de Coyote.
The curanderas won't accept you, Cristina!
That witch owl knows my name. How long until she discovers I'm an apprentice and goes after the others?
I have to warn them.
My teacher, Mamá Conchita, knows of the Owl Tribe.
Perhaps she knows how to stop them.

CHAPTER 2

THE CRISIS DEEPENS

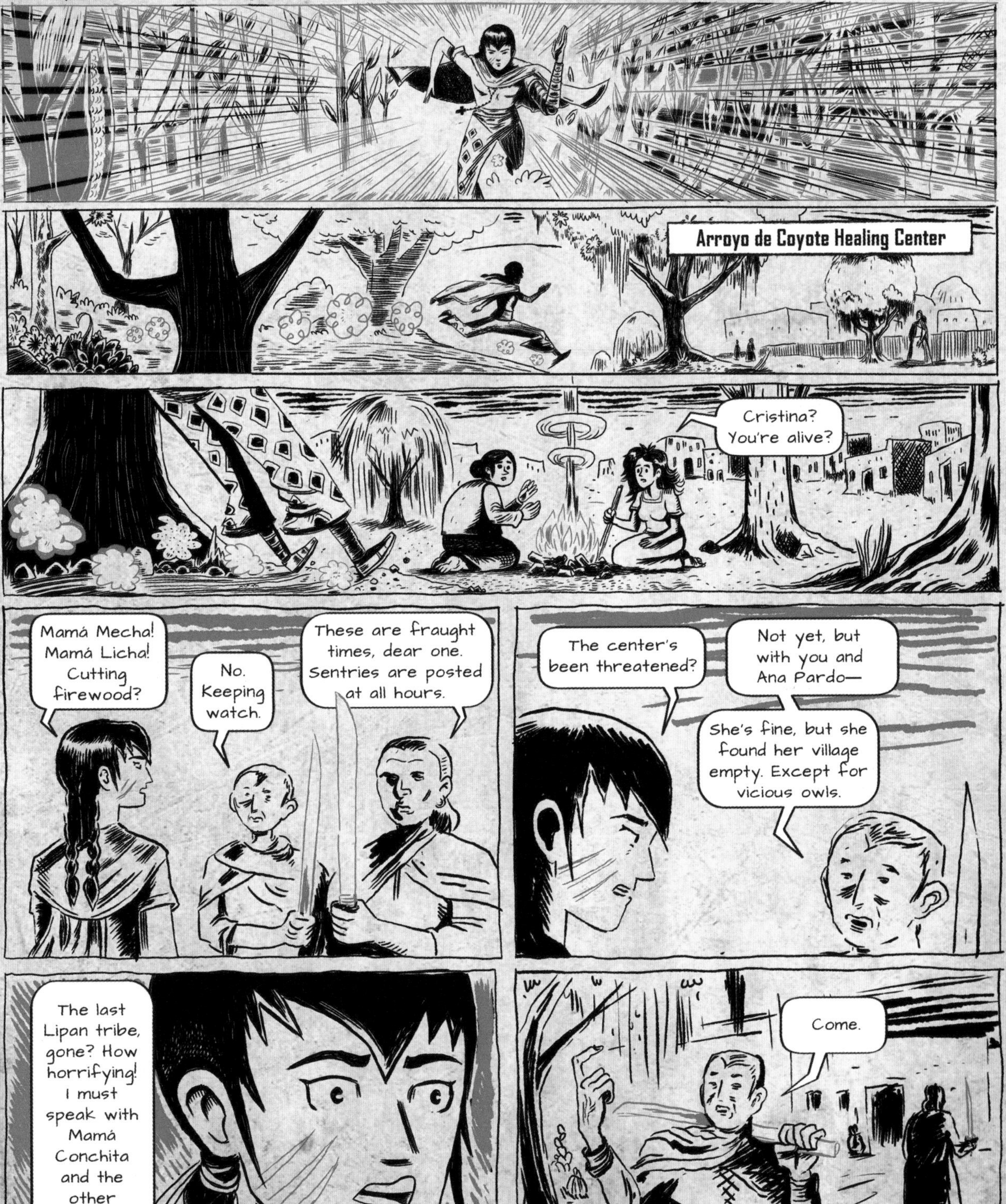
Arroyo de Coyote Healing Center
Cristina? You're alive?
Mamá Mecha! Mamá Licha! Cutting firewood?
No. Keeping watch.
These are fraught times, dear one. Sentries are posted at all hours.
The center's been threatened?
Not yet, but with you and Ana Pardo—
She's fine, but she found her village empty. Except for vicious owls.
The last Lipan tribe, gone? How horrifying! I must speak with Mamá Conchita and the other tenanches.
Come.

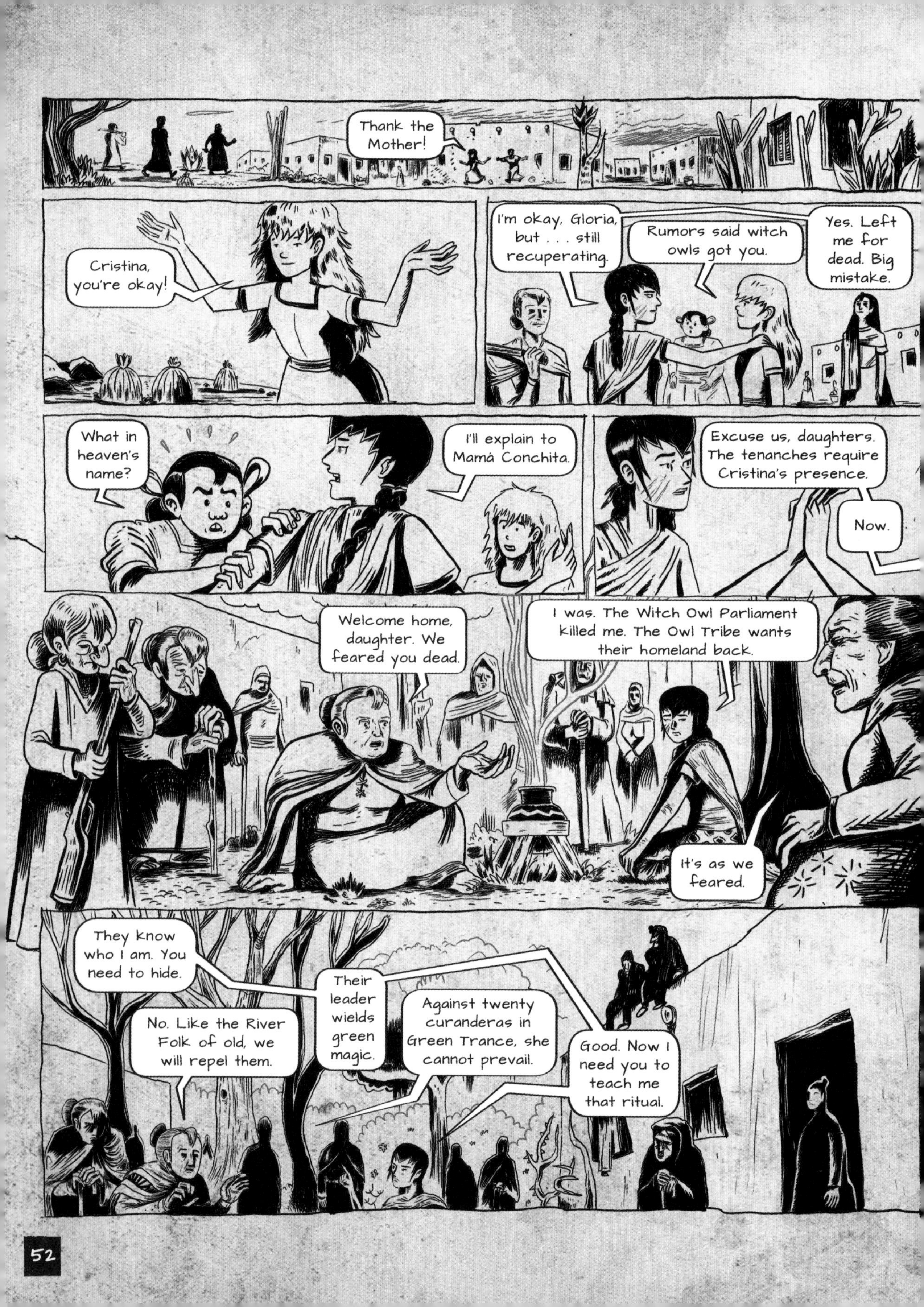

Thank the Mother!
Cristina, you're okay!
I'm okay, Gloria, but . . . still recuperating.
Rumors said witch owls got you.
Yes. Left me for dead. Big mistake.
What in heaven's name?
I'll explain to Mamá Conchita.
Excuse us, daughters. The tenanches require Cristina's presence.
Now.
Welcome home, daughter. We feared you dead.
I was. The Witch Owl Parliament killed me. The Owl Tribe wants their homeland back.
It's as we feared.
They know who I am. You need to hide.
No. Like the River Folk of old, we will repel them.
Their leader wields green magic.
Against twenty curanderas in Green Trance, she cannot prevail.
Good. Now I need you to teach me that ritual.

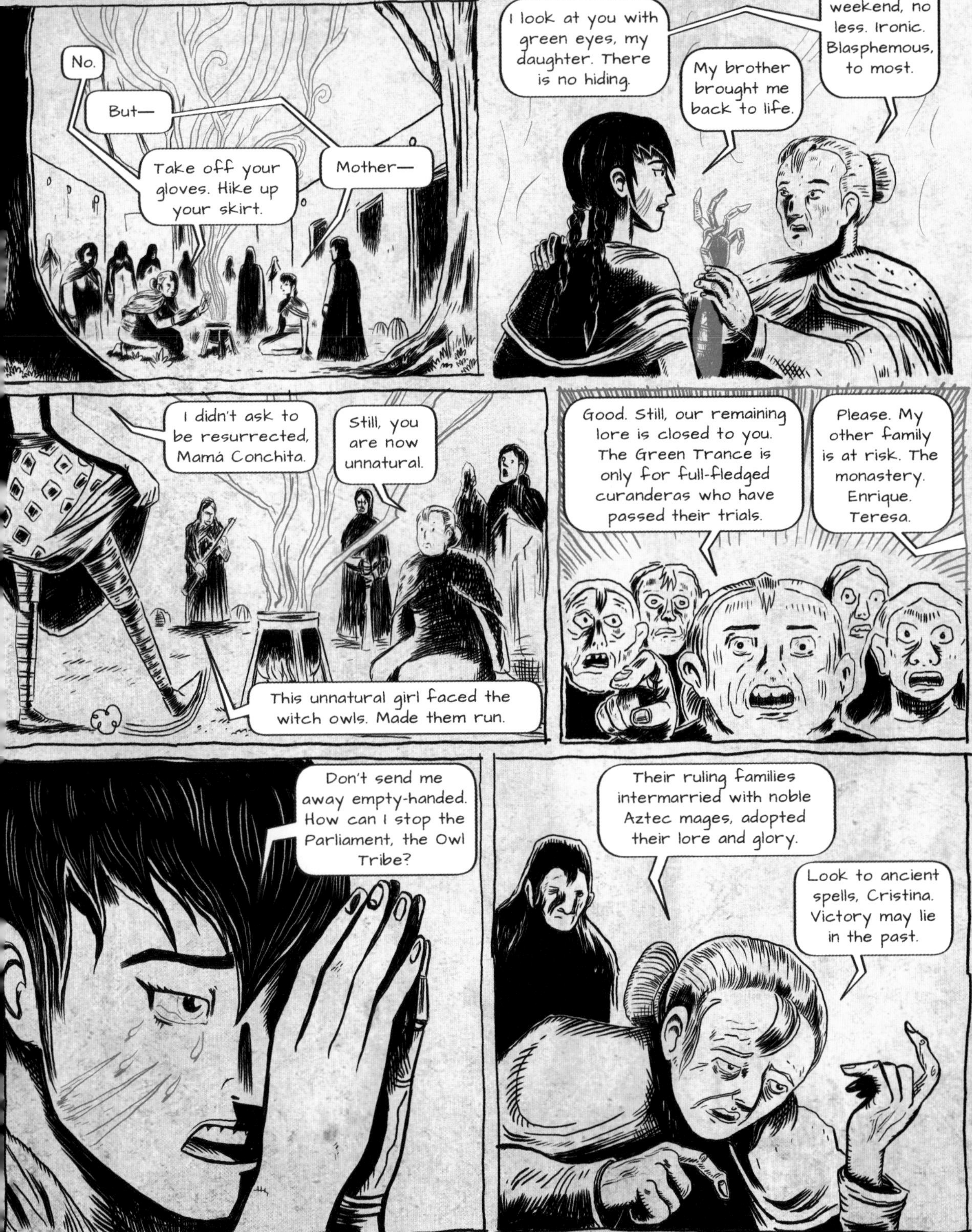
No.
But—
Take off your gloves. Hike up your skirt.
Mother—
I look at you with green eyes, my daughter. There is no hiding.
My brother brought me back to life.
On Easter weekend, no less. Ironic. Blasphemous, to most.
I didn't ask to be resurrected, Mamá Conchita.
Still, you are now unnatural.
This unnatural girl faced the witch owls. Made them run.
Good. Still, our remaining lore is closed to you. The Green Trance is only for full-fledged curanderas who have passed their trials.
Please. My other family is at risk. The monastery. Enrique. Teresa.
Don't send me away empty-handed. How can I stop the Parliament, the Owl Tribe?
Their ruling families intermarried with noble Aztec mages, adopted their lore and glory.
Look to ancient spells, Cristina. Victory may lie in the past.

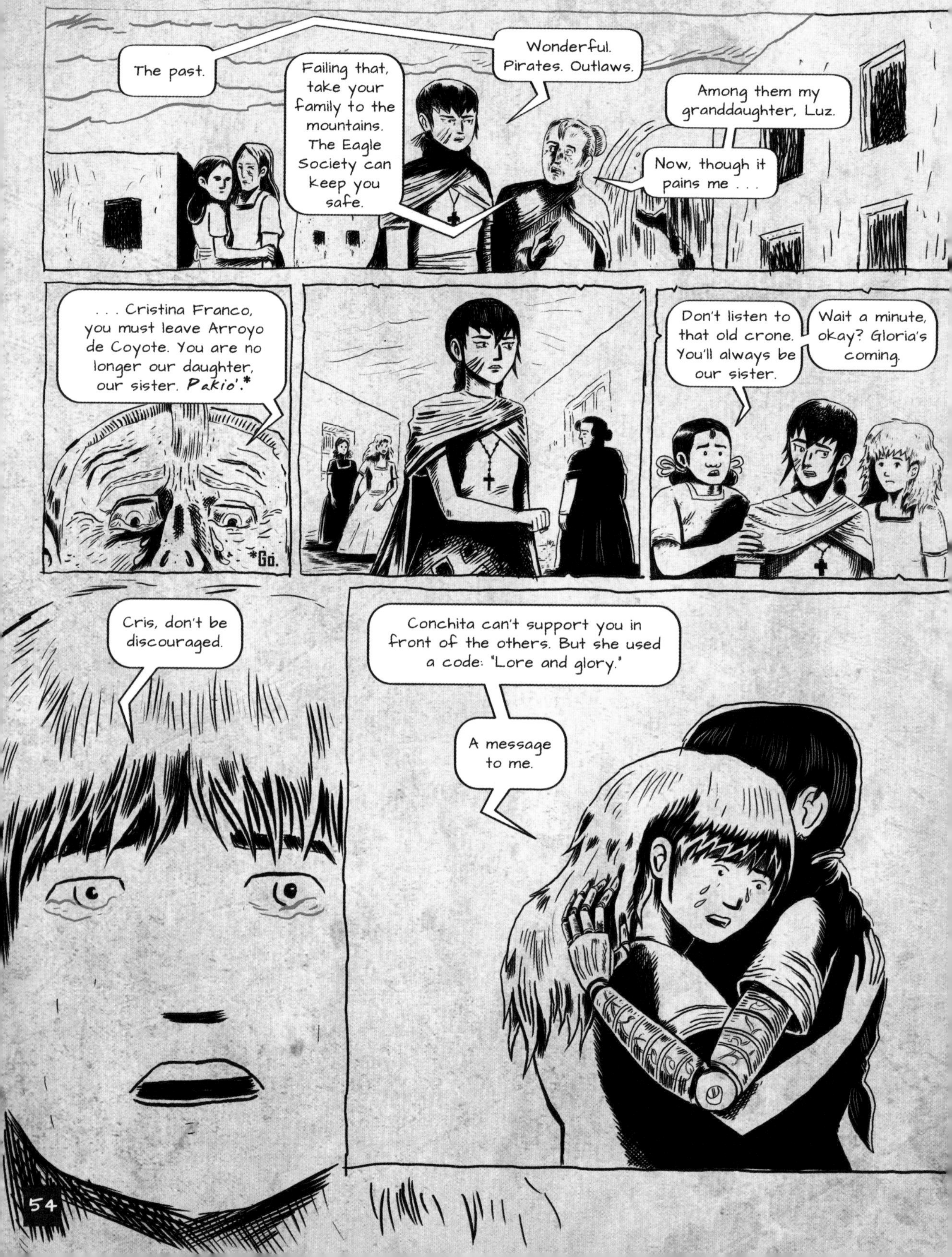

Failing that, take your family to the mountains. The Eagle Society can keep you safe.
Wonderful. Pirates. Outlaws.
The past.
Among them my granddaughter, Luz.
Now, though it pains me . . .
. . . Cristina Franco, you must leave Arroyo de Coyote. You are no longer our daughter, our sister. *Pakio'.**
*Go.
Don't listen to that old crone. You'll always be our sister.
Wait a minute, okay? Gloria's coming.
Cris, don't be discouraged.
Conchita can't support you in front of the others. But she used a code: "Lore and glory."
A message to me.

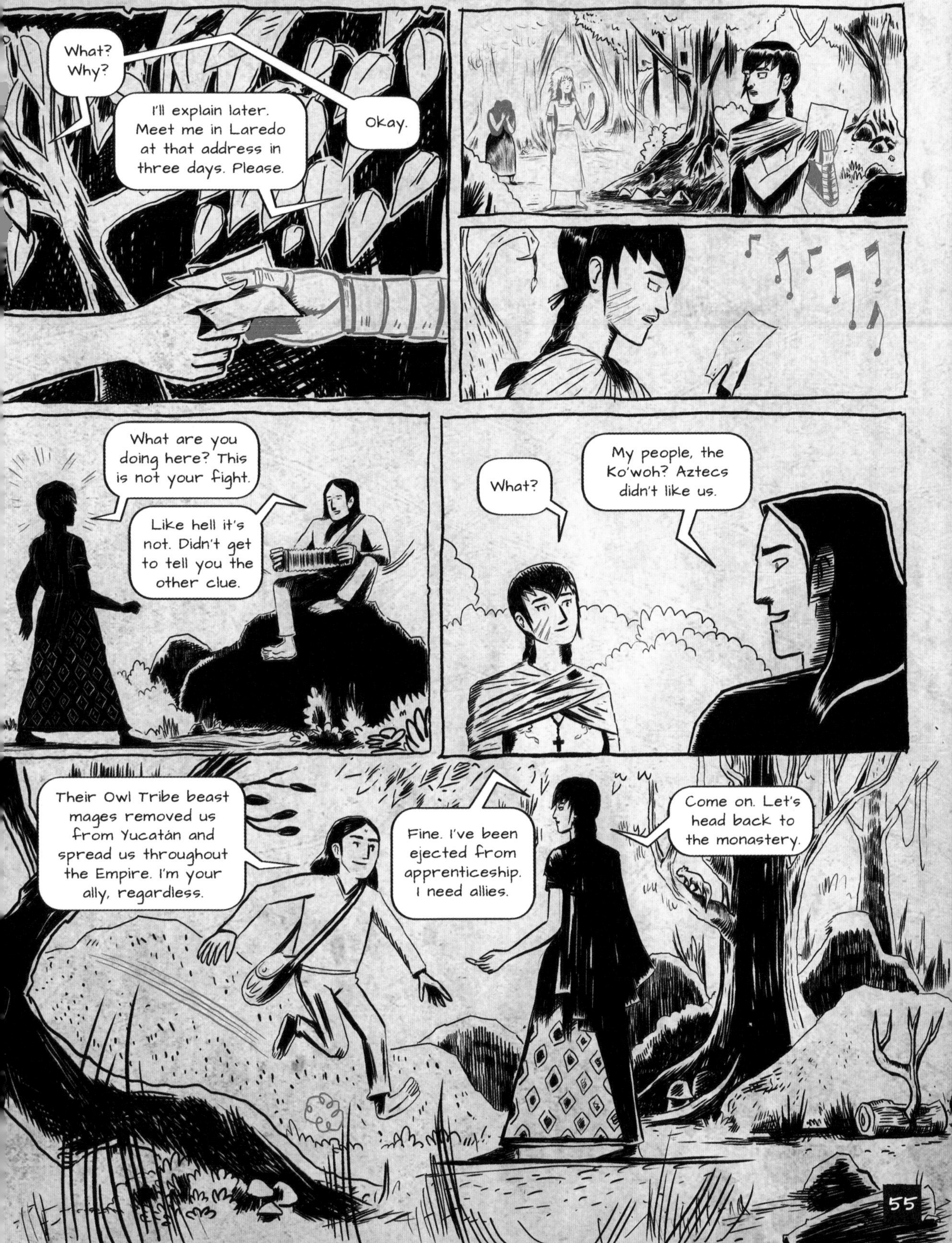
What? Why?
I'll explain later. Meet me in Laredo at that address in three days. Please.
Okay.
What are you doing here? This is not your fight.
Like hell it's not. Didn't get to tell you the other clue.
What?
My people, the Ko'woh? Aztecs didn't like us.
Their Owl Tribe beast mages removed us from Yucatán and spread us throughout the Empire. I'm your ally, regardless.
Fine. I've been ejected from apprenticeship. I need allies.
Come on. Let's head back to the monastery.

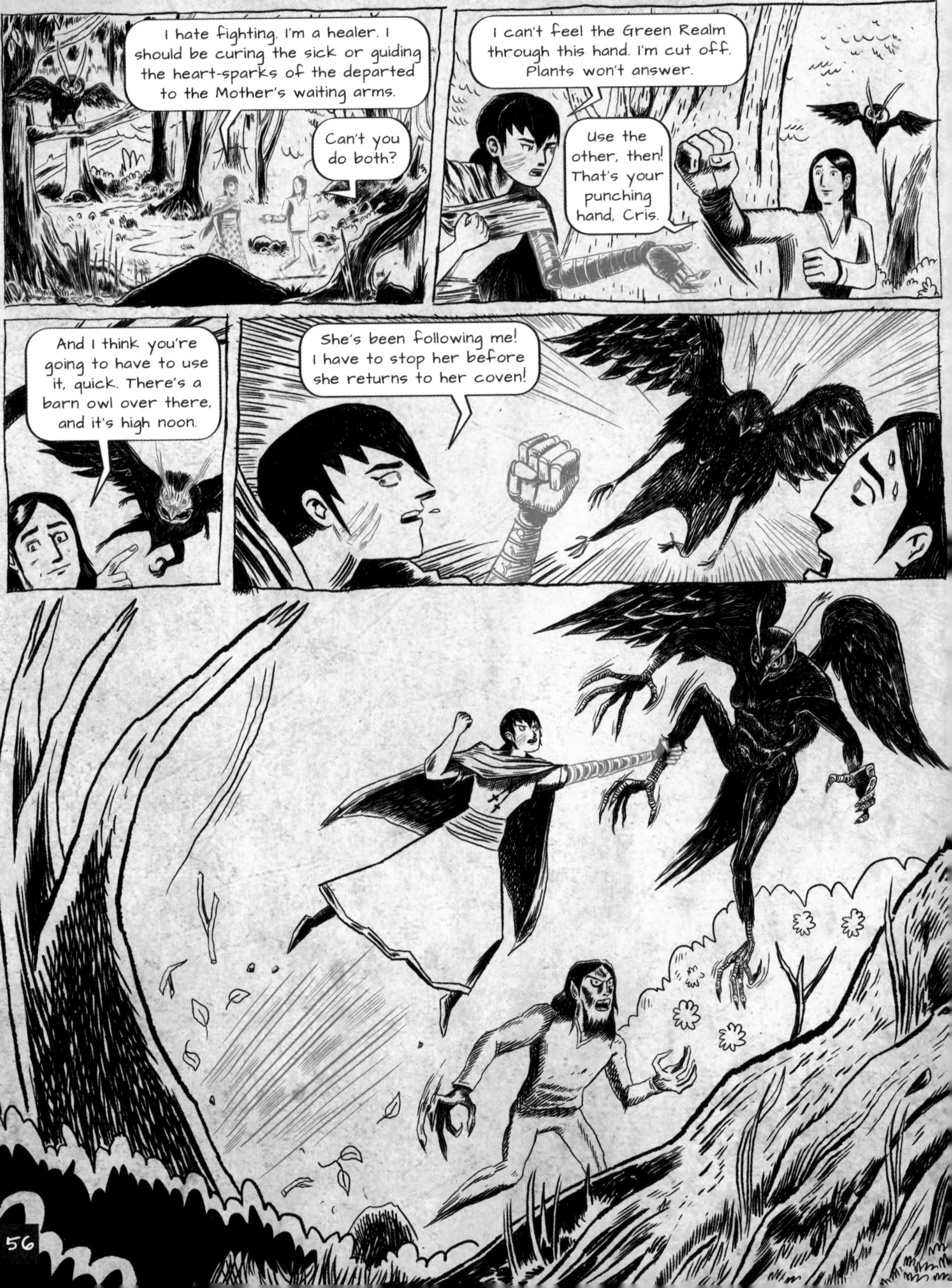

I hate fighting. I'm a healer. I should be curing the sick or guiding the heart-sparks of the departed to the Mother's waiting arms.
Can't you do both?
I can't feel the Green Realm through this hand. I'm cut off. Plants won't answer.
Use the other, then! That's your punching hand, Cris.
And I think you're going to have to use it, quick. There's a barn owl over there, and it's high noon.
She's been following me! I have to stop her before she returns to her coven!

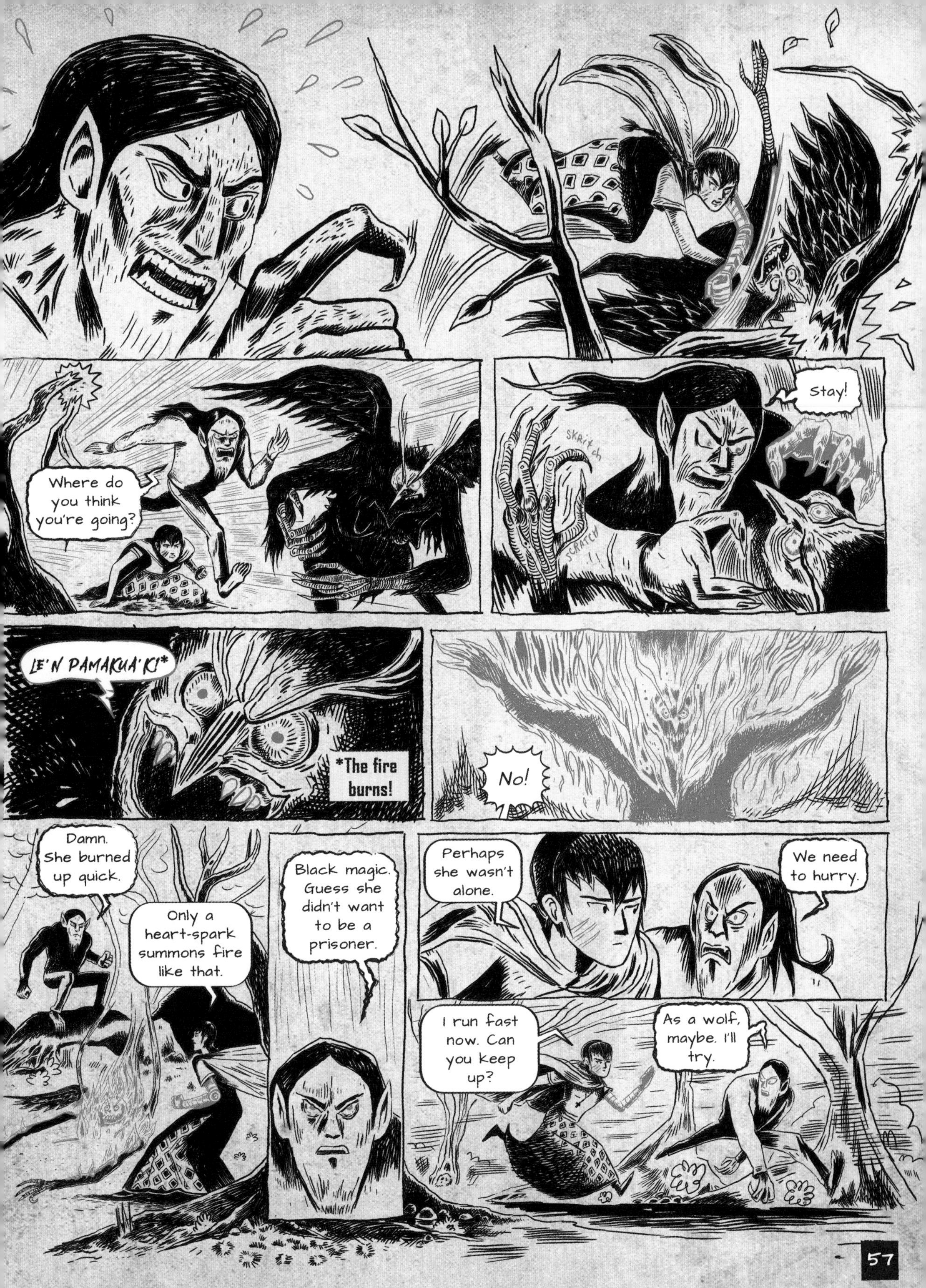
Where do you think you're going?
Stay!
SKRITCH
SCRATCH
LE'N DAMAKUA'KI*
*The fire burns!
No!
Damn. She burned up quick.
Only a heart-spark summons fire like that.
Black magic. Guess she didn't want to be a prisoner.
Perhaps she wasn't alone.
We need to hurry.
I run fast now. Can you keep up?
As a wolf, maybe. I'll try.

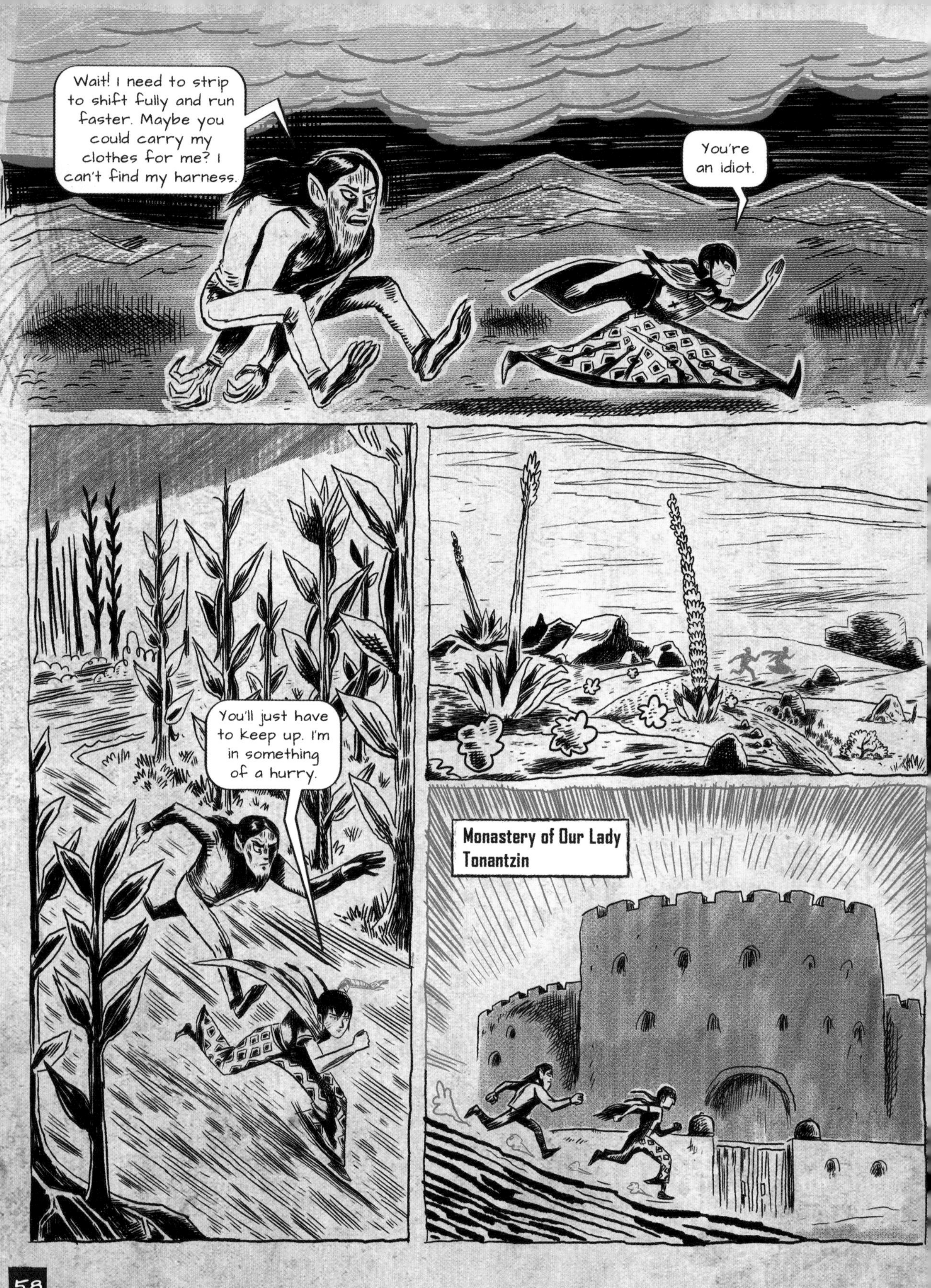
Wait! I need to strip to shift fully and run faster. Maybe you could carry my clothes for me? I can't find my harness.
You're an idiot.
You'll just have to keep up. I'm in something of a hurry.
Monastery of Our Lady Tonantzin

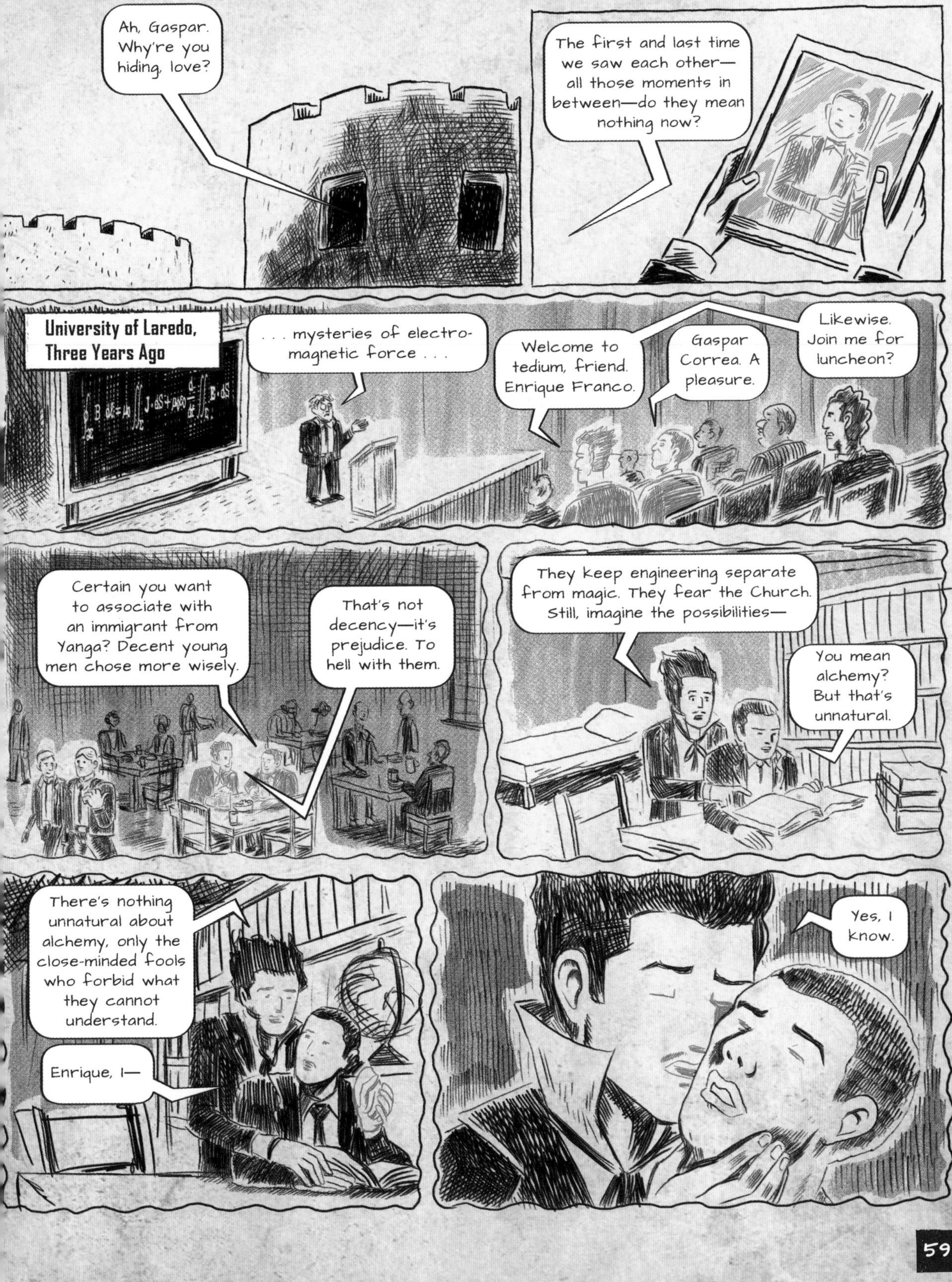
Ah, Gaspar. Why're you hiding, love?
The first and last time we saw each other—all those moments in between—do they mean nothing now?
University of Laredo, Three Years Ago
. . . mysteries of electro-magnetic force . . .
Welcome to tedium, friend. Enrique Franco.
Gaspar Correa. A pleasure.
Likewise. Join me for luncheon?
Certain you want to associate with an immigrant from Yanga? Decent young men chose more wisely.
That's not decency—it's prejudice. To hell with them.
They keep engineering separate from magic. They fear the Church. Still, imagine the possibilities—
You mean alchemy? But that's unnatural.
There's nothing unnatural about alchemy, only the close-minded fools who forbid what they cannot understand.
Enrique, I—
Yes, I know.

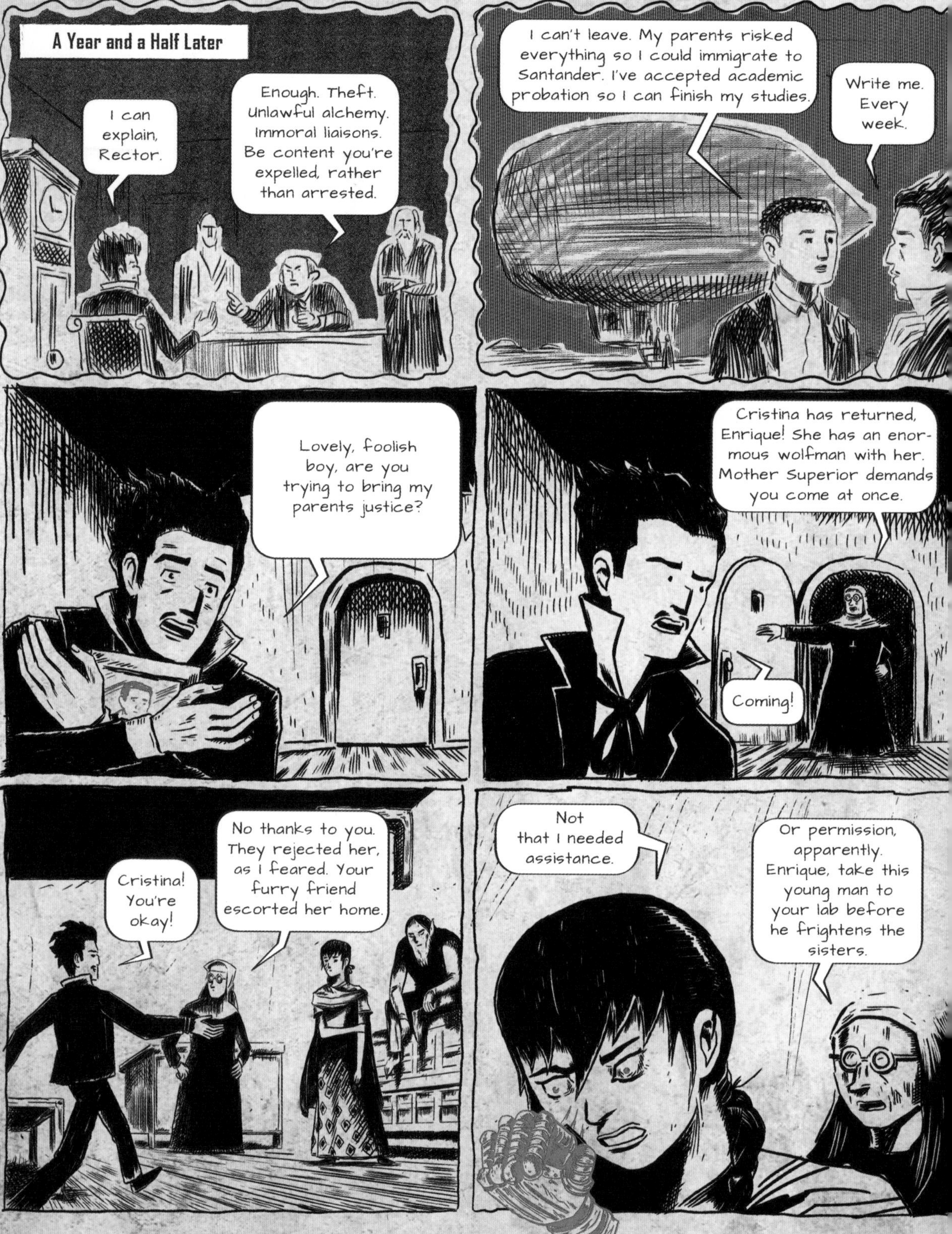
A Year and a Half Later
I can explain, Rector.
Enough. Theft. Unlawful alchemy. Immoral liaisons. Be content you're expelled, rather than arrested.
I can't leave. My parents risked everything so I could immigrate to Santander. I've accepted academic probation so I can finish my studies.
Write me. Every week.
Lovely, foolish boy, are you trying to bring my parents justice?
Cristina has returned, Enrique! She has an enormous wolfman with her. Mother Superior demands you come at once.
Coming!
Cristina! You're okay!
No thanks to you. They rejected her, as I feared. Your furry friend escorted her home.
Not that I needed assistance.
Or permission, apparently. Enrique, take this young man to your lab before he frightens the sisters.

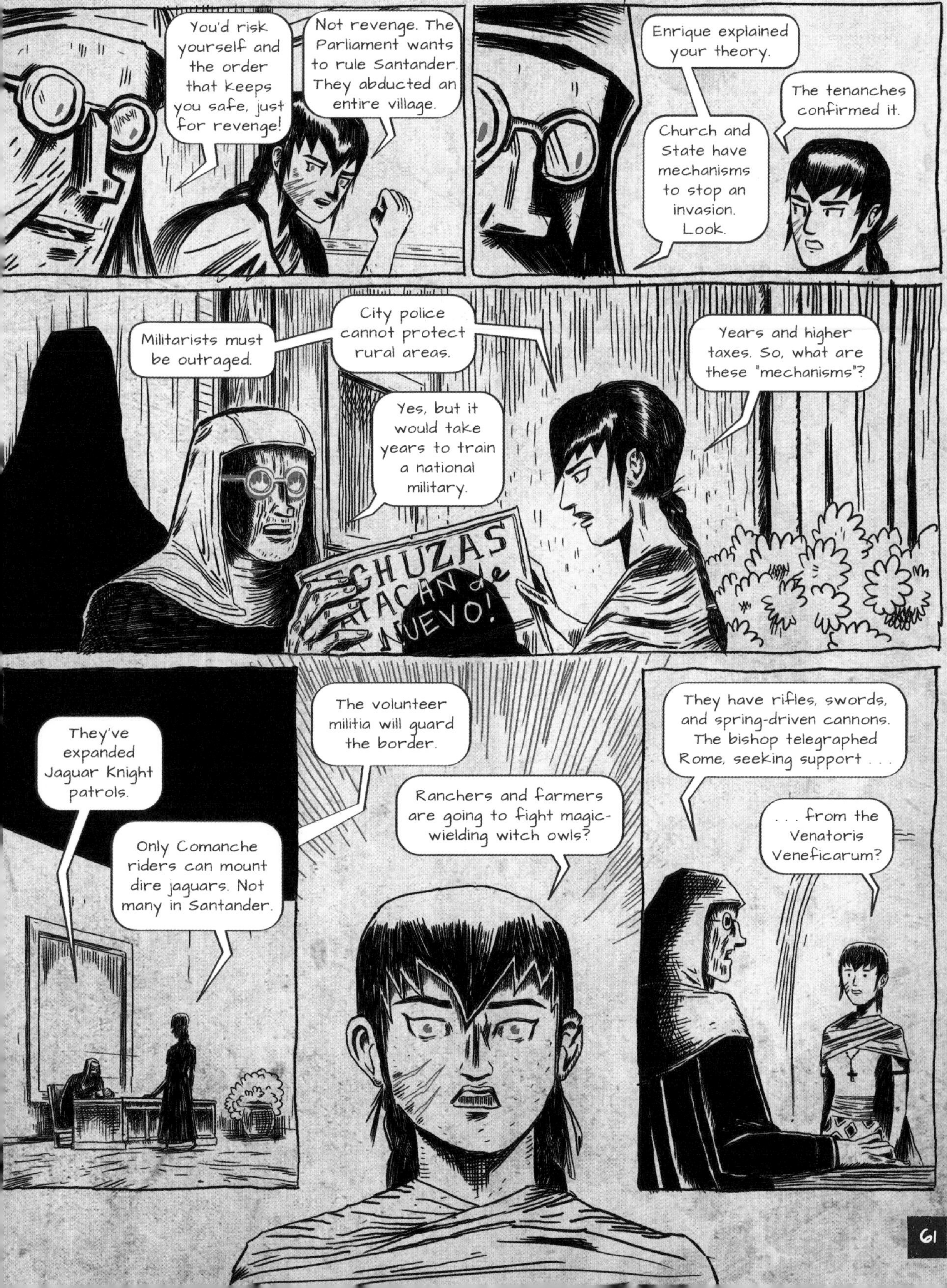
You'd risk yourself and the order that keeps you safe, just for revenge!
Not revenge. The Parliament wants to rule Santander. They abducted an entire village.
Enrique explained your theory.
Church and State have mechanisms to stop an invasion. Look.
The tenanches confirmed it.
Militarists must be outraged.
City police cannot protect rural areas.
Yes, but it would take years to train a national military.
Years and higher taxes. So, what are these "mechanisms"?
LECHUZAS ATACAN de NUEVO!
They've expanded Jaguar Knight patrols.
Only Comanche riders can mount dire jaguars. Not many in Santander.
The volunteer militia will guard the border.
Ranchers and farmers are going to fight magic-wielding witch owls?
They have rifles, swords, and spring-driven cannons. The bishop telegraphed Rome, seeking support . . .
. . . from the Venatoris Veneficarum?

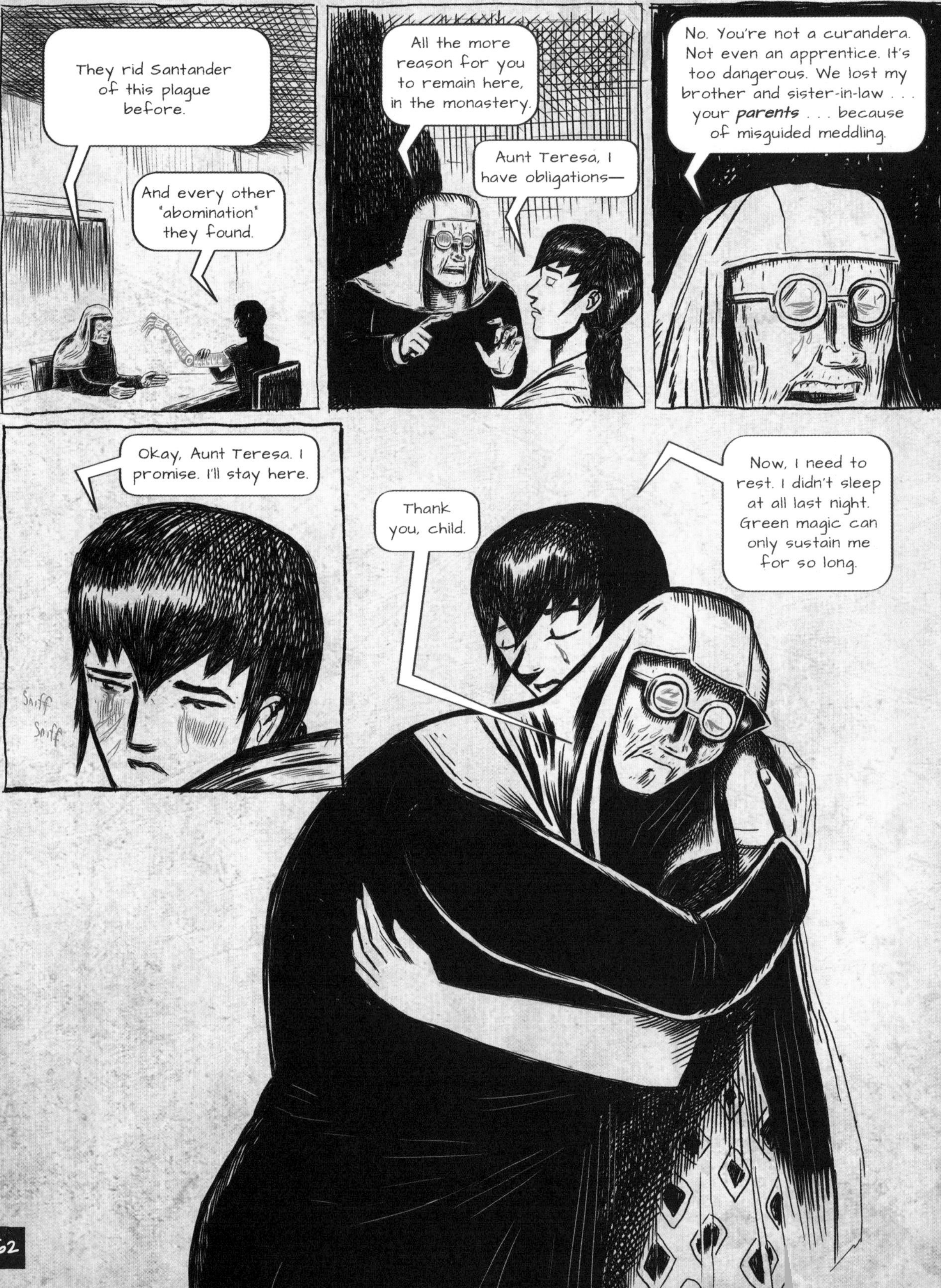
They rid Santander of this plague before.
And every other "abomination" they found.
All the more reason for you to remain here, in the monastery.
Aunt Teresa, I have obligations—
No. You're not a curandera. Not even an apprentice. It's too dangerous. We lost my brother and sister-in-law . . . your **parents** . . . because of misguided meddling.
Okay, Aunt Teresa. I promise. I'll stay here.
Sniff
Sniff
Thank you, child.
Now, I need to rest. I didn't sleep at all last night. Green magic can only sustain me for so long.

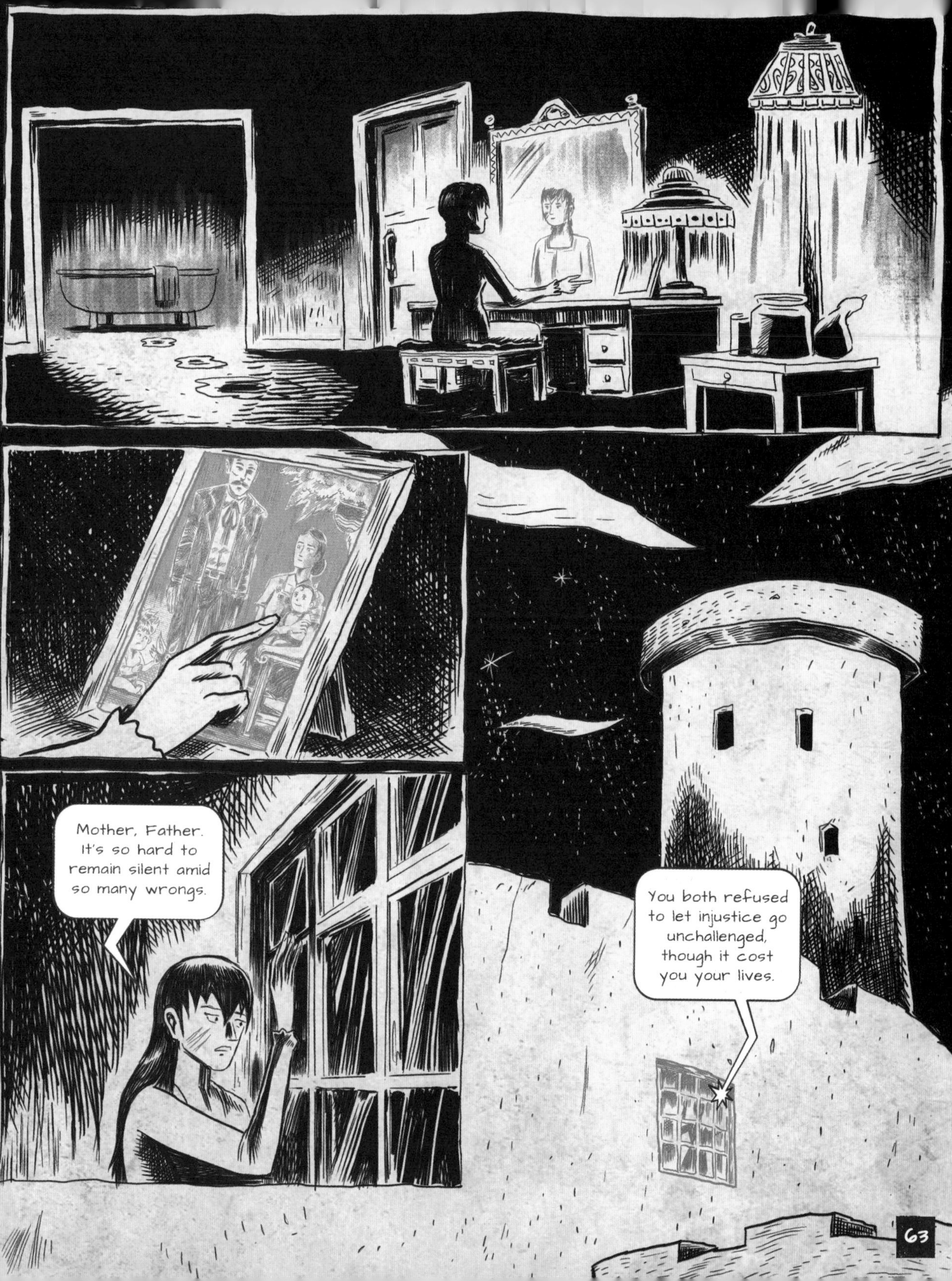
Mother, Father. It's so hard to remain silent amid so many wrongs.
You both refused to let injustice go unchallenged, though it cost you your lives.

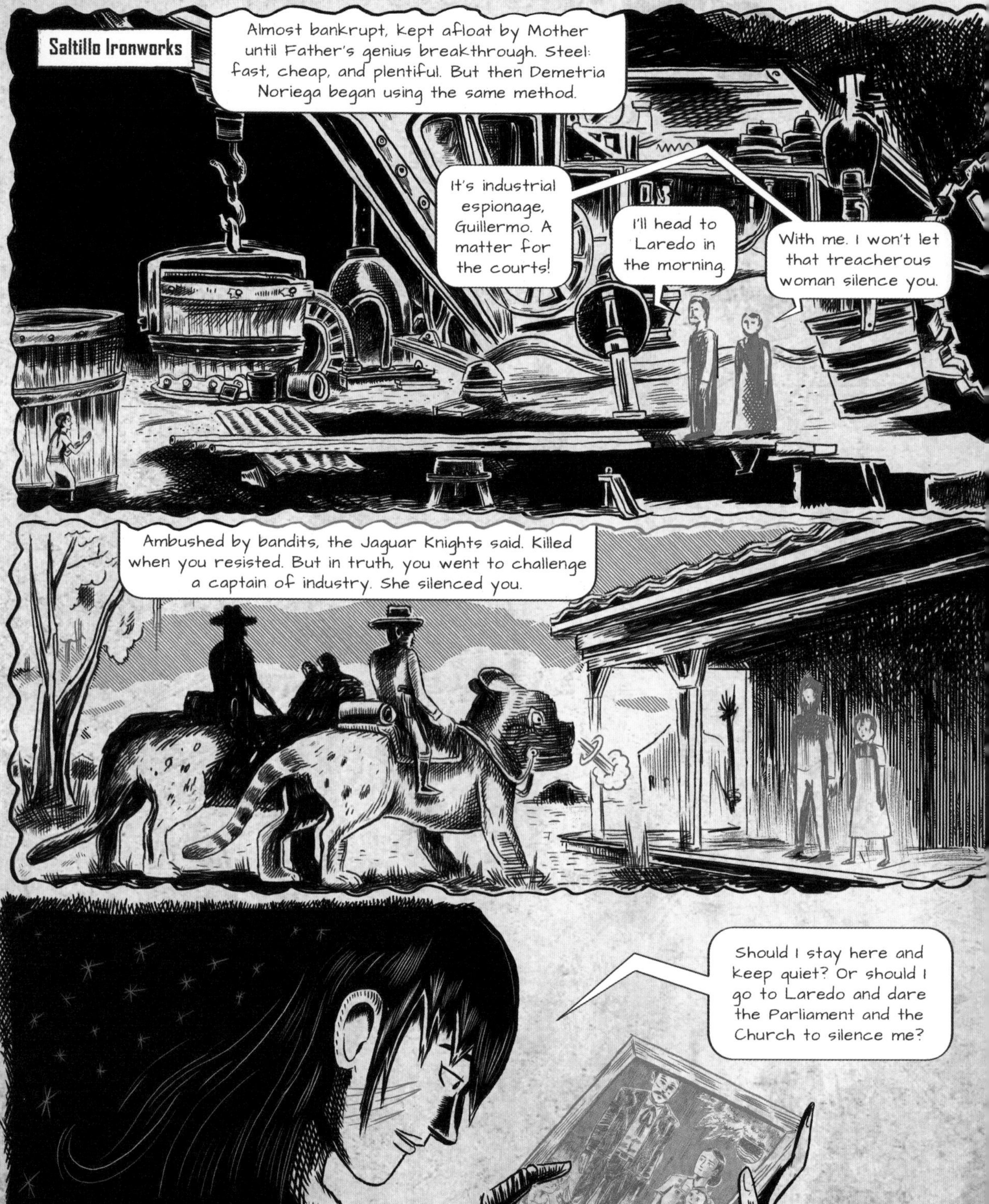
Saltillo Ironworks
Almost bankrupt, kept afloat by Mother until Father's genius breakthrough. Steel: fast, cheap, and plentiful. But then Demetria Noriega began using the same method.
It's industrial espionage, Guillermo. A matter for the courts!
I'll head to Laredo in the morning.
With me. I won't let that treacherous woman silence you.
Ambushed by bandits, the Jaguar Knights said. Killed when you resisted. But in truth, you went to challenge a captain of industry. She silenced you.
Should I stay here and keep quiet? Or should I go to Laredo and dare the Parliament and the Church to silence me?

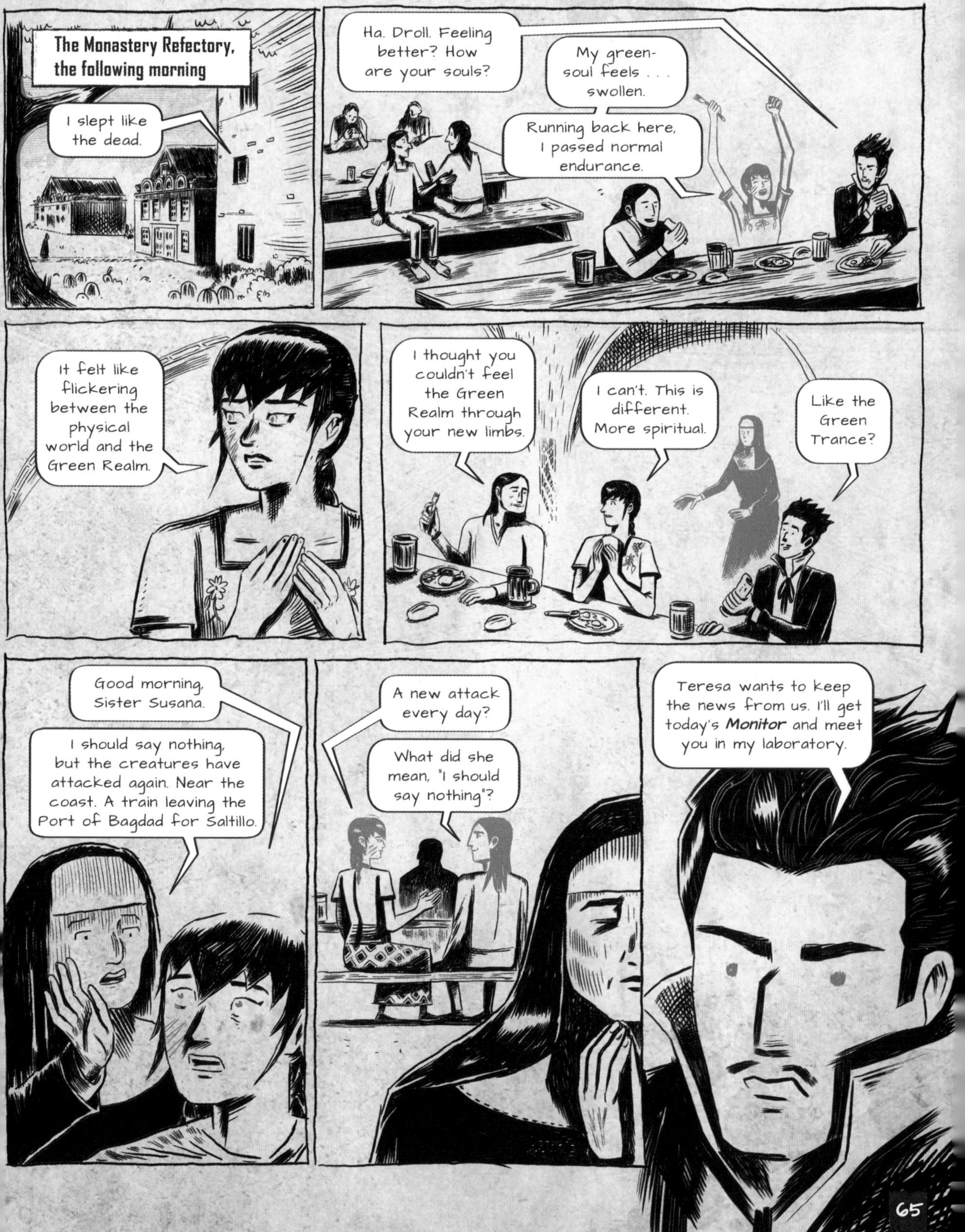
The Monastery Refectory, the following morning
I slept like the dead.
Ha. Droll. Feeling better? How are your souls?
My green-soul feels . . . swollen.
Running back here, I passed normal endurance.
It felt like flickering between the physical world and the Green Realm.
I thought you couldn't feel the Green Realm through your new limbs.
I can't. This is different. More spiritual.
Like the Green Trance?
Good morning, Sister Susana.
I should say nothing, but the creatures have attacked again. Near the coast. A train leaving the Port of Bagdad for Saltillo.
A new attack every day?
What did she mean, "I should say nothing"?
Teresa wants to keep the news from us. I'll get today's **Monitor** and meet you in my laboratory.

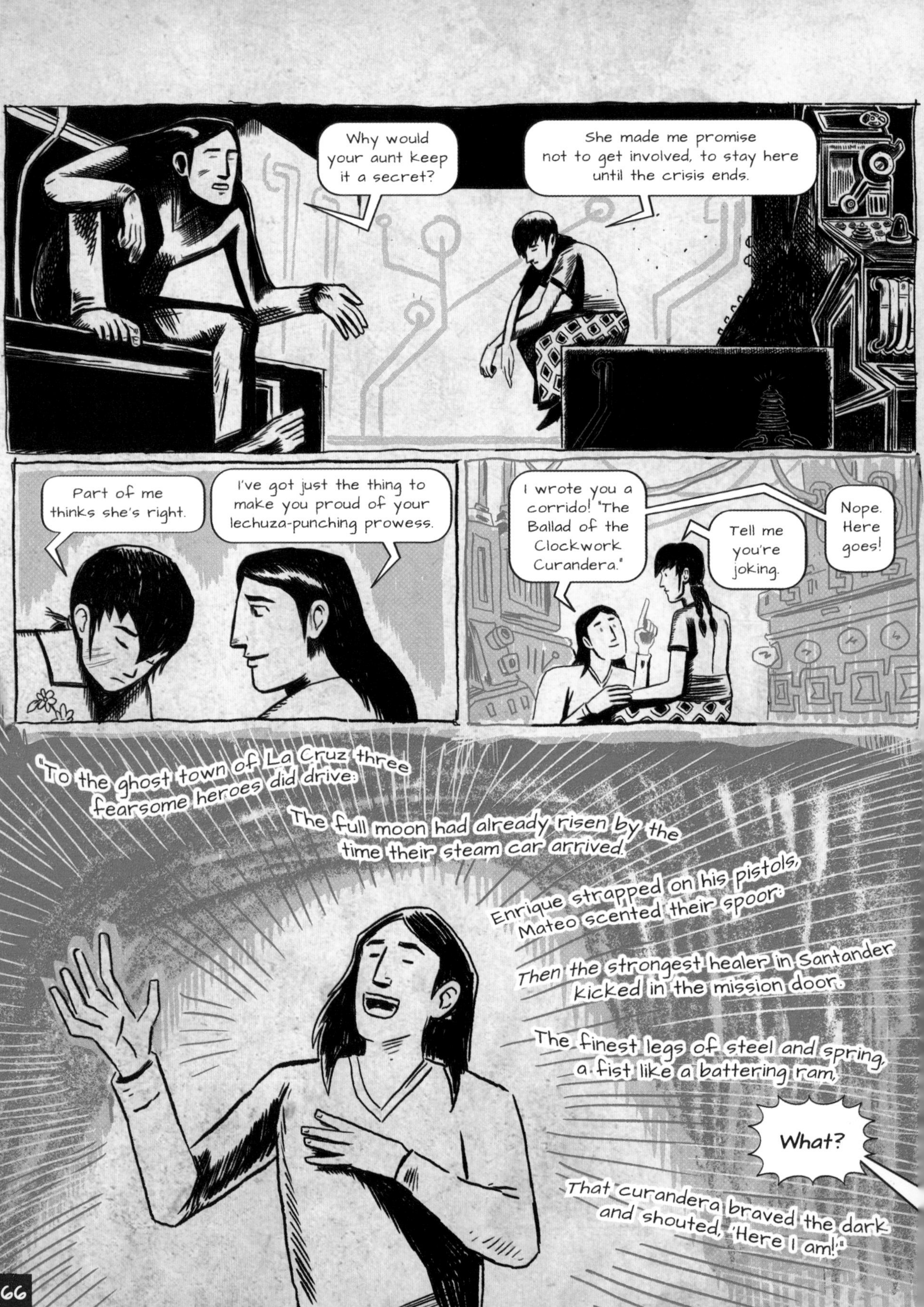
Why would your aunt keep it a secret?
She made me promise not to get involved, to stay here until the crisis ends.
Part of me thinks she's right.
I've got just the thing to make you proud of your lechuza-punching prowess.
I wrote you a corrido! "The Ballad of the Clockwork Curandera."
Tell me you're joking.
Nope. Here goes!
"To the ghost town of La Cruz three fearsome heroes did drive.
The full moon had already risen by the time their steam car arrived.
Enrique strapped on his pistols, Mateo scented their spoor.
Then the strongest healer in Santander kicked in the mission door.
The finest legs of steel and spring, a fist like a battering ram,
What?
That curandera braved the dark and shouted, 'Here I am!'"

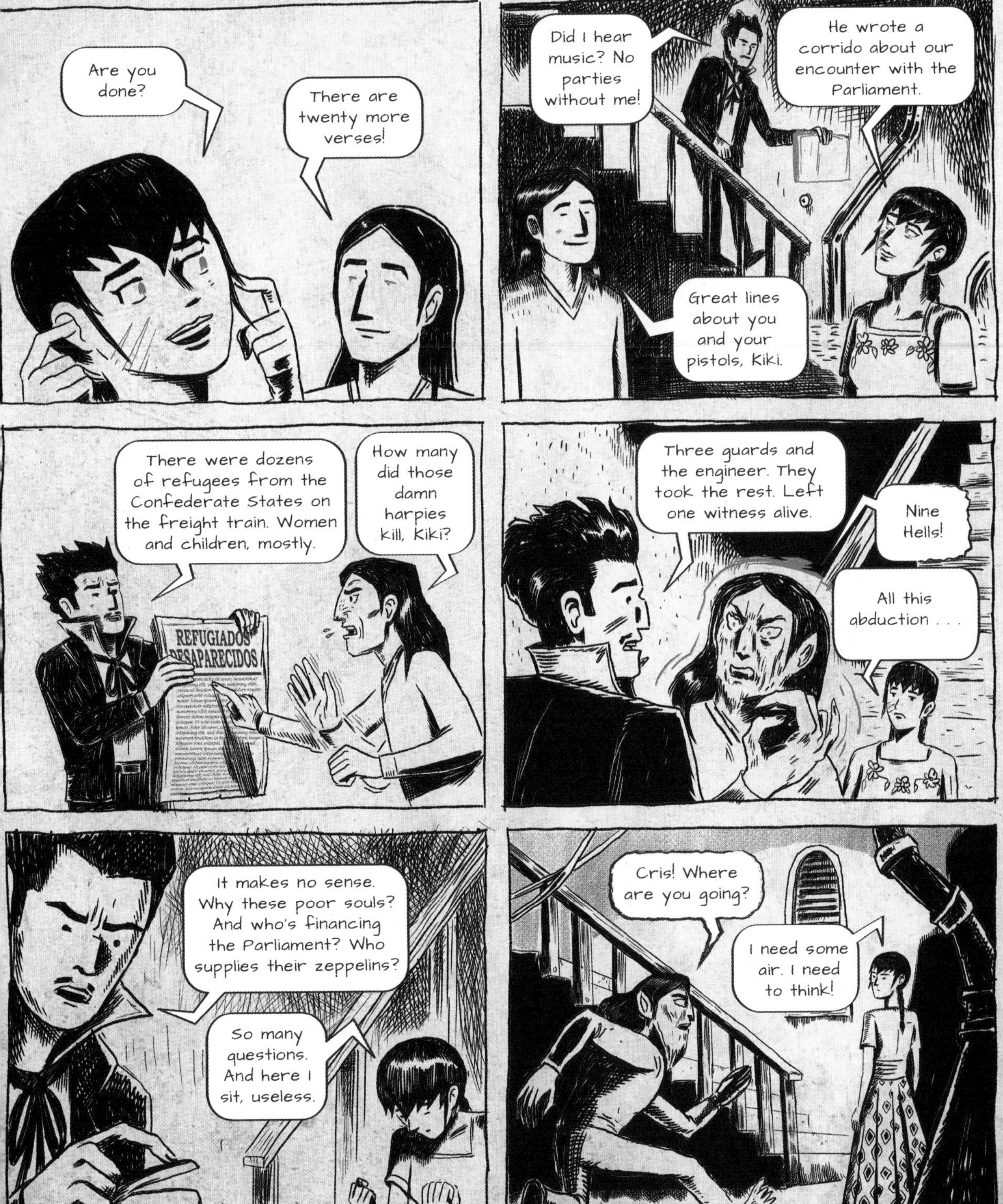

Are you done?
There are twenty more verses!
Did I hear music? No parties without me!
He wrote a corrido about our encounter with the Parliament.
Great lines about you and your pistols, Kiki.
There were dozens of refugees from the Confederate States on the freight train. Women and children, mostly.
REFUGIADOS DESAPARECIDOS
How many did those damn harpies kill, Kiki?
Three guards and the engineer. They took the rest. Left one witness alive.
Nine Hells!
All this abduction . . .
It makes no sense. Why these poor souls? And who's financing the Parliament? Who supplies their zeppelins?
So many questions. And here I sit, useless.
Cris! Where are you going?
I need some air. I need to think!

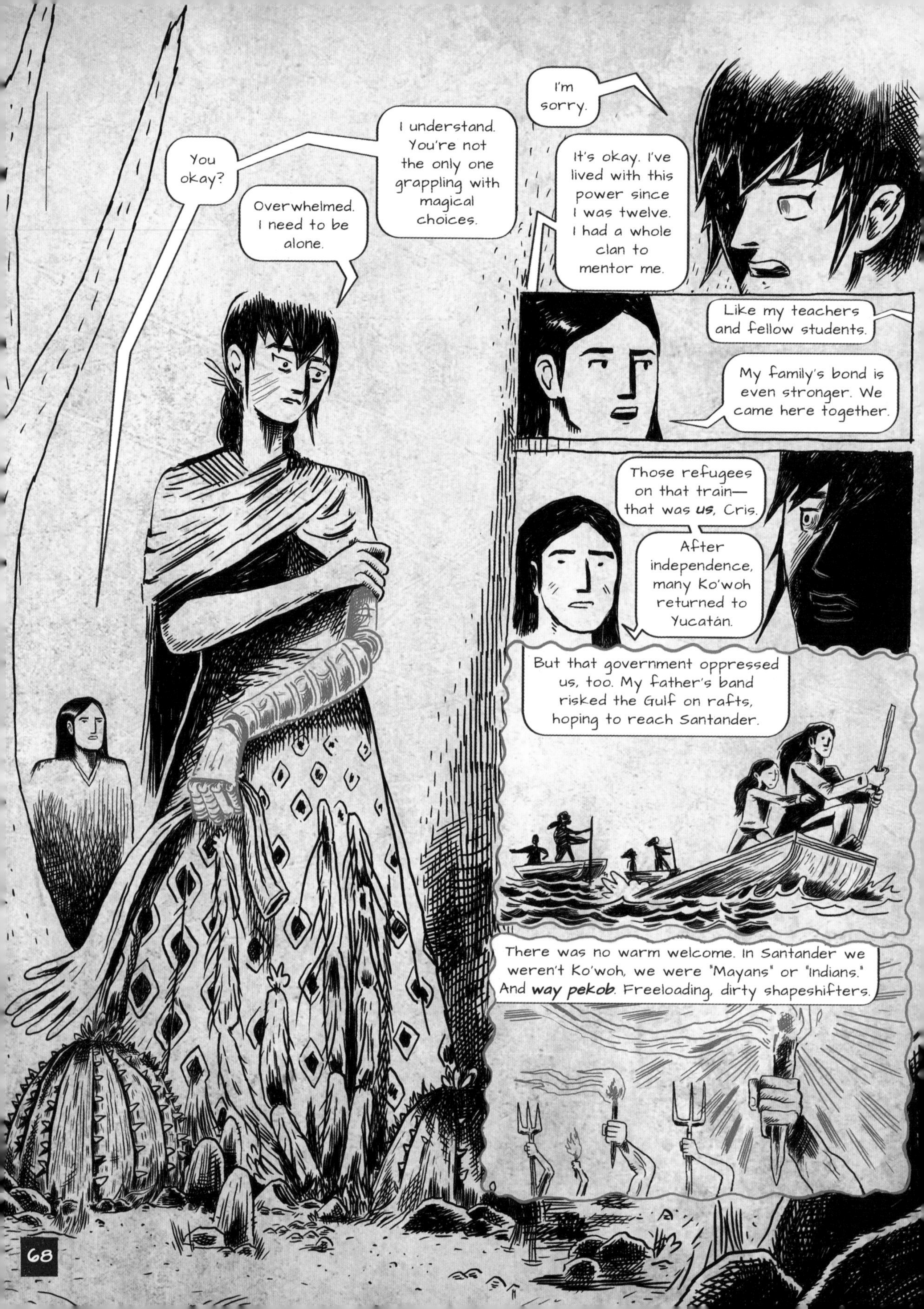
You okay?
Overwhelmed. I need to be alone.
I understand. You're not the only one grappling with magical choices.
I'm sorry.
It's okay. I've lived with this power since I was twelve. I had a whole clan to mentor me.
Like my teachers and fellow students.
My family's bond is even stronger. We came here together.
Those refugees on that train— that was **us**, Cris.
After independence, many Ko'woh returned to Yucatán.
But that government oppressed us, too. My father's band risked the Gulf on rafts, hoping to reach Santander.
There was no warm welcome. In Santander we weren't Ko'woh, we were "Mayans" or "Indians." And ***way pekob***. Freeloading, dirty shapeshifters.

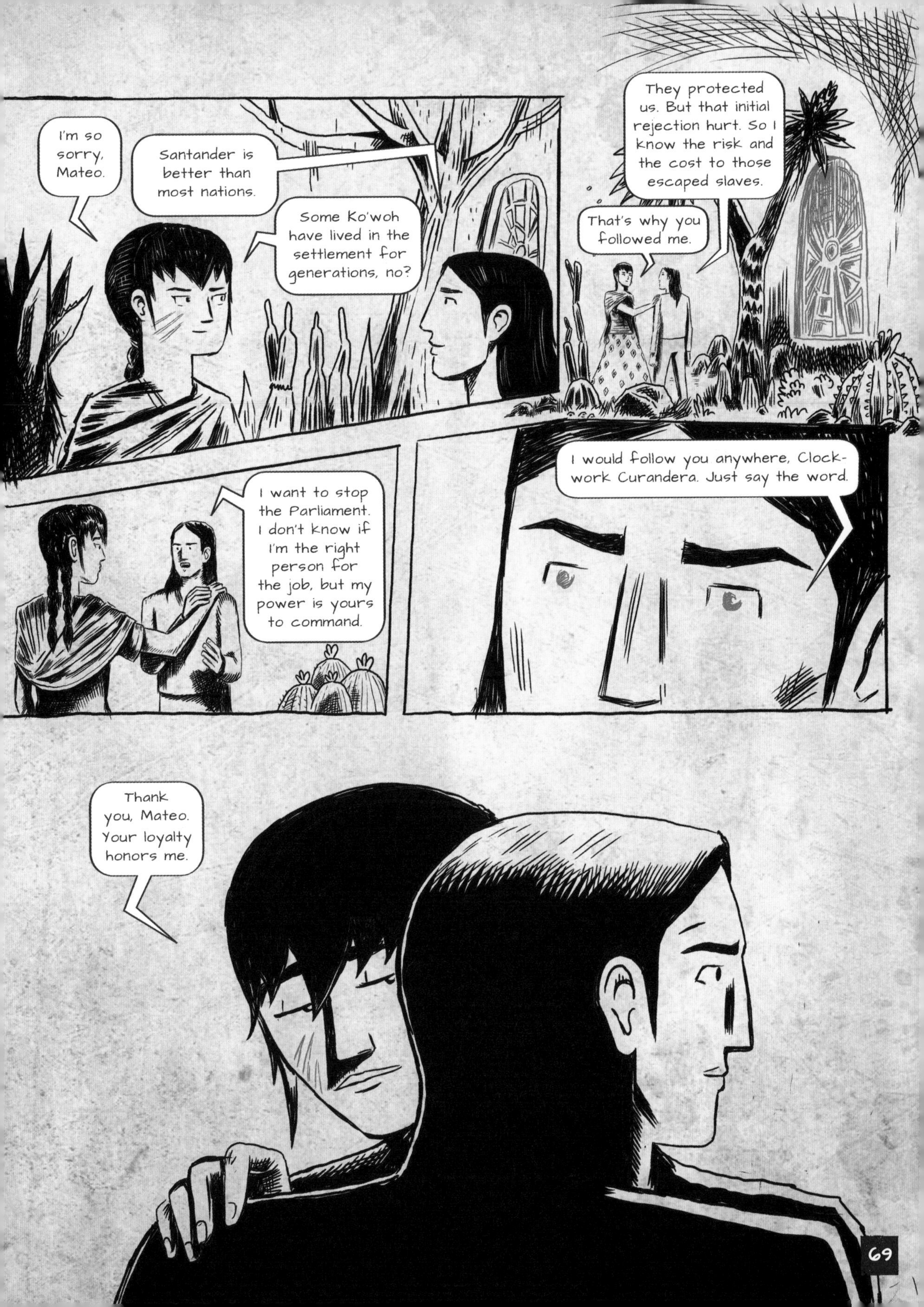

I'm so sorry, Mateo.
Santander is better than most nations.
Some Ko'woh have lived in the settlement for generations, no?
They protected us. But that initial rejection hurt. So I know the risk and the cost to those escaped slaves.
That's why you followed me.
I want to stop the Parliament. I don't know if I'm the right person for the job, but my power is yours to command.
I would follow you anywhere, Clockwork Curandera. Just say the word.
Thank you, Mateo. Your loyalty honors me.

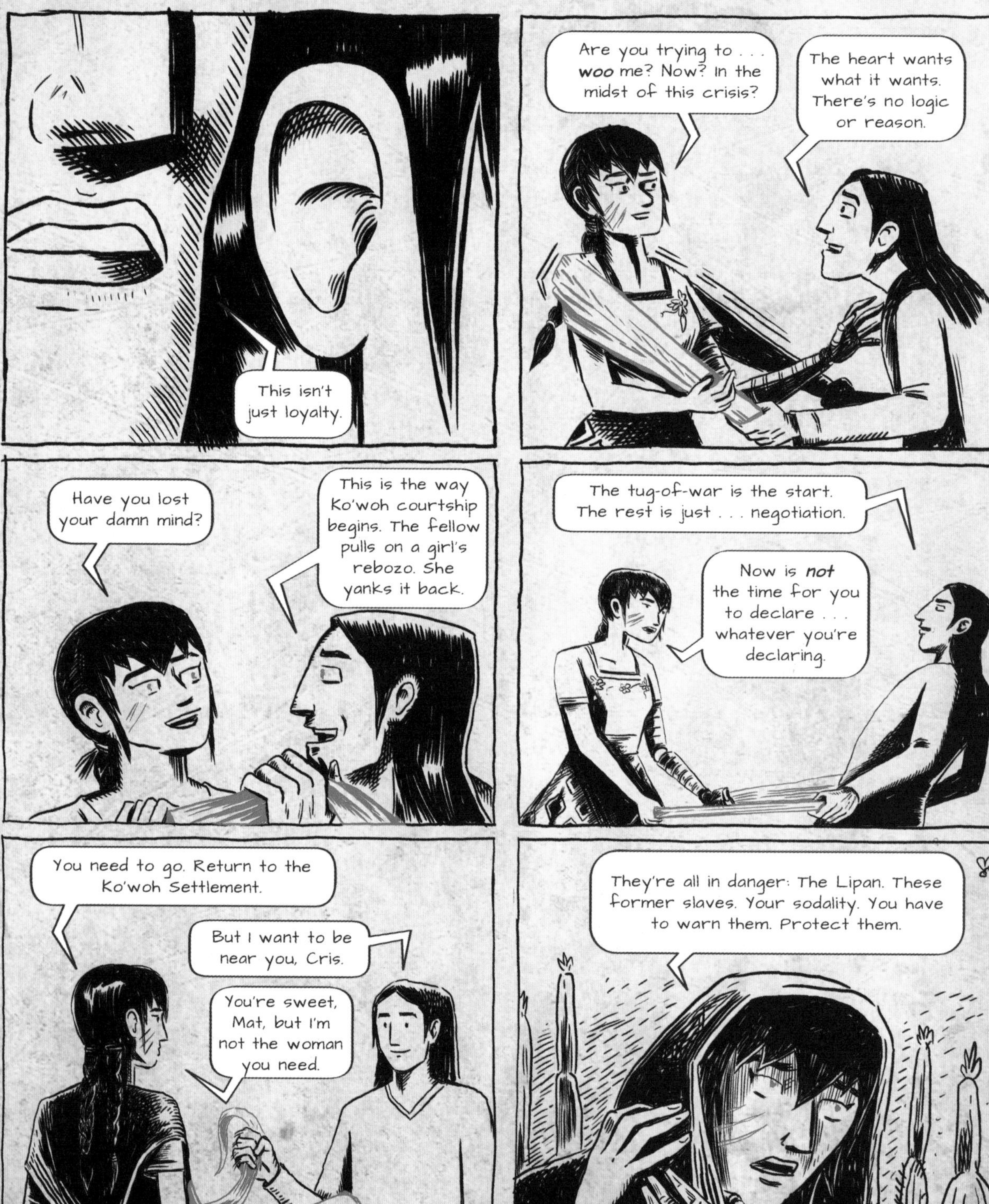
This isn't just loyalty.
Are you trying to . . . woo me? Now? In the midst of this crisis?
The heart wants what it wants. There's no logic or reason.
Have you lost your damn mind?
This is the way Ko'woh courtship begins. The fellow pulls on a girl's rebozo. She yanks it back.
The tug-of-war is the start. The rest is just . . . negotiation.
Now is *not* the time for you to declare . . . whatever you're declaring.
You need to go. Return to the Ko'woh Settlement.
But I want to be near you, Cris.
You're sweet, Mat, but I'm not the woman you need.
They're all in danger: The Lipan. These former slaves. Your sodality. You have to warn them. Protect them.

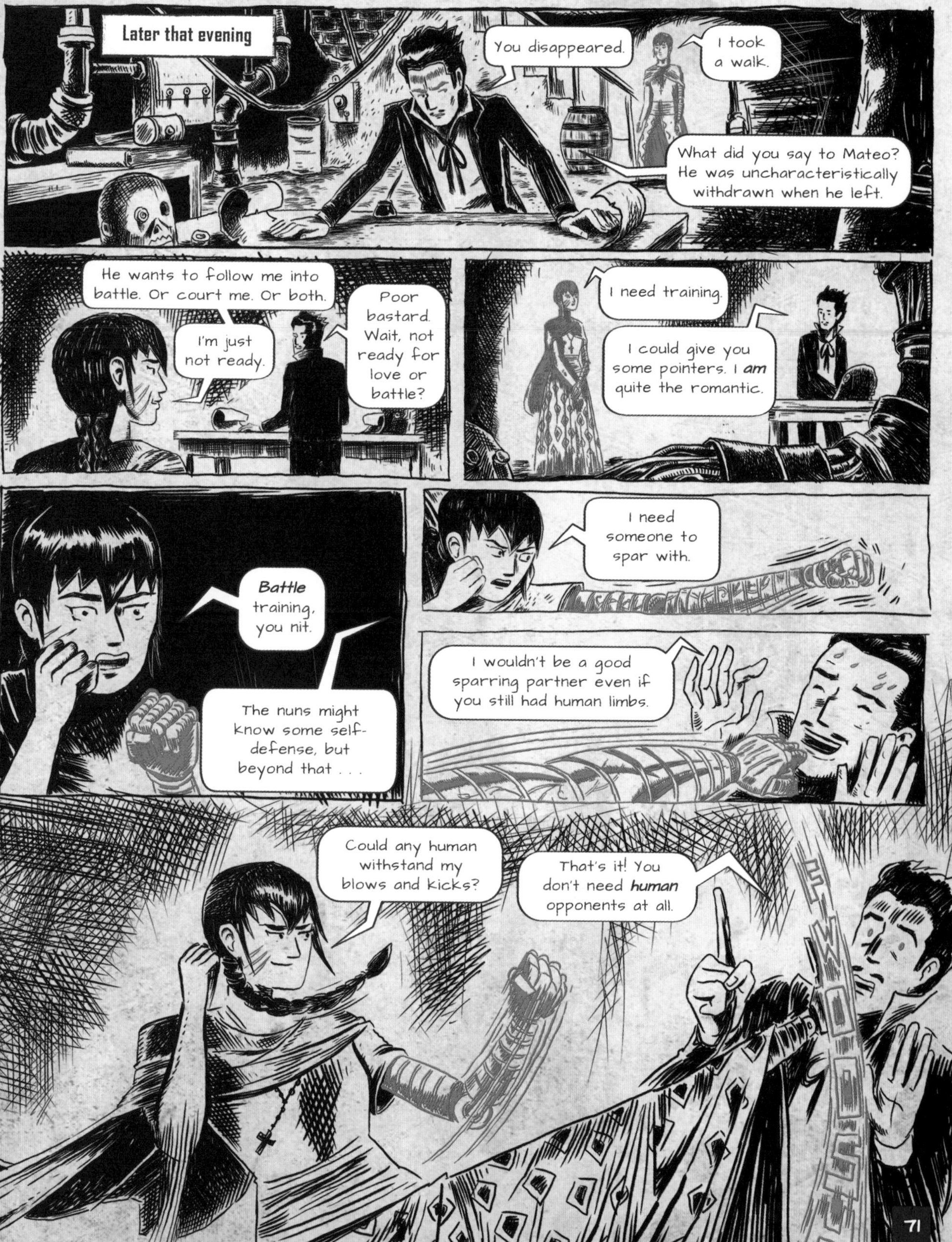

Later that evening
You disappeared.
I took a walk.
What did you say to Mateo? He was uncharacteristically withdrawn when he left.
He wants to follow me into battle. Or court me. Or both.
I'm just not ready.
Poor bastard. Wait, not ready for love or battle?
I need training.
I could give you some pointers. I *am* quite the romantic.
Battle training, you nit.
The nuns might know some self-defense, but beyond that . . .
I need someone to spar with.
I wouldn't be a good sparring partner even if you still had human limbs.
Could any human withstand my blows and kicks?
That's it! You don't need ***human*** opponents at all.

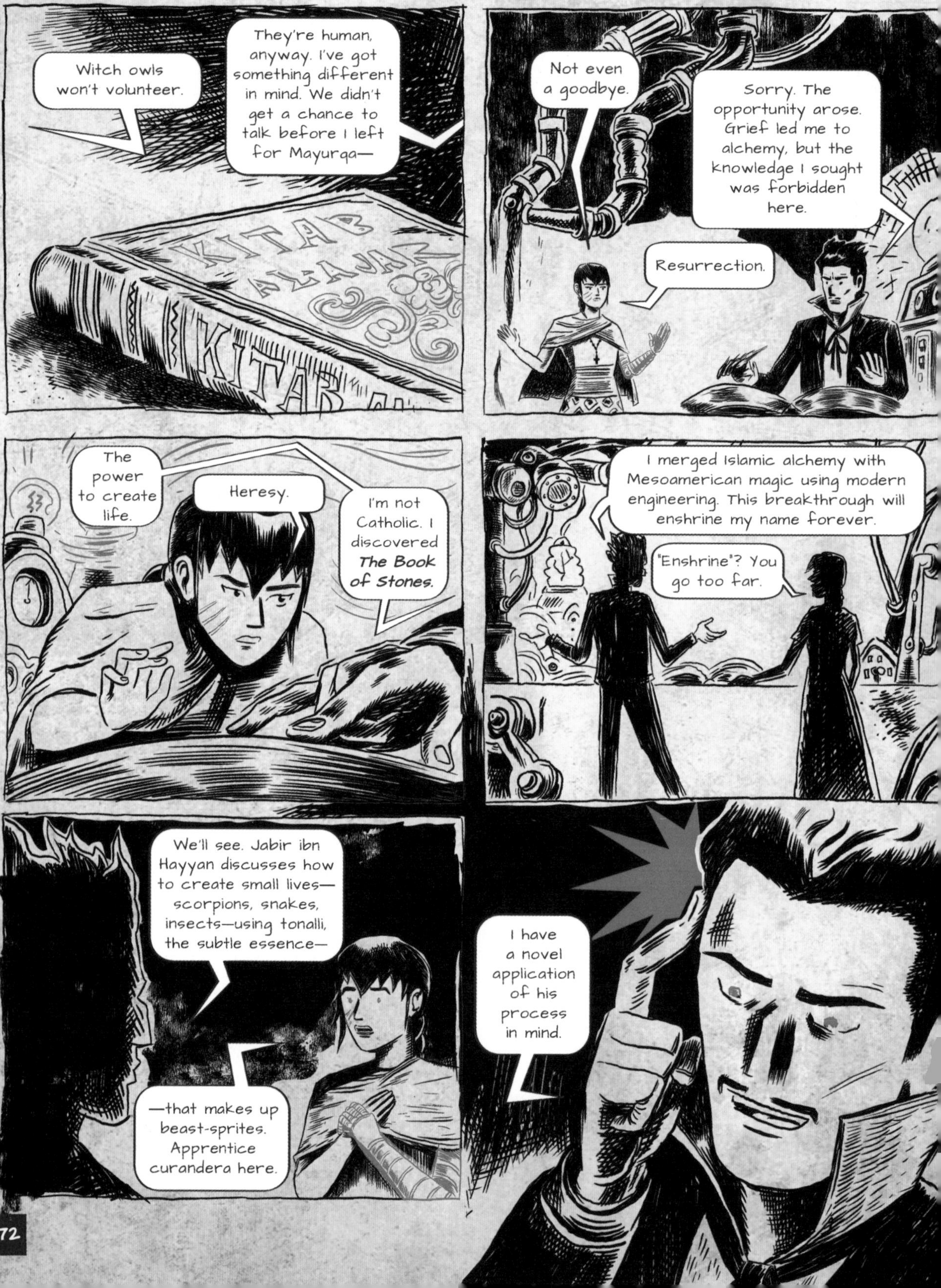

Witch owls won't volunteer.
They're human, anyway. I've got something different in mind. We didn't get a chance to talk before I left for Mayurqa—
KITAB AL-AJAM
KITAB AL-
Not even a goodbye.
Sorry. The opportunity arose. Grief led me to alchemy, but the knowledge I sought was forbidden here.
Resurrection.
The power to create life.
Heresy.
I'm not Catholic. I discovered ***The Book of Stones.***
I merged Islamic alchemy with Mesoamerican magic using modern engineering. This breakthrough will enshrine my name forever.
"Enshrine"? You go too far.
We'll see. Jabir ibn Hayyan discusses how to create small lives—scorpions, snakes, insects—using tonalli, the subtle essence—
—that makes up beast-sprites. Apprentice curandera here.
I have a novel application of his process in mind.

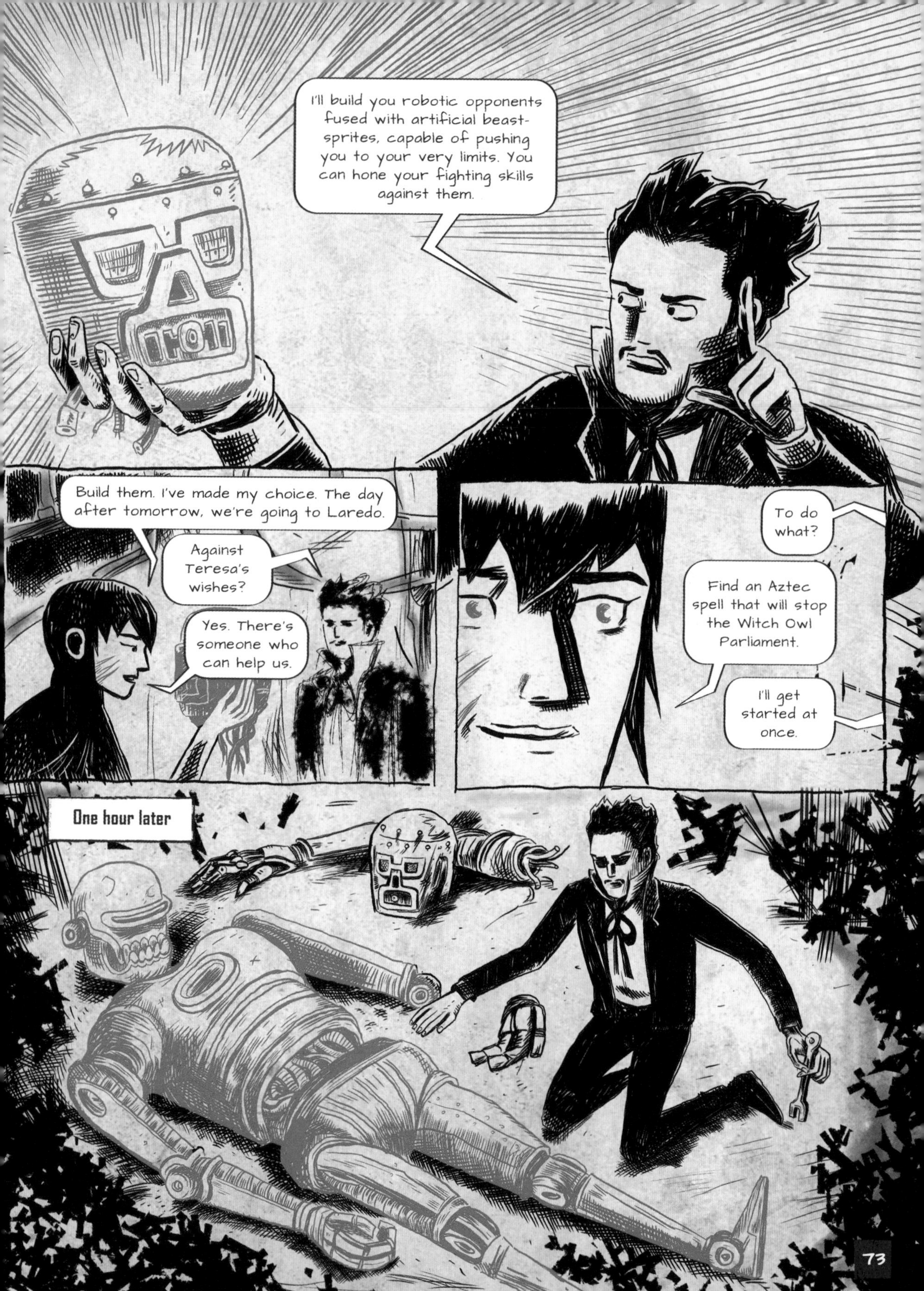

I'll build you robotic opponents fused with artificial beast-sprites, capable of pushing you to your very limits. You can hone your fighting skills against them.
Build them. I've made my choice. The day after tomorrow, we're going to Laredo.
Against Teresa's wishes?
Yes. There's someone who can help us.
To do what?
Find an Aztec spell that will stop the Witch Owl Parliament.
I'll get started at once.
One hour later

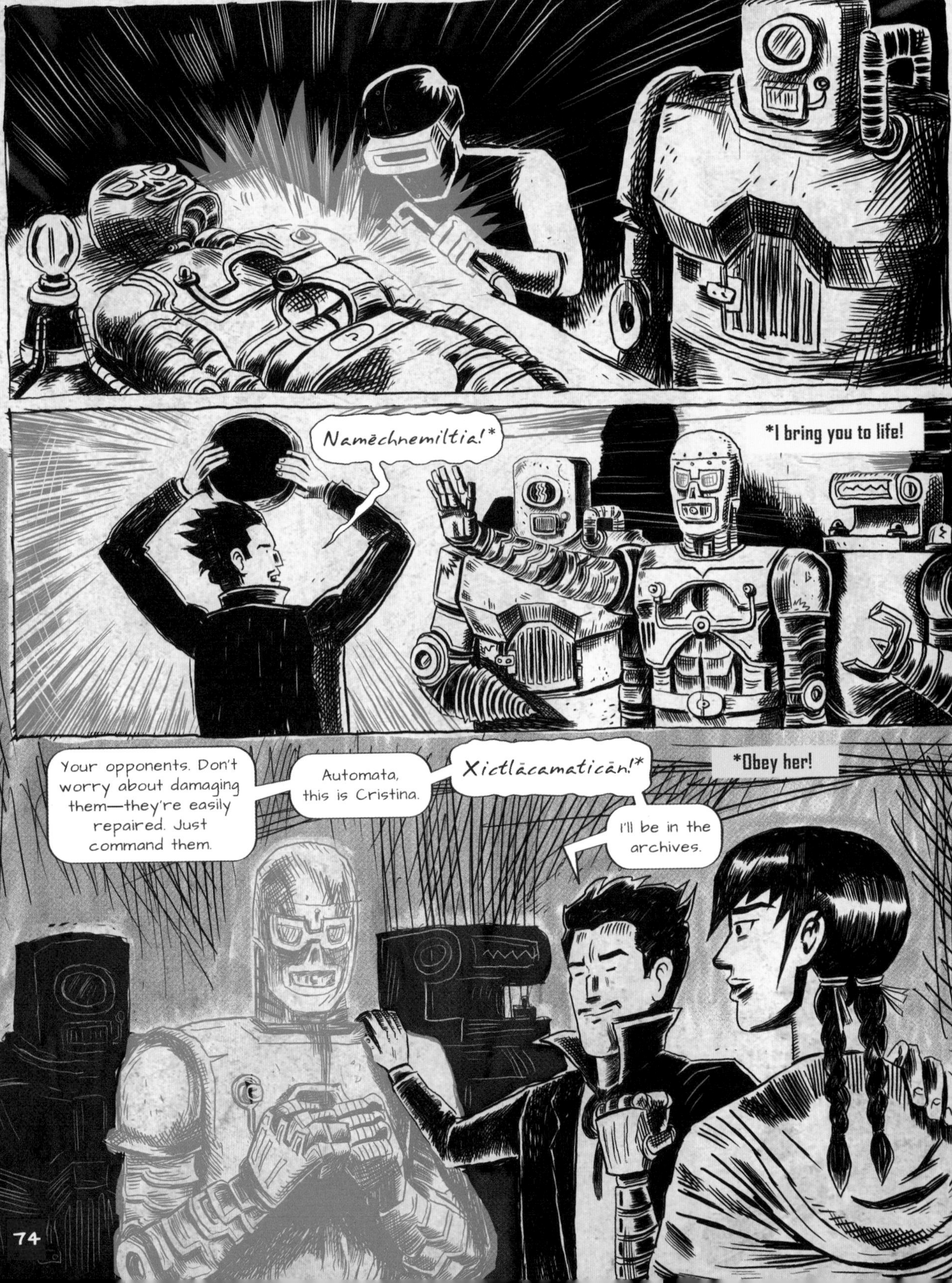
Namēchnemiltia!*
*I bring you to life!
Your opponents. Don't worry about damaging them—they're easily repaired. Just command them.
Automata, this is Cristina.
Xictlācamaticān!*
*Obey her!
I'll be in the archives.

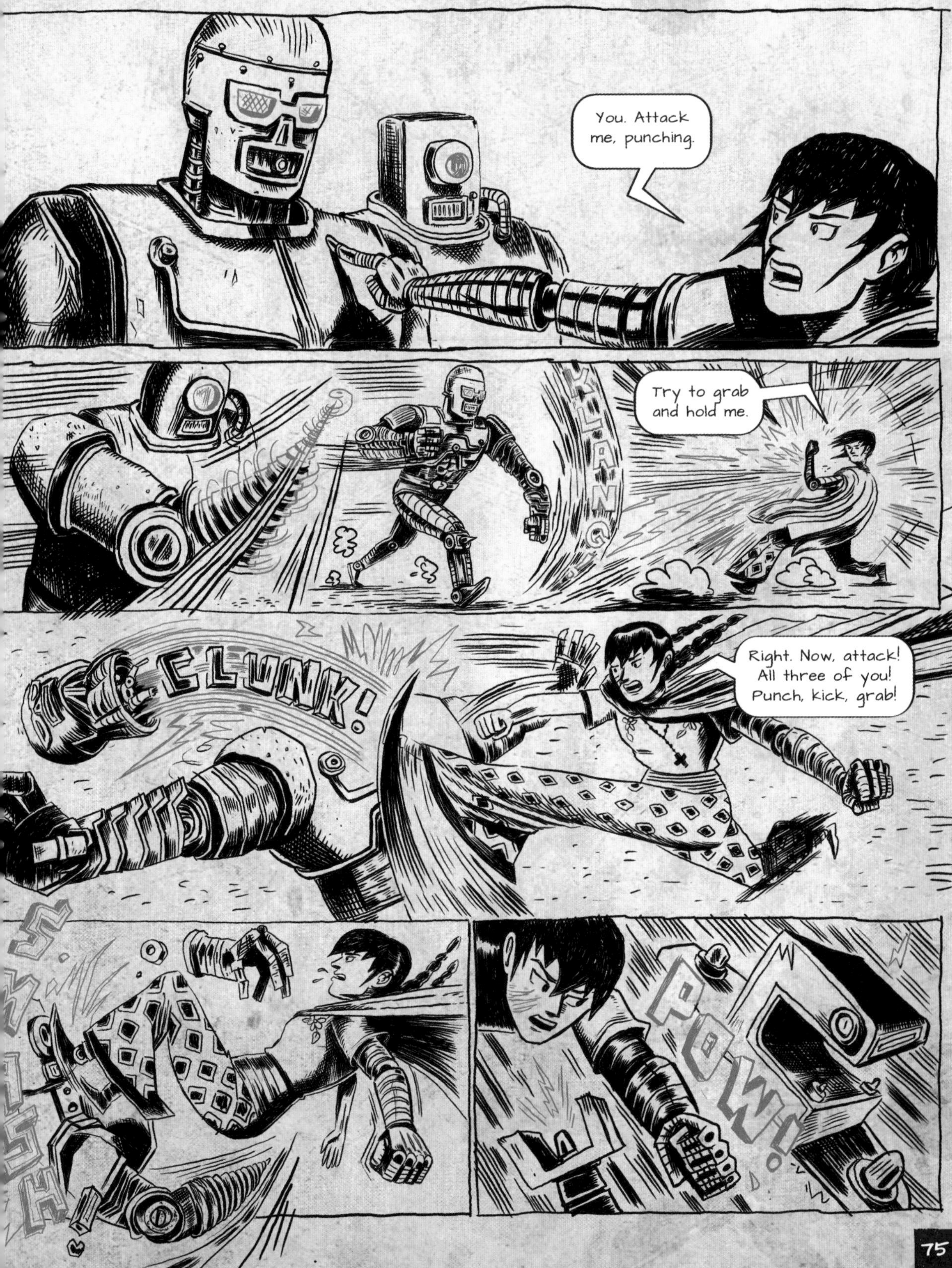

You. Attack me, punching.
Try to grab and hold me.
KLANG
CLUNK!
Right. Now, attack! All three of you! Punch, kick, grab!
POW!

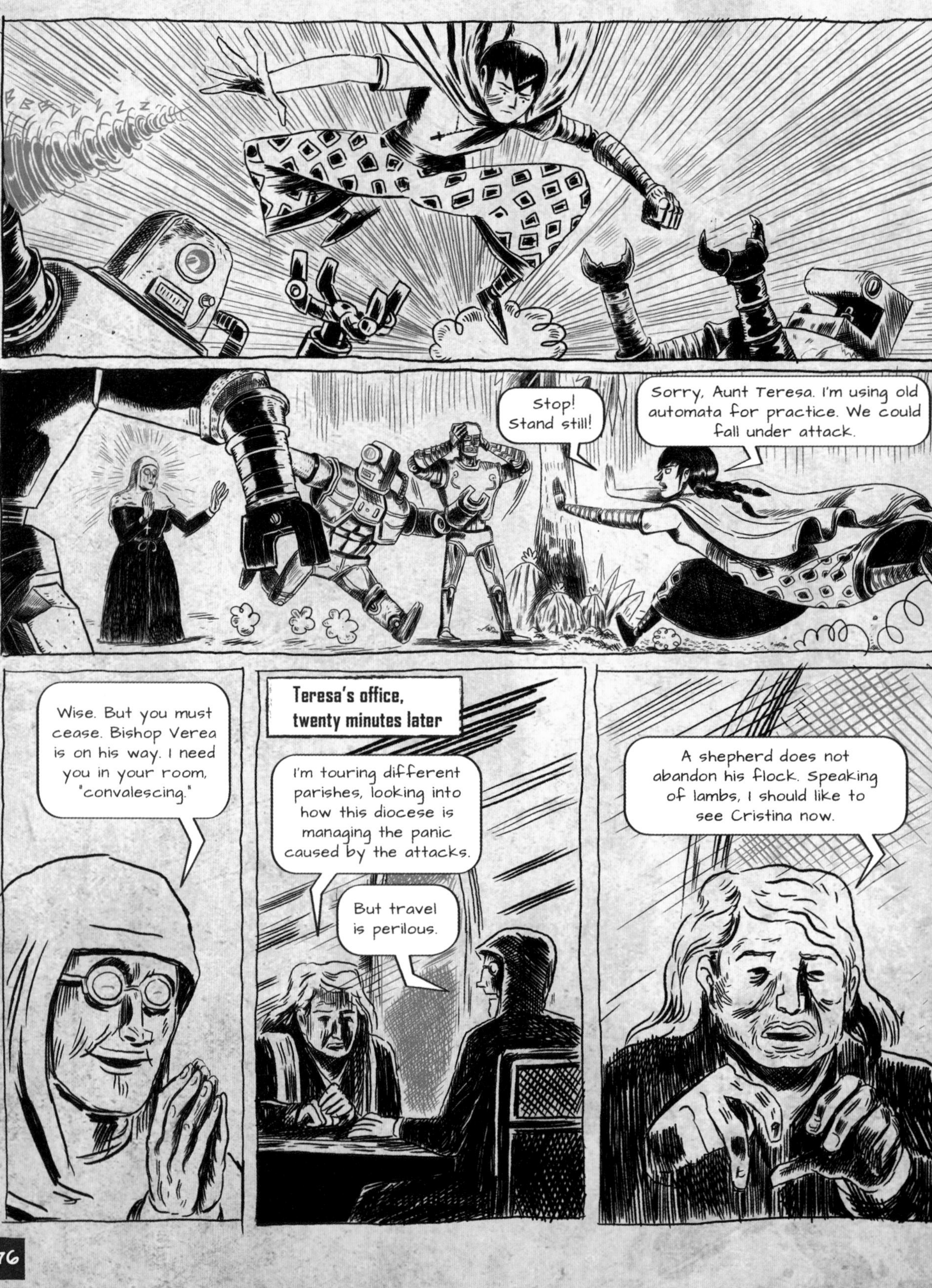
BBBZZZZ
Stop! Stand still!
Sorry, Aunt Teresa. I'm using old automata for practice. We could fall under attack.
Wise. But you must cease. Bishop Verea is on his way. I need you in your room, "convalescing."
Teresa's office, twenty minutes later
I'm touring different parishes, looking into how this diocese is managing the panic caused by the attacks.
But travel is perilous.
A shepherd does not abandon his flock. Speaking of lambs, I should like to see Cristina now.

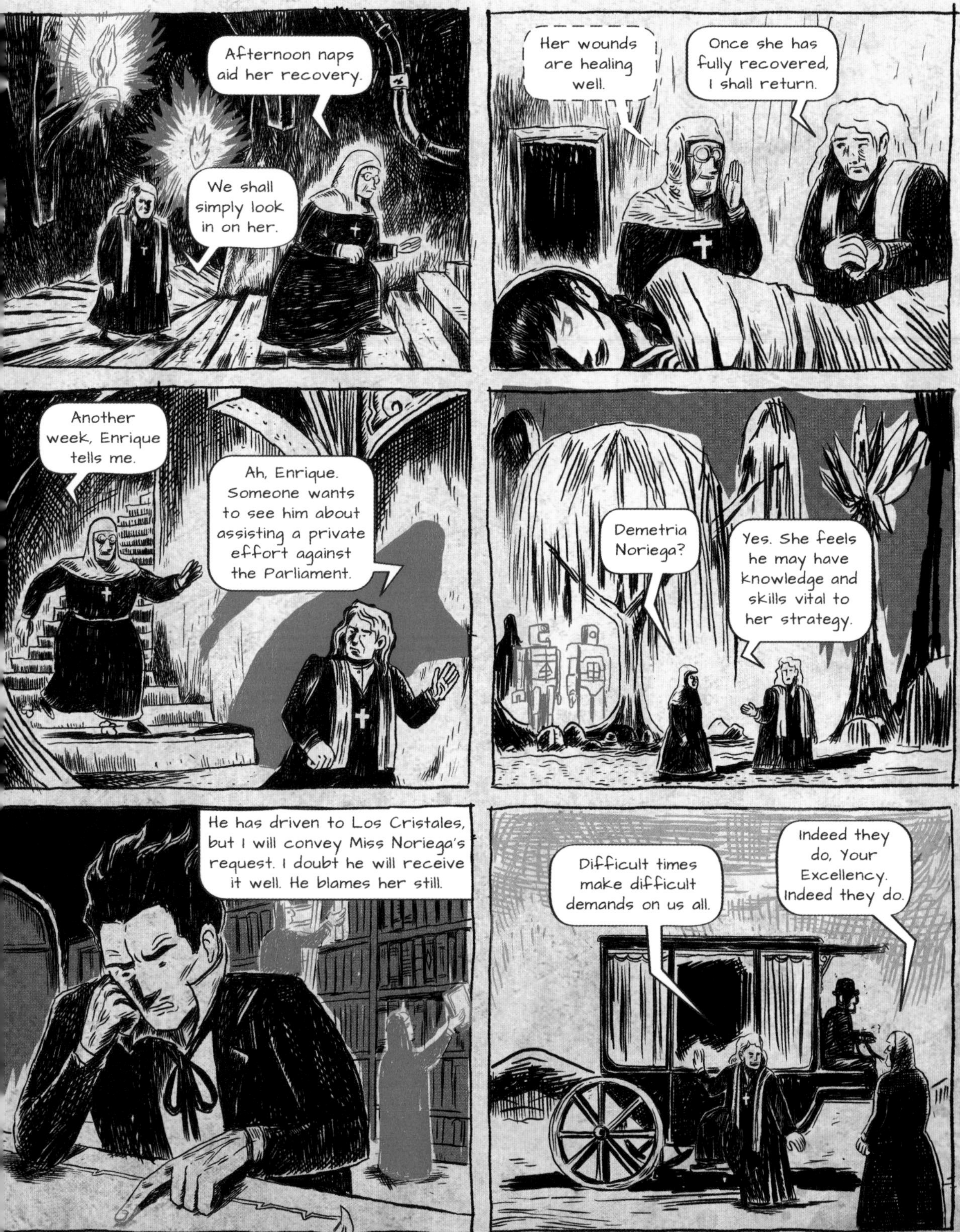
Afternoon naps aid her recovery.
We shall simply look in on her.
Her wounds are healing well.
Once she has fully recovered, I shall return.
Another week, Enrique tells me.
Ah, Enrique. Someone wants to see him about assisting a private effort against the Parliament.
Demetria Noriega?
Yes. She feels he may have knowledge and skills vital to her strategy.
He has driven to Los Cristales, but I will convey Miss Noriega's request. I doubt he will receive it well. He blames her still.
Difficult times make difficult demands on us all.
Indeed they do, Your Excellency. Indeed they do.

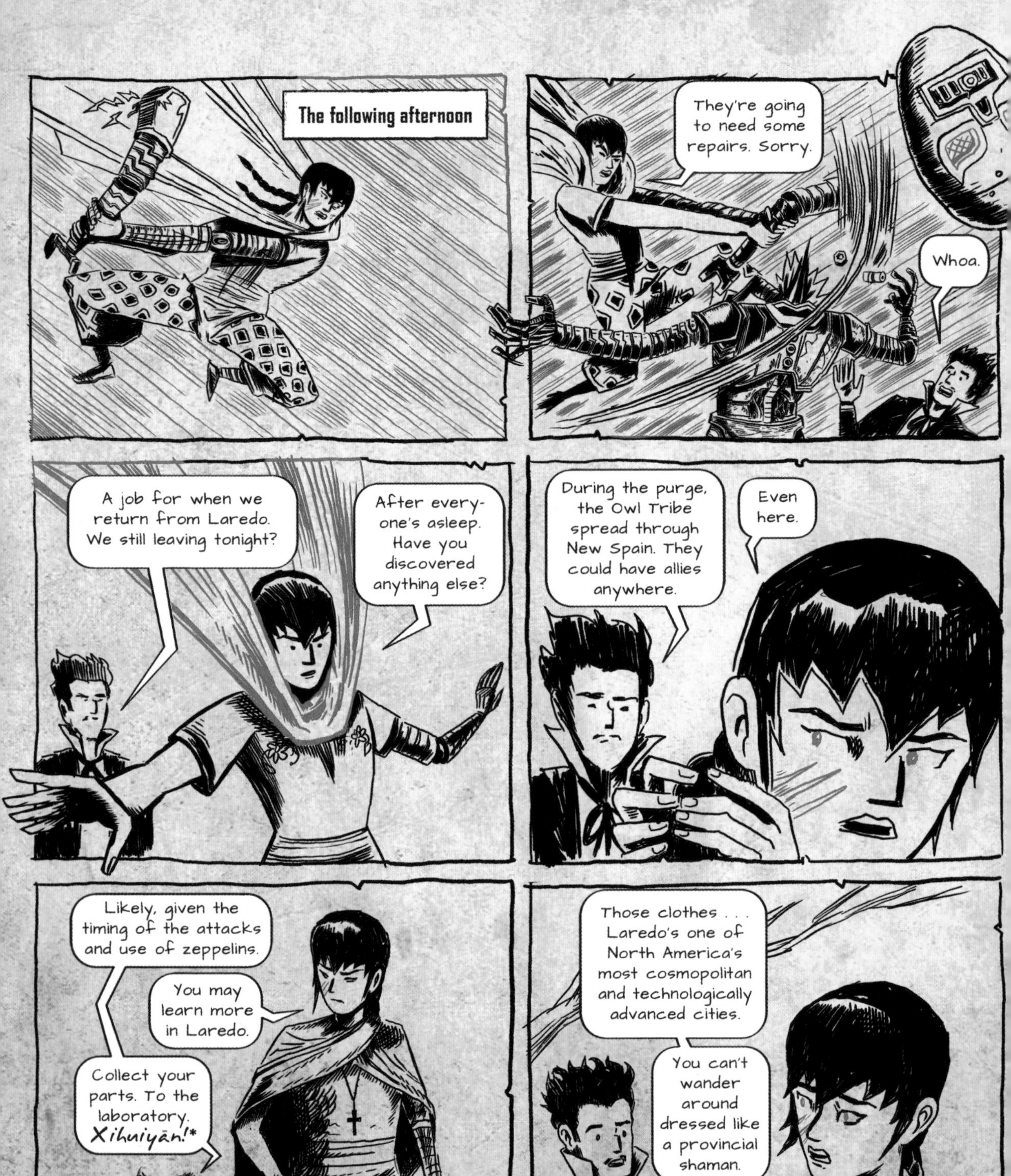
The following afternoon
They're going to need some repairs. Sorry.
Whoa.
A job for when we return from Laredo. We still leaving tonight?
After every-one's asleep. Have you discovered anything else?
During the purge, the Owl Tribe spread through New Spain. They could have allies anywhere.
Even here.
Likely, given the timing of the attacks and use of zeppelins.
You may learn more in Laredo.
Collect your parts. To the laboratory. *Xihuiyān!**
*Go!
Those clothes . . . Laredo's one of North America's most cosmopolitan and technologically advanced cities.
You can't wander around dressed like a provincial shaman.

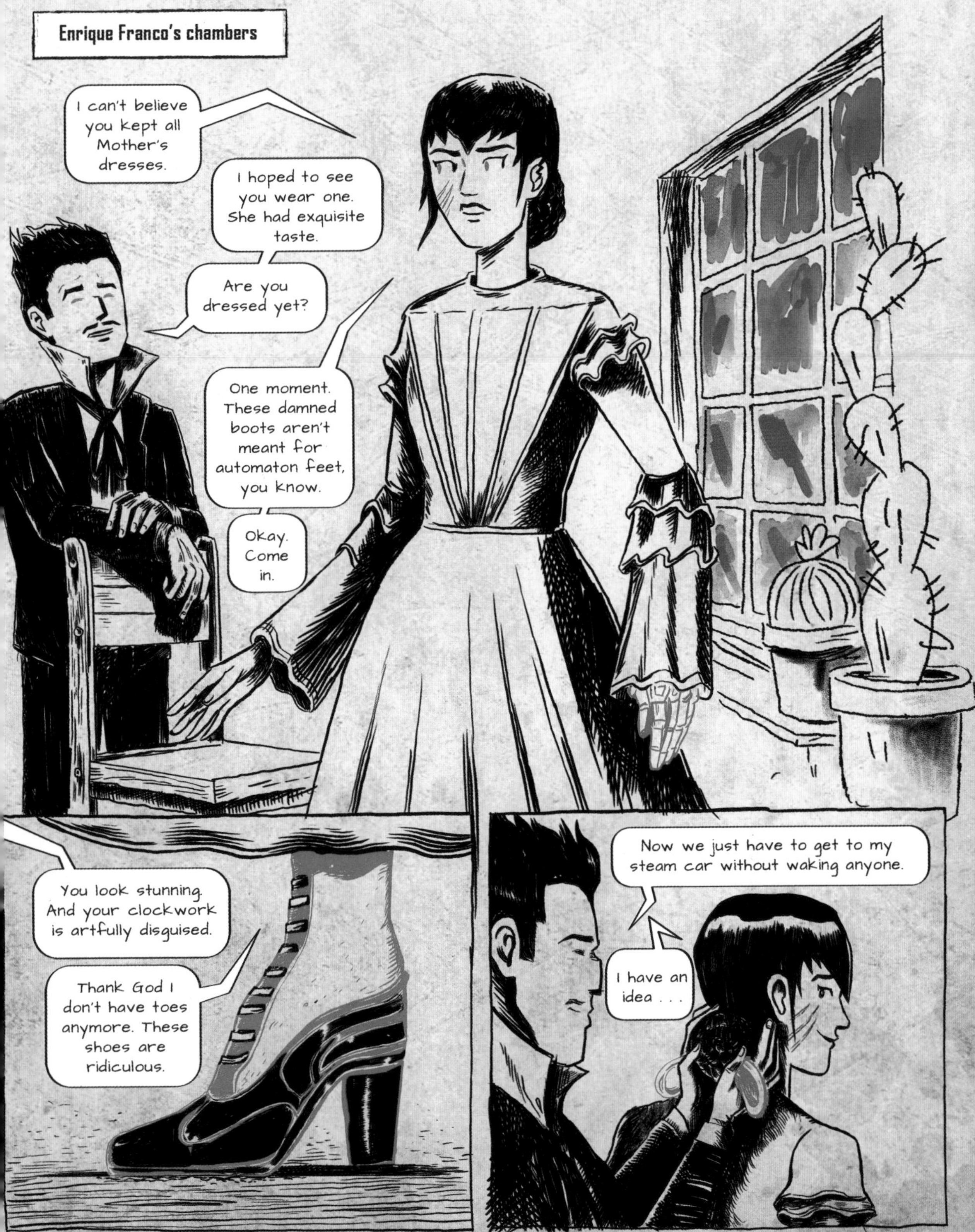
Enrique Franco's chambers
I can't believe you kept all Mother's dresses.
I hoped to see you wear one. She had exquisite taste.
Are you dressed yet?
One moment. These damned boots aren't meant for automaton feet, you know.
Okay. Come in.
You look stunning. And your clockwork is artfully disguised.
Thank God I don't have toes anymore. These shoes are ridiculous.
Now we just have to get to my steam car without waking anyone.
I have an idea . . .

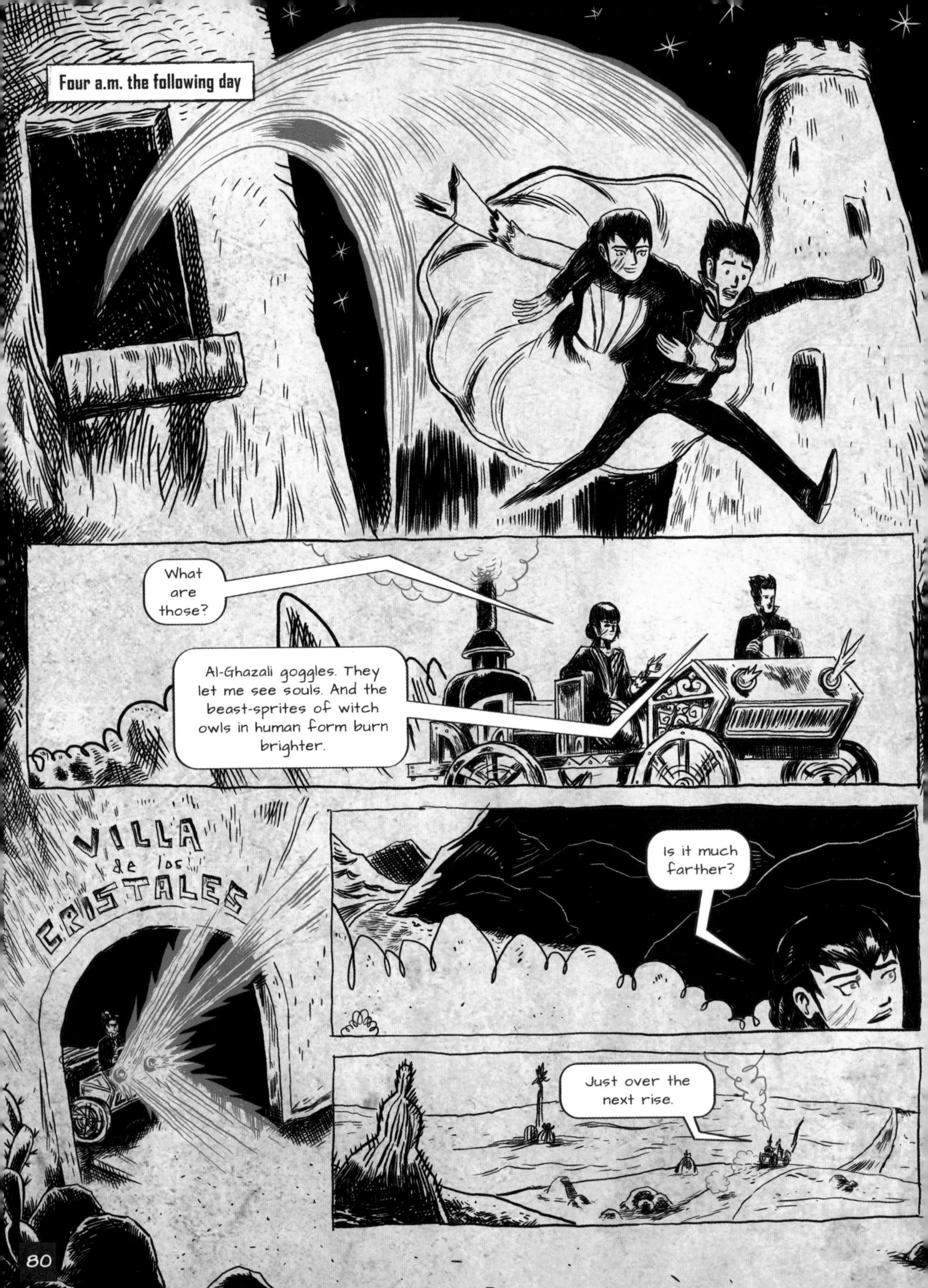

Four a.m. the following day
What are those?
Al-Ghazali goggles. They let me see souls. And the beast-sprites of witch owls in human form burn brighter.
VILLA de los CRISTALES
Is it much farther?
Just over the next rise.

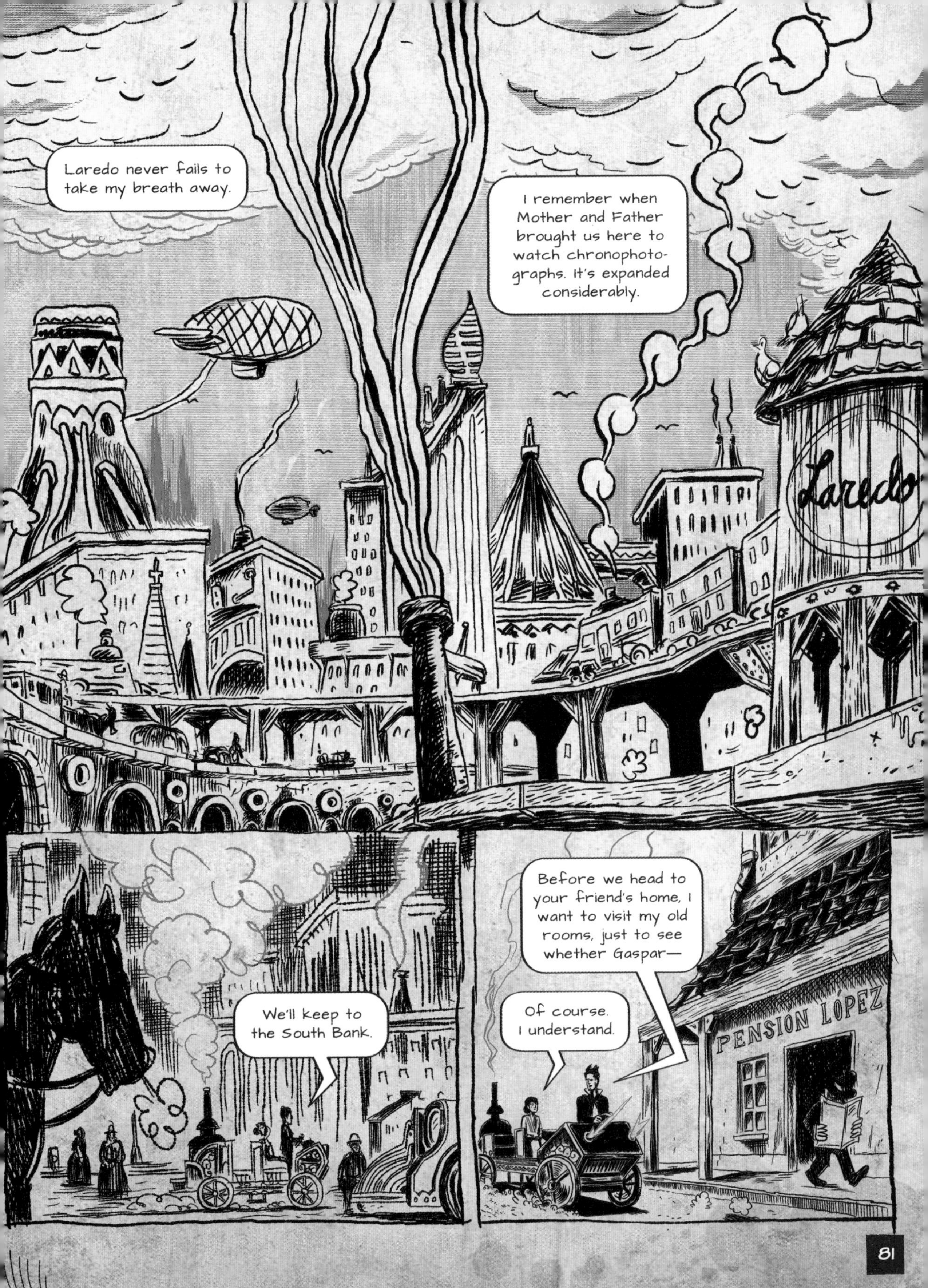
Laredo never fails to take my breath away.
I remember when Mother and Father brought us here to watch chronophoto-graphs. It's expanded considerably.
Laredo
We'll keep to the South Bank.
Before we head to your friend's home, I want to visit my old rooms, just to see whether Gaspar—
Of course. I understand.
PENSION LÓPEZ

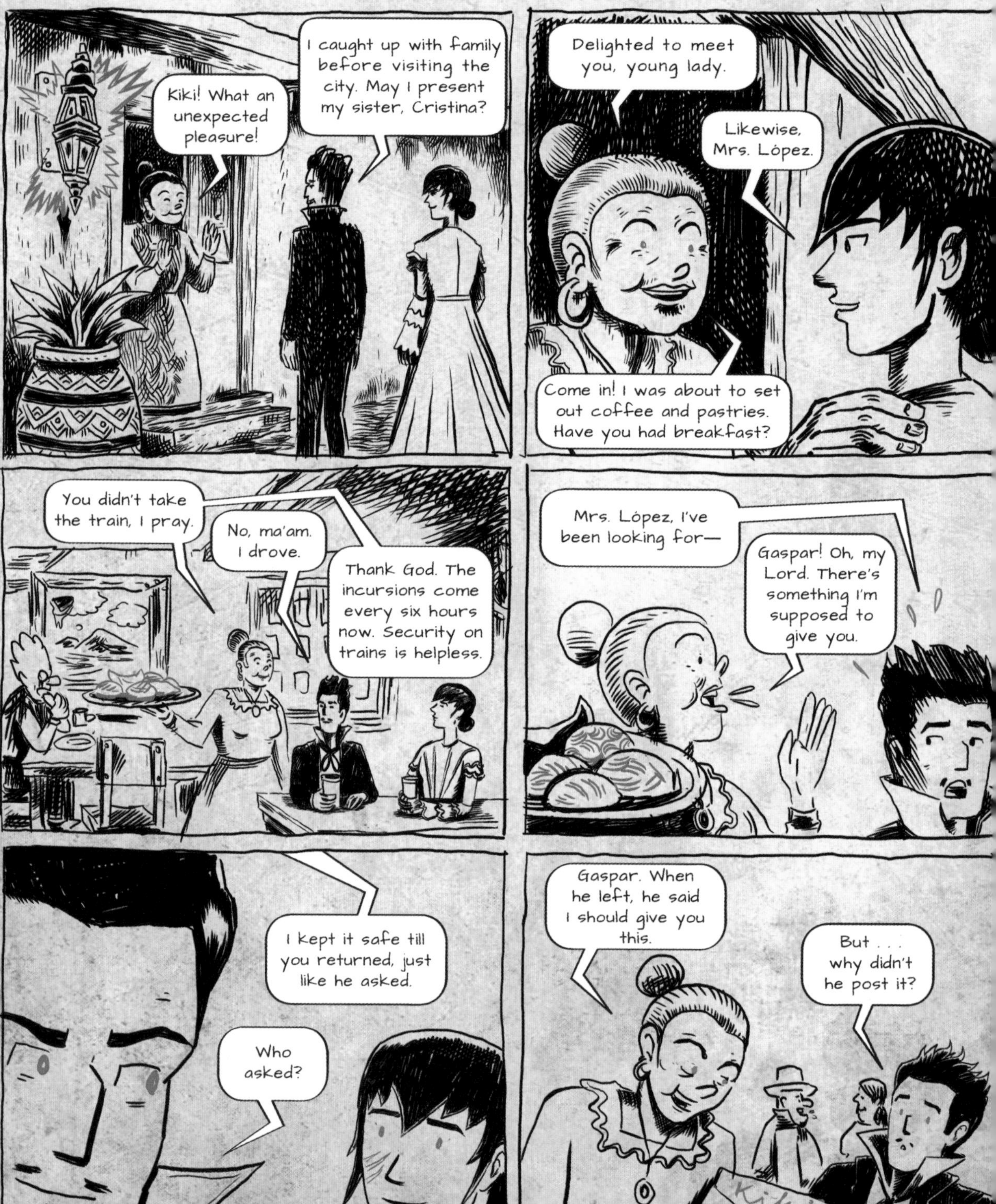
Kiki! What an unexpected pleasure!
I caught up with family before visiting the city. May I present my sister, Cristina?
Delighted to meet you, young lady.
Likewise, Mrs. López.
Come in! I was about to set out coffee and pastries. Have you had breakfast?
You didn't take the train, I pray.
No, ma'am. I drove.
Thank God. The incursions come every six hours now. Security on trains is helpless.
Mrs. López, I've been looking for—
Gaspar! Oh, my Lord. There's something I'm supposed to give you.
I kept it safe till you returned, just like he asked.
Who asked?
Gaspar. When he left, he said I should give you this.
But . . . why didn't he post it?
Kiki

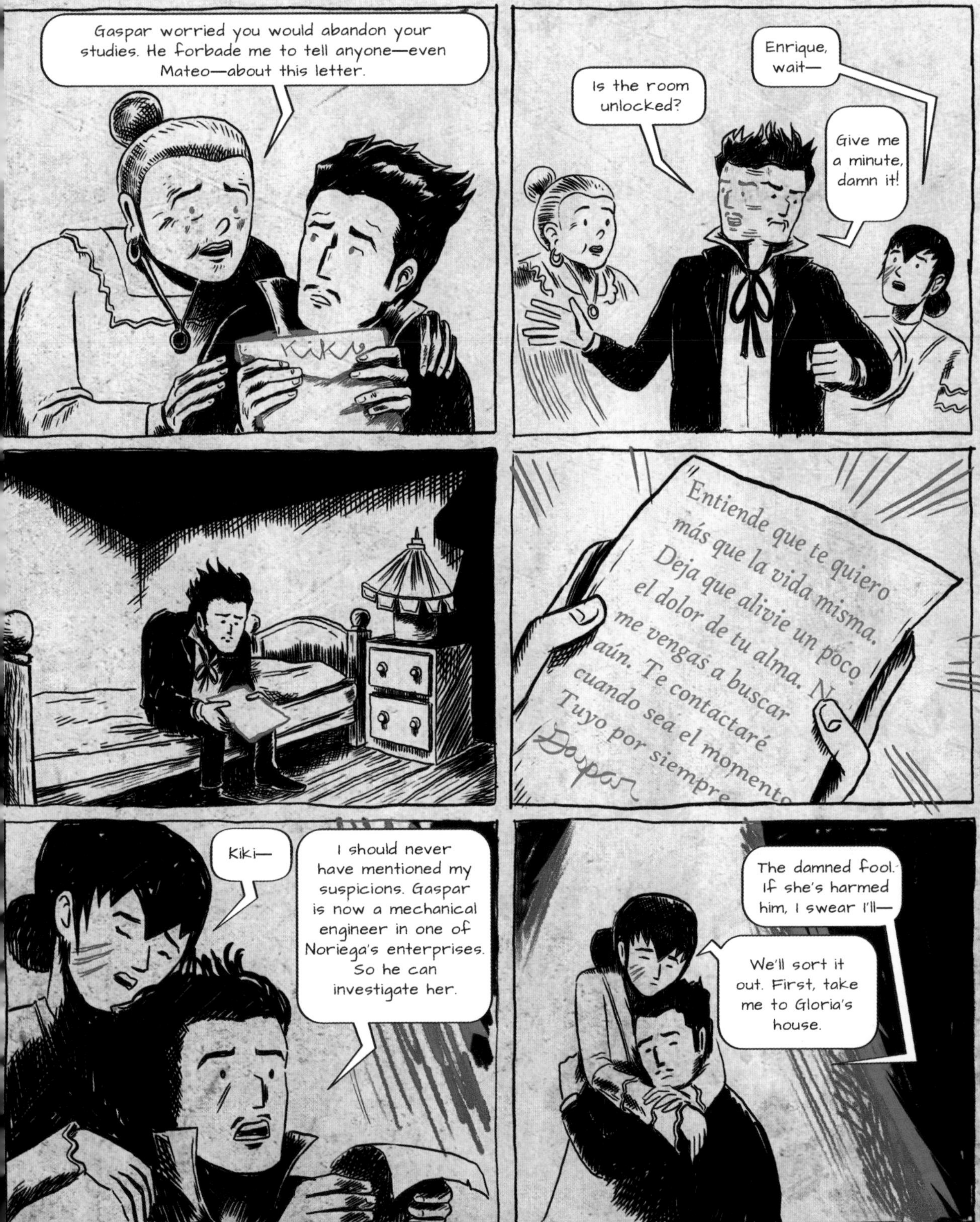
Gaspar worried you would abandon your studies. He forbade me to tell anyone—even Mateo—about this letter.
Kiki
Enrique, wait—
Is the room unlocked?
Give me a minute, damn it!
Entiende que te quiero más que la vida misma. Deja que alivie un poco el dolor de tu alma. N aún. Te contactaré cuando sea el momento. me vengas a buscar Tuyo por siempre
Gaspar
Kiki—
I should never have mentioned my suspicions. Gaspar is now a mechanical engineer in one of Noriega's enterprises. So he can investigate her.
The damned fool. If she's harmed him, I swear I'll—
We'll sort it out. First, take me to Gloria's house.

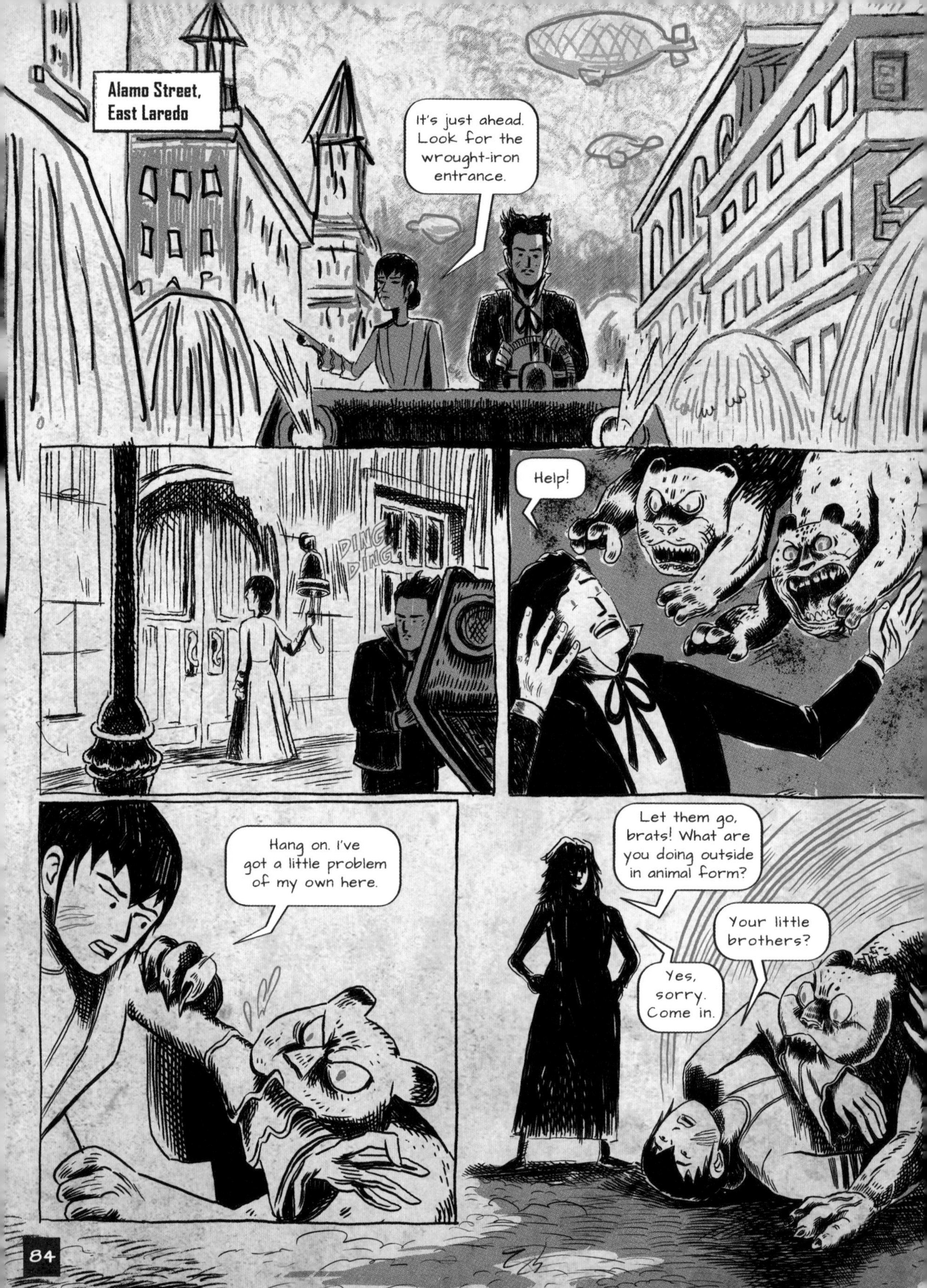

Alamo Street, East Laredo
It's just ahead. Look for the wrought-iron entrance.
DING DING
Help!
Hang on. I've got a little problem of my own here.
Let them go, brats! What are you doing outside in animal form?
Your little brothers?
Yes, sorry. Come in.

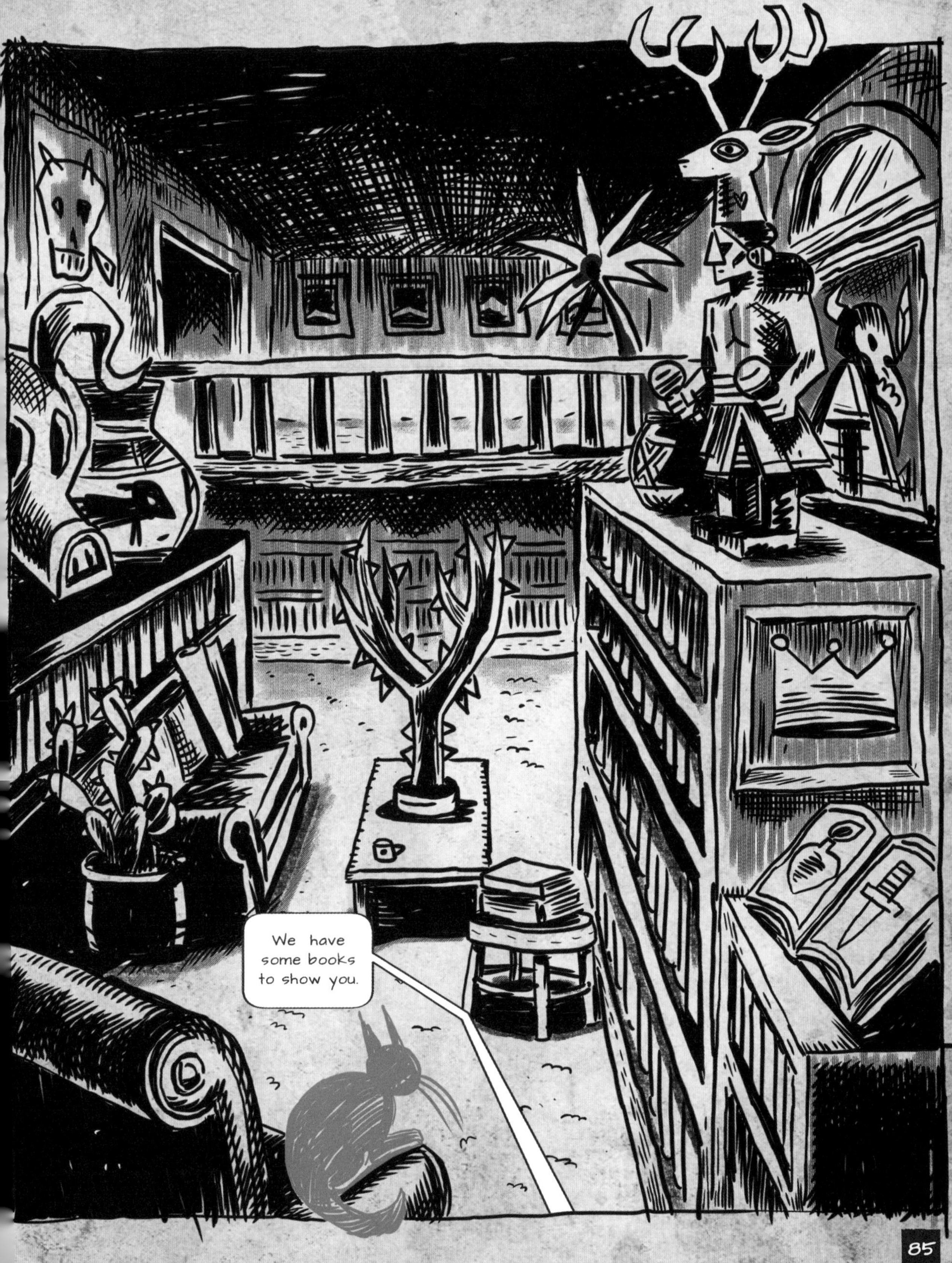
We have some books to show you.

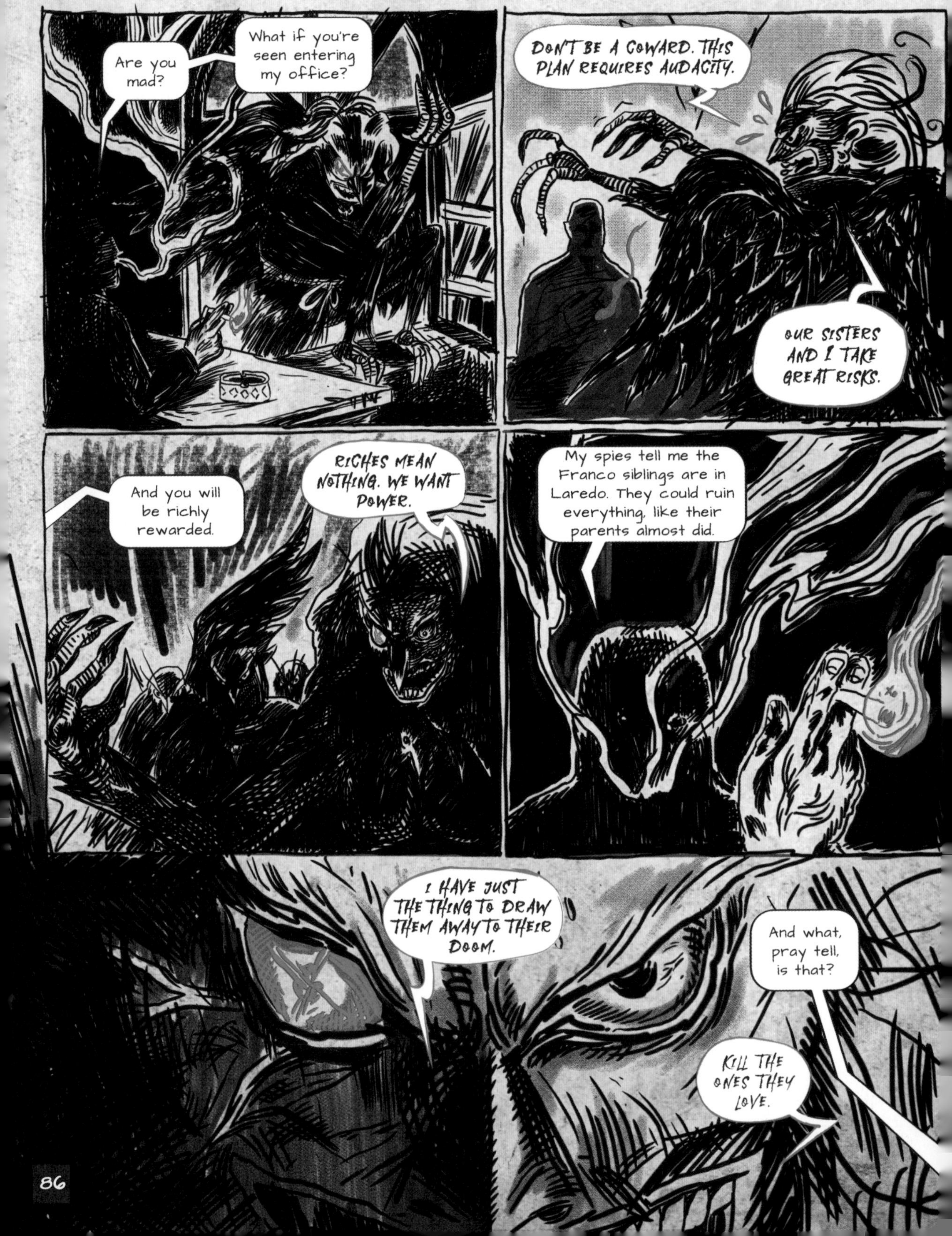
Are you mad?
What if you're seen entering my office?
DON'T BE A COWARD. THIS PLAN REQUIRES AUDACITY.
OUR SISTERS AND I TAKE GREAT RISKS.
And you will be richly rewarded.
RICHES MEAN NOTHING. WE WANT POWER.
My spies tell me the Franco siblings are in Laredo. They could ruin everything, like their parents almost did.
I HAVE JUST THE THING TO DRAW THEM AWAY TO THEIR DOOM.
And what, pray tell, is that?
KILL THE ONES THEY LOVE.

To Be Continued
In the Next Installment!

Look for Clockwork Curandera, Volume II: Robots of the Republic

Coming Soon to a Bookseller Near You!

THE PURPLE REBOZO

A *Clockwork Curandera* PREQUEL SHORT STORY

A NOISY CHACHALACA AWAKENS ME BEFORE DAWN, GOSSIP CACKLING FROM ITS beak. I may as well heed the bird's ornery call. I doubt I've slept more than three hours, so restless have I been all night with anticipation.

It's November 1, 1864. Today I become an apprentice curandera.

A glance at Gloria Palacios tells me she hasn't suffered the same insomnia. She's sprawled on her mat like an infant, snoring lightly. On the far side of the cabin, two other fifth-year students—Ana Prado and Nicolasa Maldonado—appear fast asleep as well.

Barefoot and wearing just my long huipil chemise, I slip outdoors. The cold is bracing, but my needs are too great.

"Ne ba'wus kwa'tci," I mutter, calling up the essential warmth of my beast-sprite. My skin flushes red for a brief moment, dispelling the worst of the chill as I hurry to the outhouse.

Vestiges of magical heat still cling to my flesh afterward as I walk to the Arroyo Coyote in the dawning light, the world awakening beneath the soles of my feet. The icy water of the stream breaks the spell as I wash my face and hands. Frigid needles tingle my skin all the way back to the cabin, but not even that sharp pain can dampen my spirits.

"Up, you lazybones!" I cry as I enter, slamming the door shut behind me. "Today's the big day!"

Gloria groans and rubs her eyes. "So much energy so early in the morning. You're an odd one, Cristina Franco."

I smile knowingly. By the time I've pulled my chemise over my head, my back to the other girls, and then slipped into my ceremonial huipil with its faint, delicate embroidery, all three of them are rolling up their sleeping mats and stowing their blankets.

"Don't forget your rebozos," I call out as I step into my tasseled skirt. "It's the last day we wear the blue."

The thought sends a little thrill along my limbs. *I'll be able to practice the healing arts on my own*, I think with a smile. *Apprentice, sure, but a curandera nonetheless.*

Mamá would be proud.

An hour later, having broken our fast with spiced warm milk and pastries—ritually our last meal as children, though Gloria swears she'll never give up sweet bread—our teachers walk us to the sacred place at the heart of Arroyo de Coyote Healing Center. A semicircle of old, gnarled mesquite and Monterrey cypress casts deep morning shadows over the nine seated tenanches, their green rebozos and white hair marking them as the most advanced curanderas in the Republic of Santander.

The middle woman stands as we approach. It's Conchita Ketekui, leader of the council. I momentarily loom over her short, plump figure before the four of us kneel.

From all around us, silent as opossums, the other students of the center emerge from the brush, the color of their shawls marking their year of studies.

Mamá Conchita begins to speak.

"Today is the Feast of the Presentation. When Blessed Mary was only three years old, her parents offered her to God in the temple to fulfill the promise they'd made in exchange for a child. We celebrate this feast in recognition of the holiness conferred on Mary from the beginning of her life, which transformed her into a greater temple than any made by hands, sanctifying her for a unique role in the divine plan. The magnificence of Mary enriches her children, especially those of us who have chosen the path of healing."

The two tenanches seated at either end stand and walk behind us. Gently, they lift the blue shawls from our heads and necks.

Mama Conchita continues.

"Today we present four young women here in this natural bower, this wild and pure temple beneath His watchful eye. May He sanctify each so that they can continue the earthly work of His son: easing the ailments of the flesh so that the spirit can more readily follow the Path of Light."

The next two council members get to their feet. In their hands I see a shimmer of violet. My breath catches in my throat.

"Today, you are no longer our students," Mamá Conchita says, her voice thick with emotion. I feel one of the tenanches drape the purple rebozo over my shoulders. Its soft touch brings tears to my eyes. "Rise, apprentice curanderas. Sisters. Friends."

My legs tremble, but I stand. Mamá Conchita embraces us, one by one. Then the last of the council members approach, holding four woven bags.

"The herbs and roots you've so carefully gathered and stored this last season have been transferred to your new bolsas de oficio. Within, you will also find your first assignments. Now turn and face your community."

Present at the ceremony are not only teachers and younger students, but also family and friends. Ana's kin, in their traditional Lipan garb. Easily a dozen of Nicolasa's cousins, visiting from Monterrey. And chasing after a trio of rambunctious boys tired of such serious goings-on is a lovely woman who just *must* be Gloria's mother.

No one for me, of course. Enrique is overseas. Aunt Teresa, at her convent.

Mother and Father dead.

"Go forth, daughters of Mary," Conchita says at last, "and heal the sick as God commands."

I sling the bag over my shoulder, give Gloria a tight hug, and leave without another word, without looking back. I can't bear to watch those families embrace the other girls. It's wrong of me, I know. But better I should get moving.

Focus on what lies ahead, not what you leave behind. It was the first rule they taught me when I came to Arroyo de Coyote, bereft at my parents' deaths, searching for purpose.

Pulling up my new rebozo to cover my head, I fix my eyes on the horizon and walk.

The carefully lettered note in my bag explains my first patient in broad strokes. Genoveva Garza Odoms, a widow in her late fifties, living on an old farm beside Resaca de los Álamos, an oxbow lake some ten miles north on the outskirts of Laredo.

It takes me two hours to reach those fallow fields, that dilapidated Texas-style house with its sagging eaves and faded clapboards.

The door swings open as the first porch step creaks beneath my feet. The widow emerges, and I immediately note her jaundiced skin. When she smiles weakly, her gums show slightly blue.

"Ah, Prima," she says, speaking the title often used for us apprentices. "Welcome to my home, which is your own."

"Thank you, Doña Genoveva," I reply, following her in. The curtains are all drawn. The air is musty and close.

"I made some lemonade," she tells me over her shoulder as she shuffles away to the kitchen. "Take a seat on the couch and I'll bring a tray."

I do as she asks, sniffing at the air, trying to detect whether the harmful substance is here inside. I catch a faint whiff of something. Closing my eyes, I focus on it. The odor grows stronger, stronger.

A clinking of glasses as something is set down on the table before me. I open my eyes to find the widow depositing a tarnished silver tray upon which sit two glasses full of tart liquid and a few stale cookies.

"I hope you don't mind me dispensing with the normal formalities, but today my head and stomach ache something fierce, Prima."

"Please, call me Cristina, ma'am."

She nods, easing down into a rocking chair and sighing. "I've been like this for a couple months now. Always tired. Vomiting."

I reach out to pick up my lemonade.

The wrongness is a shock to my senses. I almost drop the glass.

"The water, Doña Genoveva," I gasp. "It's contaminated."

Her eyes go a little wide, but she also sighs with relief to know the source. "Comes from the Resaca de los Álamos. John—that's my late husband—brought one of them steam-driven pumps down with him from the Duchy of Texas. That's where he's from, where my sons have gone to seek their fortune in that new oil business. Anyway, pump brings water up from the lake."

I nod, opening my bag. "Well, thank the Mother, this should be an easy enough fix. Just last summer I helped Mamá Licha purified a tainted well."

As I measure out herbs for her to boil into a tea once the water's drinkable, the widow clears her throat. "I don't quite understand, Prima Cristina. That water used to be so clear and good. Thirty years I gave it to my husband and children."

I study her feverish features for a second. "What changed, ma'am? What has been different this year?"

She scratches her patchy hair. "Well, there was that wild storm blew in off the Quetzal Sea back in September, you recall? Came right up the Río Bravo, dumped a couple feet of rain."

I do indeed remember it. Our creek swelled well beyond its banks, forcing students into teachers' cabins for the better part of a week till the water subsided.

"Likely the fault of the Arroyo del Diablo," Doña Genoveva sighs. "Little channel nearby, distributary of the river. The lake used to be part of it. The flooding joined them again for about a month."

I finish folding up the herbs into a paper packet, sealed with a drop of resin. "That must be the problem, ma'am. I'm going to perform a cleansing ritual on the lake, then you're going to drink this tea every morning and every night for ten days. I'll be back then to check on your progress."

I stand and place the packet in her hand. She clings to me for a second, a smile brightening her yellowed eyes. "Thank you, Prima Cristina. May the Mother soften your step."

"May She ease your lying down and your getting up," I respond, completing the formal leave-taking.

Outside, I follow the large clay pipe that transports water above ground to the widow's home. After a few hundred yards, I reach the edge of the oxbow lake, where a small pump house squats beside a cord of firewood. The carrizo along the lakeshore has withered more than is normal for late fall. I can sense no animals drinking nearby.

Unlike humans, clearly they know better.

Kneeling, I lay both palms against the ground, reach out with my green-soul. I root myself in the Green Realm and whisper to the reeds, the algae, the nearly invisible growing things deep in the silt.

Pull the poison from the water. Leave it clean and fresh. Thrust that wrongness deep down, into the bedrock far below.

Taking a slow, deep breath, I repeat the old words:

"A'x pakma't. A'x payesu'i. A'x paka'mle. Let this water run clean!"

Green magic thrums along the earth, into the water, drawing poisons away.

But in the midst of the spell, something *pushes back*. Hard.

I am thrown backward by a spiral of spiritual energy that twists me in the air so I smash face-first into the ground. Scrambling to stand, I kick off my sandals, digging my toes deep into the soft soil.

Once more I reach out. There's something here, a trace. Not a physical substance.

Subtle essence. Not human. Squirming. A powerful echo of pain.

My eyes scan the distance. Faint puffs of smoke. Industrial?

The certainty hits me. The Arroyo del Diablo. That's where the poison came from.

Something is suffering in its waters.

Fifteen minutes later, I'm walking along the creek bank. I sense the same poison, clearly some industrial pollutant, but not in nearly the quantities I was expecting.

Looming larger and larger before me is some sort of factory, belching clouds of smoke, strangely hued. Before long, I can make out the sign.

TEPOZTECANI FINISHERS.

I stop in my tracks. I know that name.

A few seconds of hard thought brings back the memory, like a blow to my stomach.

"At least speak to Carlos over at Tepoztecani Finishers!" my mother yells on the other side of the door I should not be listening at. But I have been ever nosy.

"And tell him what?" my father growls. "Not to sign a contract with Demetria Noriega because she's stolen my steel-making process? To forgo all those profits? He'll laugh in my face."

Apparently, whoever Carlos was, he *did* sign a contract with the woman responsible for my parents' death.

Now here sits his factory, using Mother-only-knows *what* chemicals to finish that traitorous steel, then dumping the runoff into this creek.

So why isn't it more polluted?

I crouch, lace my fingers in the weeds, sink my toes in the mud.

Carefully, I begin to probe with my green-soul. With patience and caution, I work my senses up the Arroyo del Diablo, searching for . . .

THERE! That powerful swirl of ku, close to the factory.

A'x pahuel. Water elemental. Trapped.

But how? Why?

Still crouching, I move quickly toward the magical being. It has manifested as a sort of whirlpool beneath a huge, grated outlet pipe. From inside the factory, a foul-smelling, poisonous sludge pours into the very center of the swirl.

They're making it consume the pollution!

My first impulse is the Freedom Sequence. It's not Green Magic, but I've seen it work before. I pull off my rebozo, almost startled by its silky texture.

Tying the first knot into the shawl, I shout: "Libera nos a malo!"

Second knot: "Quia tuum est regnum!"

Third: "Et potestas!"

Fourth: "Et gloria!"

Then I tie the fifth and final knot, gasping the Latin words: "In saecula! Amen!"

Nothing has changed. The elemental is trapped in its filtering swirl. I groan.

Something glints in the afternoon sunlight, distracting me from the indignant rage and frustration now filling my chest.

That's when I see them. Steel bars, arranged all around—on the bank, in the creek. Engraved with dark glyphs. Jade and emerald infused with power, embedded in the metal. Even the grating on the foul drainage pipe is part of the design.

A hex. A massive skein of magical force, meant to trap a water elemental and bend it to this gruesome task.

The ancient being senses me. I'm flooded with emotions: anger, fear, despair.

It begs for release, its voice like a crashing wave in my heart. *Free me. Or destroy me.*

Tears begin streaming down my face as I grab one of the steel bars and pull with all my might. It doesn't budge. I slam my shoulder into it again and again. Nothing.

Think, curandera. The elemental's words are shredded by agony. *You are not that frail body. Your power is not limited to that flesh and bone.*

I drop to my knees, thrust my arms up to my elbows in the marshy earth. My green-soul is a blade, piercing deeper into the Green Realm than I have ever dared.

I think of my father, toiling for years to produce steel cheaply and cleanly, only to have the process stolen by a woman who has very likely put it to this unnatural, evil use. I think of my mother, who sank her family fortune into her husband's dreams and lost everything, even her own life.

My questing heart finds the earth beneath the concrete that anchors the steel. It is rich with life that teems at my touch, quickened and obedient.

Bore me a hole, I whisper. *Deep, deep, deep. Let us hide these twisted tools from the world.*

Tilting back my head, I scream in one of the old tongues:

"Pamelpau*! Forever!"

All around, the steel bars tremble for an anxious instant. Then they drop into the ground. The hex is broken.

At first, all that happens is that the whirlpool stops spinning. The creek goes still but for the sluggish current and the discolored cascade of pollution.

Then, right beside me, the water shoots up into the air, spattering my face. Instead of raining back down into Arroyo del Diablo, the water coalesces into a human shape next to me on the bank: a young man, slightly transparent, glowing from within.

Very handsome. Very nude.

"Thank you," he says. "Another year of devouring that vile sludge, and my tide-sprite would have been extinguished."

"What will you do?" I ask. "It's too dangerous to remain at Arroyo del Diablo."

*Sink into the earth

He gives a bubbling sigh. "Indeed. After so many delightful centuries acting the devil in its waters. Yet time does flow on, does it not? I'll drift down the Great River once more, see what mischief I can stir up. But first . . . I intend to wait until evening, when the foolish men in that atrocious building leave for their dry, insipid homes. Then I will raise the waters and smash their factory to pieces."

I am an agent of order, creation, healing. I should take no pleasure in destruction. Yet at his words, I cannot help but feel a thrill of vengeance twist my belly.

"I must be getting back," I say. "May the Mother guide you true."

His smile is like the sun upon the water, golden and blue. "Flow forever, curandera."

I lean close to him and whisper fiercely, "Leave no stone standing. Make those bastards pay."

Before he can answer me, I spin on my heel and hurry off. The water elemental chuckles behind me, his laugh like a burbling brook.

As I trudge back to the farm to collect my sandals, untying the knots in my rebozo, I hear him in my mind one final time. His whisper is like melting ice.

"May you too one day get your revenge. I only pray you are not made to suffer first."

I shudder and cross myself.

I've suffered quite enough.

AUTHOR'S NOTE

Let me be clear in case you don't know: curanderas are real.

I grew up on the border between Texas and Mexico. My childhood was marked—as was my father's and grandfather's—by visits to these capable healers. With weird-smelling herbs and quirky prayers and oils that warmed my muscles beneath their deft hands, the curanderas cured me again and again, no matter what ailed me.

Not just physical sickness, understand. They knew how to grapple with my emotional or psychological issues as well, providing ancestral therapy that rivaled any counselor or psychiatrist.

And of course, there was the spiritual side of their craft. Many promised they could remove curses or counter attacks by dark forces. Time and again, they seemed to prove their powers to our community.

Curanderas struck me as more than human. They were living, breathing superheroes.

Now, I was a huge comic book fan as a kid. I was particularly drawn to magical, horror-tinged DC series like *House of Mystery*, *Swamp Thing*, and *Hellblazer*.

Then cyberpunk manga like *Akira* and *Ghost in the Shell* began to get published in English, and I had found my new love. By the time *Battle Angel Alita* came out, I was a convert.

All along, I was reading the greats of science fiction, including the mother of the genre: Mary Shelley's *Frankenstein*. And when the steampunk genre steamed down the tracks of popular culture, I was an early adopter of the aesthetic.

As will happen in a mischievous mind like mine, all these elements eventually came together, morphing slowly in the recesses of my subconscious.

One day, an idea bubbled to the surface.

What if a curandera—whose power to heal comes from her connection to nature—had to become a cyborg to survive? How would she deal with that new identity?

What if she lived in a steampunk version of the nineteenth century, not in some industrial European city, but here where my family has existed for centuries, in northern Mexico and south Texas?

I couldn't get her out of my head, this Clockwork Curandera. When I shared my ideas with illustrator Raúl the Third, he got her, immediately. His incomparable art captured her spirit and strength, her dedication to community, her desire to heal even as she fights to protect.

What a delight that Tu Books saw in Cristina Franco and her world a story they wanted to foster and bring to readers like you.

I hope you've enjoyed your time in the Republic of Santander, among its deserts and monsters, its monasteries and cantinas. There's so much more to see when you return. Robots and airships, shapeshifters and thunderbirds. Quite an adventure.

And like the curanderas of my childhood, Cristina will be there, too, ready to fend off the darkness. Ready to heal our hearts and minds as well as our bodies.

Until then, dear friends—steer clear of the screech owls.

—David Bowles

SKETCHES

IN-PROCESS ART BY RAÚL THE THIRD

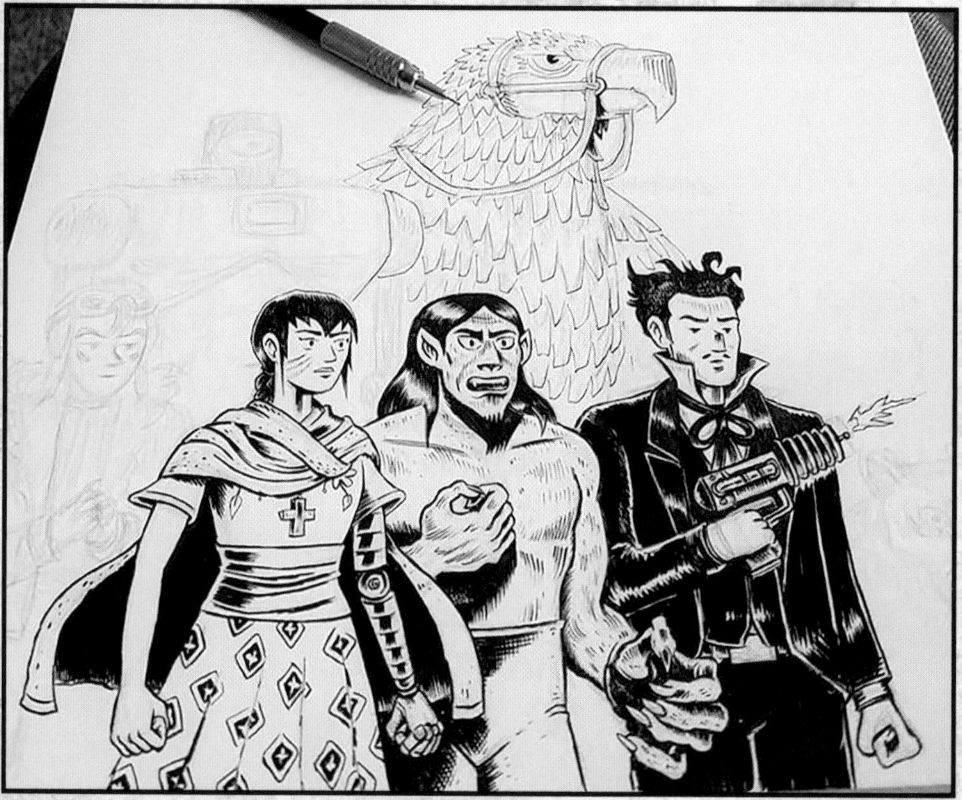

Character design sketch by Raúl, including allies coming in future installments.

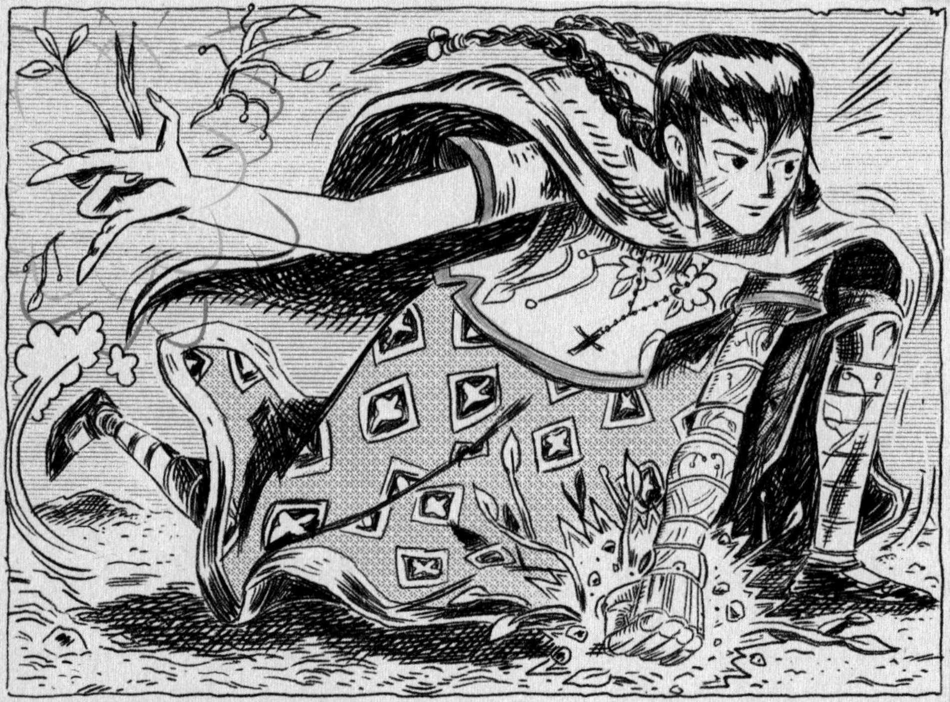

Cristina uses both her robotic and magical abilities.

TWO TABLETS! THREE YET ONE! FOUR EVANGELISTS!

Initial test panels by Raúl from the Prologue. He would go on to streamline Cristina's appearance.

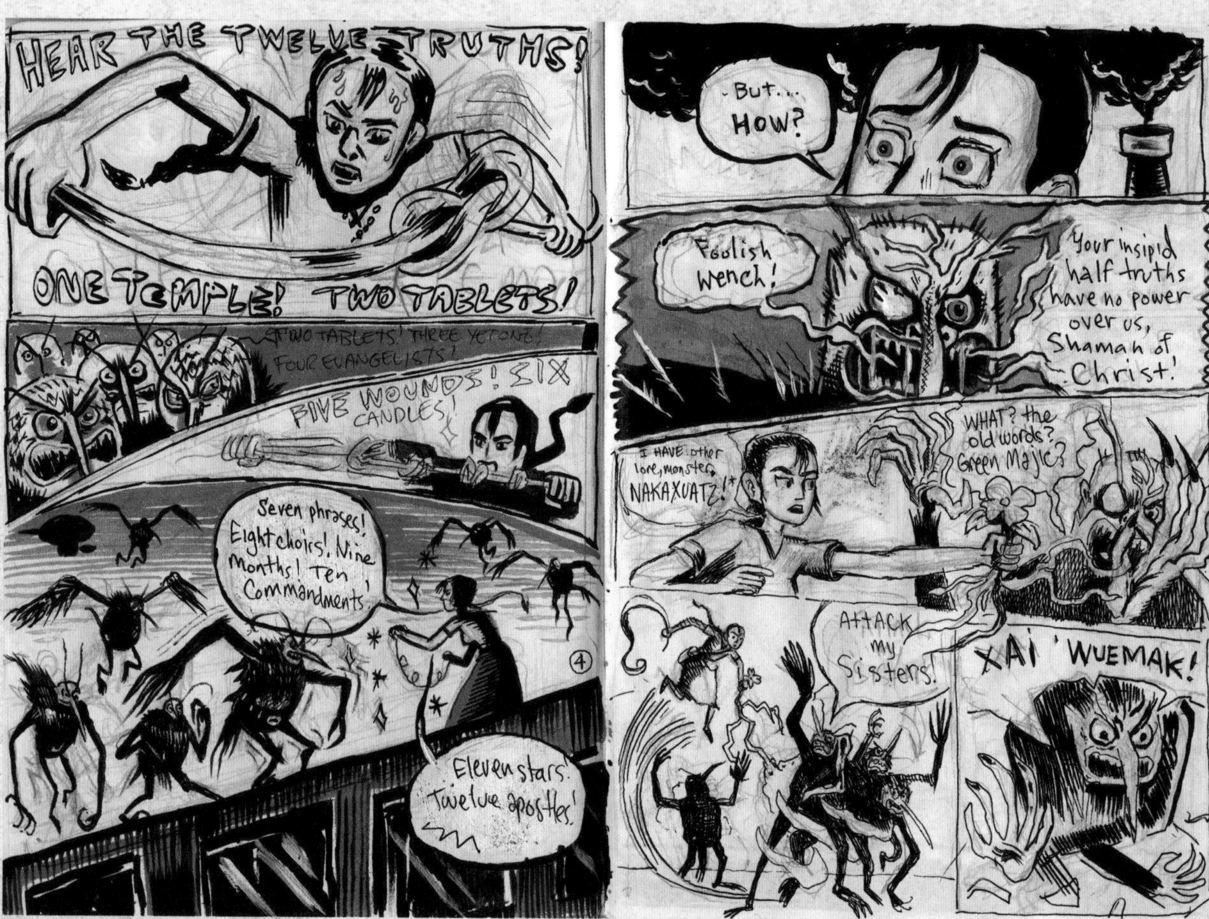
HEAR THE TWELVE TRUTHS!
ONE TEMPLE! TWO TABLETS!
TWO TABLETS!
FOUR EVANGELISTS!
FIVE WOUNDS! SIX CANDLES!
Seven phrases! Eight choirs! Nine months! Ten Commandments!
Eleven stars! Twelve apostles!
4
But... HOW?
Foolish wench!
Your insipid half truths have no power over us, Shaman of Christ!
I HAVE other lore, monster, NAKAXUATZ!
WHAT? the old words? Green Majic?
ATTACK my Sisters!
XAI 'WUEMAK!

Thumbnails of Cristina's first encounter with the Witch Owls.
Illustrators create thumbnails to help decide the best layout of each scene.

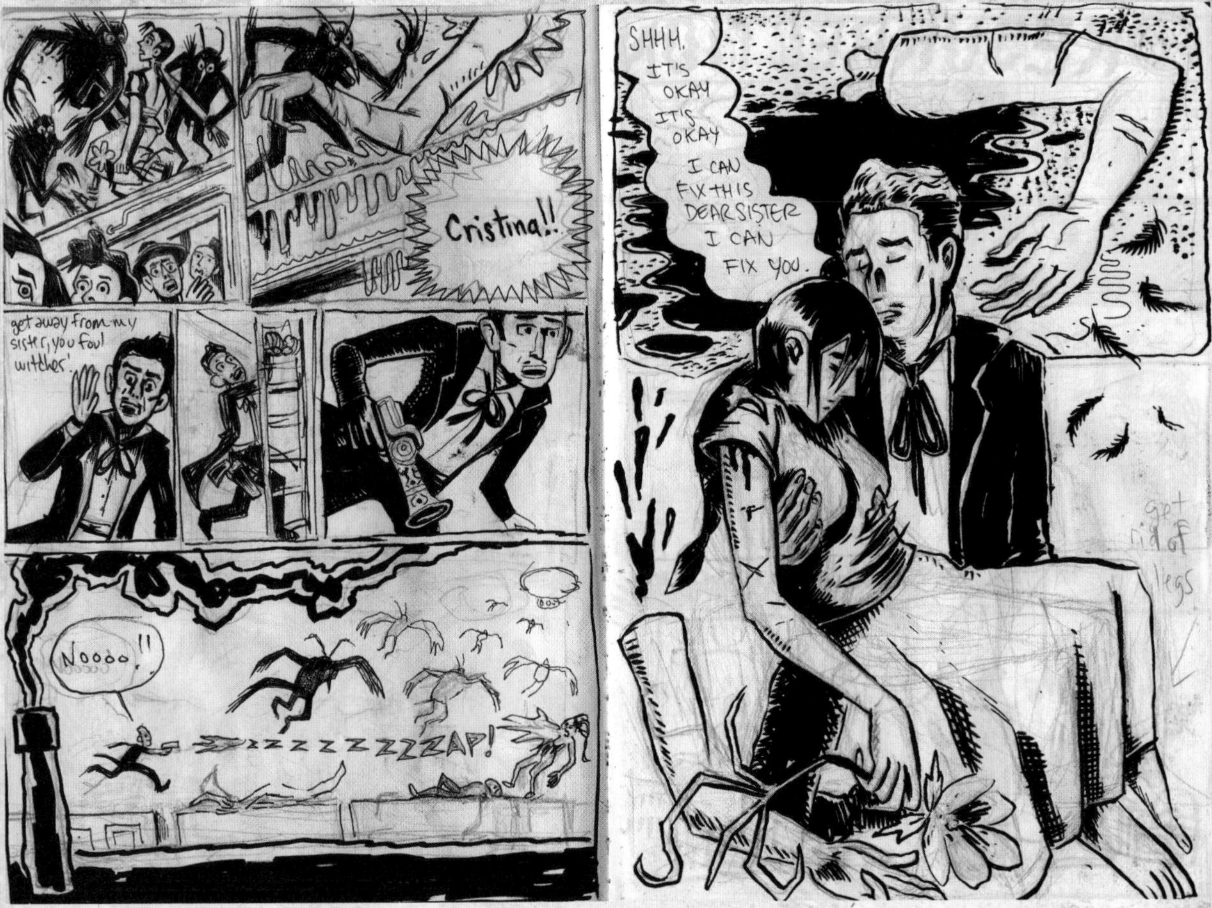
Cristina!!
get away from my sister, you foul witches!
Noooo!!
ZZZZZZZZZAP!
SHHH.
IT'S OKAY
IT'S OKAY
I CAN FIX THIS DEAR SISTER
I CAN FIX YOU.
get rid of legs

Thumbnails of Enrique's attempt to rescue his sister, including a few panels that Raúl ultimately decided to cut.